WEIRDOS WELCOME

Published by River Grove Books
Austin, TX
www.rivergrovebooks.com

Distributed by River Grove Books

Subjects: BISAC: YOUNG ADULT FICTION / Neurodiversity | YOUNG ADULT FICTION / Social Themes / Emotions & Feelings | YOUNG ADULT FICTION / Romance / Contemporary

Design and composition by Greenleaf Book Group
Cover design by Greenleaf Book Group
Cover images ©Adobe Stock/sensay; ©Adobe Stock/artyway
Pitbull icon ©Adobe Stock/martialred

Publisher's Cataloging-in-Publication data is available.

Print ISBN: 978-1-966629-70-2

eBook ISBN: 978-1-966629-71-9

First Edition

FOR ROBERT AND HARRISON

WEIRDOS WELCOME

CYNTHIA BASEMAN

RIVER GROVE
BOOKS

1
BRADEN

My cousin Connor liked to call me an "awfulist."

This time, it wasn't because I'd been fixated on my friend Hojun's death at a party almost two years ago, or because I thought the mole on my right thumb might morph into malignant melanoma, or even because of my nagging worry that I'd never get a girlfriend. He called me an awfulist because I blew off an invite to another one of his kickbacks.

"What do you mean, you're not coming?" Connor asked as we breezed past the school library on our way to first period. He and I were born four months apart and have the same dark hair, large feet, and round cheeks. That's where the similarities end.

"I'm behind on my history reading," I explained as Connor stared at me, clutching his Styrofoam cup. "Way behind. Gonna take me all weekend to catch up."

"Seriously, Braden? Why you gotta be such a goddamn awfulist?"

Lately, Connor had claimed that my definition of fun had strayed ever since we started junior year. He still lived for kickbacks—sneaking beers, playing poker with friends—while more and more, I craved being alone.

On some level, Connor knew that I was wound tight, that I was someone who obsessed over things and made excuses to avoid social stuff. I don't think he knew the extent of it, though. The stomachaches. The need to check things over and over. The sense of impending disaster. Compared with Connor's laid-back, skateboarder attitude, I looked like a nerdy, overachieving nut.

Near my locker, we ran into Zach, who pulled me into a half hug. "Tonight's gonna be big!" he yelled. "Nothin' but net!"

"Definitely." I flashed what I hoped was a convincing smile. No sense letting on to the captain of the basketball team that the prospect of tonight's game made me nauseated. It's best not to be the freak.

Sure, I loved wearing the Pacific Crest uniform and the status of being on the team. Go Vikings! But I loved less the pressure to win—and the jerks on the other team who would trip you on purpose or elbow you in the kidney if they thought they could get away with it.

To be honest, I dreamed of quitting basketball.

But *quitting* did not appear in the Bernstein bible. *Thou shalt not give up*, on the other hand, did. Many of Dad's sermons—I mean "father-son talks"—centered on this theme.

"You look thrilled," Connor commented between sips of coffee.

"Must've left my pom-poms at home," I deadpanned, closing my locker.

Connor smirked, and we headed our separate ways.

As I swung open the door to class, Kennedy and Taylor—the student government goddesses—rushed up and air-kissed me. The scent of their perfume lingered on my cheek.

"We're getting to the game early tonight," Taylor informed me, rapidly blinking her unnaturally long, dark lashes.

Kennedy smiled, and her teeth gleamed. "We want good seats."

Before I could respond, an alarm rang over the loudspeaker, jarring the entire class. Then came the vice principal's voice, instructing us to exit the building.

Bomb threat.

My heart pounded. Blood rushed in my ears. But in the face of imminent destruction, the girls just dawdled, lazily adjusting the straps of their backpacks.

"Move it!" I snapped. "Move it like there's a sale at Prada!"

They giggled.

If it wasn't for my kid sister, Jenji—a devout vegan who once staged a protest at the store on Rodeo Drive for selling leather rather than pleather—I wouldn't know Prada from Pringles. But at least I managed to get Taylor and Kennedy moving toward the exit.

The hallway was overflowing. I pushed through the zombies—hordes of them, what seemed like all of Pac Crest High School's roughly sixteen hundred students, snaking through the halls and spilling out onto the front lawn.

There! I spotted Connor in the crowd and made a fast break. "Hurry up!" I urged. "In case the Science & Technology Building bursts into a fireball!"

He swatted me away. "Chill, Braden. It's gotta be a hoax."

Maybe, I thought. *Or maybe they'll be scooping up body parts from the pavement.*

We were instructed to form lines and head south along the sidewalk until we reached the designated safe area: Will Rogers Park. Along the way, we caught tidbits of teachers' conversations: *suspension . . . waste of police resources . . . espresso's probably gone cold . . . .*

Most teachers seemed calm enough, but even as a second-semester junior, I still found some of them hard to read. The good ones had trained themselves to maintain that zen look even when a disturbed kid hurled his desk across the room. The not-so-good ones never really expressed any emotion but apathy.

One of the vice principals abruptly pulled a kid out of line for laughing. Connor and I shared a look.

The Pacific Crest cops had moved quickly. Three black-and-whites, lights flashing, were parked by the front lawn. Officers lurched out of them, advancing toward the building on foot. Another officer, stationed at the corner, held back four lanes of traffic while we crossed to the park.

I hated it there.

I'd grown up playing basketball with Hojun at Will Rogers Park. I'd also attended his memorial service there. And no matter how hard I tried, I could never really accept that the goofy guy who could outsmart, outplay, outdance me seven days a week was, in fact, dead. Now here I was again at Will Rogers, half expecting an explosion to rock the ground beneath my feet.

Connor and I walked deeper into the park, passing the stoners, the band kids, the cheer girls. I glanced over my shoulder at campus. From this distance, I calculated, we could still suffer burn blisters and third-degree burns.

"How do they know when it's safe?" I asked.

Connor shrugged. "They're trained."

His trust in the police didn't derail my worry train. Only one thing could. And like a mirage, there he was—sitting cross-legged, back against a nearby tree, potbelly spilling over the waist of his jeans.

Lucas Cruz had a gap between his front teeth, black-framed glasses thick as the Mexican Coke bottle he was drinking from, and the usual expression on his face—the one I found endlessly fascinating: pure nonchalance. If an artist were commissioned to sculpt a piece titled *Looking for a Fuck to Give*, featuring a pudgy Filipino guy with an attitude, they'd model it on Lucas.

I plopped down next to him, already feeling my teeth unclench and my limbs relax. "Lucas! How's it going, man?"

"Any better and they'd throw my ass in jail." He had a way with words—a good thing, considering he was in Advanced Journalism with me. Both of us lived to write about sports, and we collaborated on stories sometimes.

"Think it's a hoax?" I asked him.

"Uh, yeah?" Connor kicked my foot. "Duh? Third one since February. They'll catch him."

"Or her," Lucas suggested, sipping his soda and swallowing a burp in the back of his throat. "Could be anybody." He nodded in the direction of a girl slouched in the shadows of a giant palm tree.

She was alone, blue hair tucked behind her seashell-shaped ears, nodding to whatever music was coming from her headphones. I'd seen her before and wondered what her deal was. She was kind of pretty, I guess, if you could look past the baggy black sweatshirt, the dark sunglasses, the black jeans. Could she be the one calling in the bomb threats?

I watched her for a while. Settled on top of a picnic table, she was scrolling on her phone. Alone. She kept shoving the sleeves of her sweatshirt up to her elbows and sweeping her hair out of her eyes. A couple of students sat down at the table—on the bench part, that is—and she didn't even look up. I couldn't get a sense of whether she was brimming with self-confidence or a sad loner.

Either way, the Girl in Black was a definite contender.

"May I have your attention!" The vice principal's voice crackled loudly over her electronic bullhorn as she announced instructions for returning to campus: seniors first, then us juniors, then everyone else. "Please return to your second-period classrooms!"

The three of us stood up to go. Connor finished his coffee and tossed the cup into a nearby trash can.

"Why do you always have to use Styrofoam?" I asked.

"I'll plant a hundred trees to make up for it," he overpromised.

"Or you could just get yourself a reusable cup and stop making excuses. Like the people who want to recommission that oil and gas platform." I nodded my chin toward the abandoned drilling rig next to the school track. "As if by giving our school money, somehow it's okay they're poisoning the air."

On the corner, waiting for the light to change, we all stared up at the two-hundred-foot oil tower. "Curious if it really is dangerous?" Connor asked.

Lucas pushed his glasses up on his nose. "You think an oil well's dangerous? Try living in Manila."

"Didn't a bunch of people with cancer try to sue the city over that rig?" I asked. An image of cancer cells invading my thyroid came to mind.

"If the vigilantes don't kill you in your sleep, then the pollution will," Lucas continued. "Kid at my old school fell into the Pasig River, and his skin turned green and smelly as a rotten zucchini."

My skin crawled. "Seriously?"

"I swear to god."

"That's disgusting." I was so creeped out.

Lucas started laughing so hard, his eyes watered. When I punched him on the shoulder, he only laughed harder.

An officer motioned at us to cross the street. Back to school. Where someone claimed to have planted a bomb. Somehow, I was supposed to sit through class. Joke with friends. Pretend I loved playing basketball.

Today the bomb threat was a hoax, but tomorrow—who could say? Two years ago, no one could have imagined that Hojun would be gone forever. I decided enough was enough. Class was nonnegotiable—I knew I couldn't get out of that. But no way did I have to compete anymore.

I pulled my phone from my pocket. "One sec."

Lucas and Connor waited on the sidewalk while I typed a quick email to Coach Sanchez and my guidance counselor, Ms. Nguyen:

> I think it's best if I withdraw from my spot on the basketball
> team. I'm finding it hard to manage my time, and I'm con-
> cerned about my grades.

To me, that sounded better than what I really wanted to say: *I feel a sense of doom. At times, it's a hum beneath the surface, at other times, it's a roar.*

2

RAE

Sheep! That's what they all looked like—my fellow students, huddled together and shambling in a mindless herd across Sunset Boulevard, back toward campus. Truthfully, the bomb threat was more annoying than scary. But they were still victims, and they didn't even get it.

I flinched when a girl with red hair brushed against me, too close for comfort. The herd had me boxed in at the crosswalk, with no place to move. Damn sheep!

Where are you, Arman? I wondered, repositioning my headphones.

When the alarm had sounded over the loudspeaker, I had fled homeroom, hoping for a glimpse of Arman—my bestie and fellow drama kid.

Loud voices jarred me now as the herd of students pushed down the sidewalk. I turned up the volume on my headphones—my buffer from sensory overload—and tried not to keep looking around like some kind of lost animal myself.

Maybe Arman was hiding out in the boys' bathroom with Spencer? Not that I would've blamed him. He'd been crushing on

Spencer since before the auditions. Before that, it was James. Before that, Seth. Arman was kind of a horndog.

The redhead bumped me again, so I scowled at her. She whispered something to her friend—about me, obviously. They probably bought into the rumors that I carried a weapon to school.

I slipped my hand into the front pocket of my hoodie, trying to make it look like I was holding a combat knife. When I peeked down, it looked more like I was holding a grapefruit.

A car honked, piercing through my headphones and making me jump.

I wished time would speed up past Math, past English, past all the rest of it, and deliver me straight to Drama Lab—my comfort zone, where all of us were weird. On the whiteboard, our drama teacher had written: *If you're not making mistakes, you're not trying hard enough!* Mr. Barsanti was one of the few teachers who seemed to understand kids like us.

The heavy sweatshirt had been a mistake. Trudging along the sidewalk, I could already feel the dampness beneath my armpits. *Wait, do I stink?* I wondered. Yes, I had forgotten deodorant again. The weight of the hood against the back of my neck was giving me a headache, but it was too late now to take it off. Now that I had pit stains, I'd have to wear the damn thing all day.

A tall boy with a crewcut kicked the back of my shoe—accidentally on purpose, most likely. I whirled around to face him, consumed by rage. He took a step back and glanced at his friend, a Filipino guy I'd seen smoking cigarettes in the alley behind school.

"Sorry!" the crewcut boy sputtered. "Really. I'm so sorry!"

"Over-apologizing is a sign of low self-esteem," I informed him, dodging away.

Hurrying along, I avoided making eye contact with anyone else, and instead gazed into the distance at nothing. Then the gloomy oil tower came into focus, wrapped in its washed-out, flower-patterned shroud. Mom had been stressing about that thing for months. The owners had gone bankrupt, and now a petroleum company wanted to take over and get the oil well running again.

Mom worked every day—not like a regular job, but for the Pacific Crest City Council. She'd even worked during our vacation in Hawaii, although that didn't stop her from pestering me to reapply sunscreen every two hours. We had the same fight over and over.

"I'm getting too old to have someone tell me what to do," I complained.

"But your skin burns so easily!" Mom worried.

"Maybe I'm part vampire."

She always laughed when I said that. What I really meant was, I didn't fit in. Nor did I want to.

Mom was the one who organized all of my appointments: the psychologist, the occupational therapist, the educational consultant, the math tutors. I hated her for it, even if all she wanted was to make life easier.

Girls on the spectrum don't get "easier." Not that I knew any other autie girls at school—just boys. It would have been really nice to find other girls who understood what it's like to be on the spectrum. Obviously, in a high school the size of Pacific Crest, statistically I couldn't be the only one. But many girls go undiagnosed, and a lot of parents live in denial. Like my dad.

Undiagnosed girls have to pretend they're just like everyone else. As long as they don't make trouble, their parents can continue on like it's normal for their daughters to constantly read instead of making friends—to avoid eye contact and get hyper-focused on special projects and have meltdowns. That made it hard to tell the difference between neurotypical girls and those on the spectrum.

Other than my online friends, I had no idea how I'd ever find my tribe.

The internet is an awesome place for weird people like me. That's another thing Mom and I argued about: online friends versus IRL friends. Mom didn't get how incredible it was to connect with other autistic people—an expression she detested.

"You're high-functioning, brilliant," she would say. "It's not the same!" Only it is. It's exactly the same.

I. Am. On. The. Spectrum.

Finally back on the front lawn of school, I took a deep breath and let the music encircle me, in the midst of a loop of my favorite songs: Taylor Swift, SZA, Beyoncé, Florence and the Machine, Ella Mai. The police were leaving. One of the officers had a German shepherd at her side. I suddenly wanted to sit down on the grass next to the police dog and rest.

I stopped walking, but no one else did. Students bumped and jostled me, swirling around me on their way back to class. Colored lights pulsed on top of the police car. Sunlight glinted off the school windows. "Freak," someone hissed.

Then a soft voice said my name. "Rae?"

I instantly brightened. *Arman. My best friend.* His voice was always comforting. But he looked concerned. Or sad. I have trouble distinguishing between the two.

"You understand it's eighty-eight degrees out," he said quietly, "and you're dressed like a Goth chick who lives at the North Pole?"

"You understand you're the only openly gay junior, and that makes you a target for every homophobic loser who has nothing better to do than torture you?"

Arman Golshan was Jewish, Persian, and gay—a triple threat. *Three minorities in one*, I frequently teased him. His tawny complexion was made even warmer by golden undertones. And his eyes were the ones I should have been born with: hazel with yellow flecks in each iris, like a wolf's. I'm the one whose last name is Wolf, but my eyes are blue.

Turns out I was right: Arman *was* concerned. He made me drink most of his electrolyte-enhanced water and walked me to Math class. Then he promised to meet me at lunchtime at our usual place, a secluded passage in the Science & Technology Building.

I had to ask. "Where were you, anyway? Boys' bathroom with Spencer?"

He just waved goodbye with a funny look on his face. Like maybe I was right about him being sad too.

3
BRADEN

Nestled in a corner of the vice principals' office, Ms. Nguyen's room was exactly what you'd expect from a guidance counselor: a closet-sized space packed with piles of file boxes, its walls covered in colorful college pennants. I shimmied past a tower of boxes and squeezed myself into the seat facing her desk, hoping she wasn't going to ask too many questions about my schedule request.

"You're sure about this?" Ms. Nguyen repeated, a kind smile lighting up her face. She was one of those perpetually joyful people, but not in an irritating way.

I nodded. "One hundred percent."

"Okay, Braden," she continued. "I checked all the electives, but since the new semester has begun already, unfortunately it's slim pickings. Let's see. If I swap Spanish to seventh period, this could work. And you could start today—next period, if you skedaddle. How does being a student aide in the Life Skills classroom sound?"

"What would I be doing?" I asked, thinking I could stand to learn a few life skills myself.

"Helping kids with different needs."

Tutoring. Chill. "Sounds fantastic. Really! Thank you!"

Ms. Nguyen tapped her pen and nodded. "Feels like a good fit. You're that guy who can talk to anyone, unlike *some* student athletes I know."

"Correction: former student athlete." A mountain of weight lifted from my shoulders.

I never say this out loud—too afraid to jinx my good luck—but was I celebrating internally? Hell, yes! As Ms. Nguyen handed me the schedule change, I may have even done a little victory dance.

I took a detour to the gym building so I could clear out my locker before tonight's game. I ducked past Zach and a few other basketball players. They were laughing about a girl on the track team whose pubes were visible when she did crunches. Cruel jokes—and looking up girls' shorts—I wouldn't miss.

Out of the corner of my eye, I saw Zach slam shut his locker and give the combo lock an impressive spin before he and his buddies piled out. I finished emptying my locker and, in a lame attempt to spin my own lock, inadvertently tweaked my wrist. Massaging my metacarpals and concerned about soft tissue damage, I hurried away in search of the Life Skills classroom.

Turning a corner in an unfamiliar hallway, I almost bumped into Connor.

"You giving your hand a hand job?" he joked.

I gave him a courtesy laugh and stopped rubbing my sore wrist.

Why couldn't I be more like my cousin? Nothing rattled him. Two years ago, when Hojun was struck by a hit-and-run driver, Connor had stayed by his side until the paramedics showed up. That day took its toll on all of us who knew Hojun, only Connor never actually seemed destroyed by losing him—not like I was. For as long as I could remember, I'd expected bad things to happen. Hojun's death just solidified that belief.

The passing bell rang.

"Later, man," I mumbled before taking a sharp turn down a stairwell, feeling lost in more ways than one. As I trotted down the stairs, I heard a man's loud voice echo from below.

"*Goddamn it*, Andrew!"

I stopped in my tracks.

"How many times do I need to explain this to you?" the voice barked. "Are you stupid? Weak? Are you a weak person?"

Another voice replied—a kid. A scared kid. "I'm sorry."

"This is important! If you screw this up, our entire family suffers."

I couldn't make out the rest, but I froze in place, not wanting any part of that argument. After a while, I ventured noiselessly down the stairs, thinking the coast was clear. It wasn't.

A kid sat slumped on the last step, his head in his hands, silently crying.

I walked around him, trying to give him space. When he looked up, his eyes were bloodshot and wet. He turned away in a flash, but not before I recognized him: Andy Jennings. Someone—his dad, probably—had just ripped him a new one.

I finally found Life Skills class in a quiet corridor beyond the textbook room. Just as I was about to push open the door, I heard a long wail that sputtered into silence. I worried someone had burst their appendix or been rejected from their "reach" school.

On edge, I swung open the door.

Seven or eight students, all boys, crowded around a table. They sounded more like twenty kids, all talking at once. One of them caught my eye: a short kid with an unusually small head. Another had an iPad set up—a good-looking dude, but clearly too old for high school. The iPad guy's hands moved nonstop, touching his tab-let, his ear, his T-shirt. He glanced at the screen, then at a bottle of water, then at his fingers, like he was counting them or something. He made a repetitive noise that sounded like *tree*.

My knees felt weak, and I leaned against the door for support. The door was wood, so I knocked on it for luck. It made me feel better—no, more than that. It bestowed mythic protection against somehow ending up like iPad Guy.

Seated cross-legged on top of her desk and wearing old leather sandals was Ms. Hinojosa, the teacher. She waved me over, and the beaded bracelets stacked halfway up her arms made a clacking sound.

I peeled myself off the door and shuffled in Ms. Hinojosa's direc-tion, passing two adults who were obviously *real* aides. One had a Russian accent and appeared to be translating for iPad Guy, whose eyes landed on me for a split second before jumping elsewhere.

Behind Ms. Hinojosa's desk was an open door to an adjacent supply room where a girl hunched over, gathering notebooks. Sun-glasses were perched on her head, pushing blue bangs off her face. When she straightened, I recognized her from earlier at the park: the mysterious Girl in Black.

She strode over the threshold with an armful of notebooks and right past me, obviously uninterested.

Ms. Hinojosa, on the other hand, greeted me. "Did you need Google Maps to find us? Everyone does. We're so glad you're here." She beamed at her class. "Hey, everybody." The noise magically died down. "We have a new student aide. He's super excited to be here. Welcome, Braden!"

One kid mumbled, "Welcome, Braden."

Another kid clapped.

Then someone began wailing.

"Hey." I slapped on a smile and shifted my weight from one foot to the other, causing the wood floor to creak. I didn't know what to do with my hands, so I put them in my front pockets. "Hi."

Ms. Hinojosa nodded toward the Girl in Black. "You can shadow Rae today. She'll give you the lay of the land. And I'm always here when you have questions."

I had a million of them: *How much land we talking? Can you turn up the AC? Will that crying kid ever quit? If these are my fellow students, why haven't I ever seen them before?*

My scalp felt itchy.

A husky, freckled kid in a Spiderman T-shirt approached me. "Who do you like better?" he asked. "Batman or Spiderman?"

Shadowing him was the other adult aide, a college-aged guy with a beard and a UCLA hoodie. "Hey, man, how about introducing yourself? Like, 'I'm Simon. What's your name?'"

The Spiderman boy stuck out his hand. "I'm Simon. Who do you like better? Batman or Spiderman?"

"Spidey."

The aide grinned at me. "Welcome to Life Skills, Braden. I'm Noah, and now you've met . . . ."

Simon shoved his phone in my face. On the screen was a scene from one of the *Spiderman* movies, where Mary Jane screams. Simon laughed like a maniac, which caused me to crack up too.

"You're weird." The Girl in Black had materialized by my side. "You're going to do great here."

"Okayyyy," I said. Just a few hours earlier, she'd accused me of having low self-esteem because I apologized for bumping into her. We stood there, awkward. "I'm Braden."

"Yes. Ms. Hinojosa established that." Her voice was flat, and she had trouble looking me in the eye, like she found me mildly repulsive.

"So, what happens in here, uh—Rae? Is there a syllabus? What are we supposed to do?"

Rae answered quickly. "That's three questions."

I blinked a few times, not sure how to respond. Did she have some sort of rule about questions? Or did she just find me boring?

She started to gently scratch at her hip with dark blue fingernails, hiking up her sweatshirt a few inches. On her smooth, pale skin was what looked like a fresh tattoo that said, in curling script, *T-Rex*.

"Oh, nice tattoo," I said, like all my friends were getting inked. "What's it mean?" I deliberately kept it to *one* question.

"T-Rex was the name of my first dog." She swiped at her phone until the screen showed a photo of a little black mutt. "He died in October." Then she scrolled down to a photo of a white fluffball.

"Very cute," I said. "What's *his* name?"

"Brontosaurus."

"You've got a thing for dinosaurs, don't ya?" When she didn't answer, I nervously launched into a description of my robotic farting dinosaur from preschool.

Rae must have thought I was incredibly immature, because she didn't even crack a smile. She just picked at her shirt collar. "I only call my dog Brontosaurus when he's naughty," she said finally. "His full name is Fredrickson Noodle Brontosaurus. Noodle for short."

"My pit bull's name is Sparkle." I rolled my eyes and pulled up a photo on my phone. "My sister's idea. I call her Spark."

Rae's eyes met mine. "I absolutely love bully breeds. Especially pit bulls." Then she glanced down again, scrolling through my photos of Spark.

"I volunteer a couple times a month at a dog rescue," I said.

Her face lit up. She rattled off a bunch of statistics—how many dogs were in shelters, how many were euthanized—and character traits of bully breeds.

I smiled. "Did you write the pit bull section for Wikipedia?"

"No." She didn't seem to get that I was trying to make a joke.

Across the room, Simon kept tapping a boy's shoulder. Another kid picked something from his ear and ate it. I fumbled in my backpack for hand sanitizer and squirted a glob into my palm, attempting to wipe away the ick factor.

At the table, iPad Guy spread his fingers and fluttered his hand. "What's his deal?" I asked Rae, lifting my chin toward him.

She just looked at me. "His deal?"

I shrugged. "He doesn't talk?"

"Thirty percent of people on the spectrum are nonverbal like Jerome."

On the spectrum. She was talking about the autism spectrum. "So, he"—I corrected myself—"so, Jerome *can't* talk?"

"Sometimes he'll say a word or two when he's stimming."

That was a new one. "Stimming?" I asked.

"Flapping his hands. Self-soothing when he's anxious. Some auties will rock or spin or repeat words to help relieve their stress." She shrugged. "It's a way we regulate. As long as he isn't hurting himself, it's perfectly acceptable."

How she remained so calm was a complete mystery to me. "I've got to be honest. It's way too intense here for me. I mean, I don't know how long you've been doing this, coming to the Life Skills room, but I don't think I can handle being around these kids."

"*I'm* one of these kids."

"Wait. What?" I asked, genuinely confused.

"I'm autistic."

Mushroom cloud. Death and destruction.

She had said it so matter-of-factly: *I'm autistic.* But she didn't look autistic—not that I knew what someone who's autistic was supposed to look like. She was actually kind of . . . hot.

But I did know for certain that she wasn't trying to make a joke. I mumbled an apology, feeling just awful, and waited for her to flip out.

Another craptastrophy.

4

RAE

om was late. Again. There was no point bitching about it. I'd stopped bothering with that the day she innocently suggested I get a ride from a friend's mother.

Mom, Mom, Mom. I shook my head. She still thought I should be that girl with a posse of friends. As if that could ever happen.

Resigned to my wait, I sat on the low brick wall by the athletic field. Nearby, a herd of sheep handed out flyers to students leaving school for the day and parents waiting at the curb. "Save our school! Save our school!" Their mindless bleating made my hair follicles ache.

Their leader looked like he belonged on a yacht, with a pressed, pastel polo shirt and freckles scattered across his nose. When he thrust a flyer into my hands, I recognized him from the stage crew: Andrew Jennings.

"Why'd you give one to her?" a girl next to him sneered.

"Don't you know who her mother is?" Andrew replied. "Councilwoman Wolf." He pointed to the new gym facility across the street, the one with my family's name written across it in hideously large letters: WOLF FAMILY FITNESS CENTER.

The girl's eyes got wide. "Your mom's the enemy," she said to me. "You get that, right?"

I struggled to read her meaning. Sarcasm? Metaphor? I scanned the flyer for context clues. Tacky clip art of oil wells and dollar signs bordered the text, which supported a project that would bring "millions of dollars" to the school district. The flyer listed the merits of a new club called Save Our School that was looking for members. Andrew Jennings was president.

Of course he was.

When I looked up from the flyer, he shrugged and said, "We have a few weeks before the vote. It'd be cool if we could be on the same team, doing something to actually make a difference around here."

It clicked.

Mom was skeptical of the "drill, baby, drill" executives at the petroleum company, who kept touting the supposed benefits of resurrecting that retired oil and gas rig. She was worried about its effects on the school and the medical high-rise on the other side. Others, like Mr. Jennings—and Andrew, apparently—were vocally supportive.

Andrew studied me. Even though his dad served on the city council with my mom, we had rarely exchanged more than a "hi" before.

"What are you gawking at?" I snapped, peeking over the rim of my sunglasses. Then I pulled on my headphones as Andrew and his bitchy friend moved on down the sidewalk. The exchange had left me twitchy.

Seeking escape, I drew my phone from my pocket and went to the Angel City Dog Rescue website. The dogs' sweet smiles and eager eyes captivated me as usual. Every evening, I reposted pit bull listings on my social media. Scrolling through photos didn't substitute for petting a warm, breathing animal, but it certainly helped.

Reading through the current adoptable dog list, I stopped on a pit bull with crooked teeth and lopsided ears. The description said her name was Georgina, and she urgently needed a volunteer to pull her from a San Pedro shelter. She was in danger of being euthanized within forty-eight hours.

Using Google Maps, I calculated it would take fifty-two minutes to get there. There was no time to waste.

My brain flung me back to earlier that day: Braden had a pit bull, and he volunteered with rescue dogs. Could he drive me to San Pedro? Would he foster a dog?

Then my brain dumped me back in the present. *Yeah, right*, it said. I'd started to think Braden was okay, but after I told him I was autistic, he got really quiet. Now I didn't know what to think.

After what had happened with my last boyfriend, my therapist told me to take it slow. I trusted Jill. I just didn't always listen to her.

Like when she'd asked me if Zach had really been a boyfriend. I mean, he didn't take me on dates—we just had a thing. He invited me over after school a few times, and we'd make quesadillas in the toaster oven. Amazingly, he had the brand of cheese I really like. After our snack, he'd faithfully honor my request to play the same Rolling Stones songs over and over on his electric guitar, which he thought was funny and not weird. Then we'd end up naked.

The smell of the detergent his mom used on the sheets gave me a headache, so we just got to it. When we were done, I didn't linger. Three weeks later, he stopped asking me over after school, and I quit listening to the Rolling Stones.

Somebody tugged off my headphones. Unsettling traffic noises and jarring voices invaded my head as I crash-landed into the present.

A soft voice calmed me. "You've got resting bitch face." Arman blinked at me with his amber-colored wolf eyes and handed back the headphones.

I pressed my lips together in an effort to be more expressive. There: relaxed grin, no teeth showing.

Arman nodded. "Better." Then he cocked his head toward the gym, where a stocky guy in a baseball uniform leaned against the railing—Miguel something. "Hotness. And yes, my kind."

"He's gay?" I asked.

"Not officially. But he likes what he sees."

"How can you tell?"

Arman shrugged. "I just can."

"If he likes you and you like him, why can't you guys just tell each other?"

"How do you think the guys in the locker room would feel if they knew? They'd be all weirded out, wondering, 'Ooh, is Miguel looking at me?' That would just about kill him."

Neurotypicals make life so much harder than it needs to be.

When Mom finally pulled up to the curb in her shiny, white Tesla, I scooped up my backpack and slumped into the car.

"Arman! It's been a while. How was spring break?" Mom always knew what to say. "I hope you had a Fast Pass for Disneyland."

Arman complimented her outfit: a fitted white blazer with a flowery scarf and designer jeans. People loved my mom, always telling her she was "reverse aging."

While they chit-chatted, I closed my eyes and wished for a girl like me to hang out with—a friend who knew what it was like to be me. As much as I loved, loved, loved Arman, he didn't know what it was like to miss the joke, to be hopeless about reading the room.

"I'm tired," I interrupted. "Can we please go?"

Mom started to object, but Arman waved his hand, jingling his car keys. "That's okay."

As he turned in the direction of student parking, Mom asked me, "Hey, did you ever finish that driver's ed course?"

Ugh. "I'm tired!" I said instead of answering. I had begun the online course over break, but it had bored me to tears.

Mom sighed and carefully pulled into traffic. "Well, I'm starved. Should we grab something to eat?"

"Mom, do we have time to drive to San Pedro?" I asked, turning up the AC.

She glanced at me. "What's in San Pedro?"

"An animal shelter." I showed her the photo of Georgina. "She loves other dogs."

Mom took a deep breath and turned her gaze back to the road. "We can discuss this at Burger Lounge."

I closed my eyes and sighed dramatically, letting the cool air hit my face.

"And bring a to-go patty home for Noodle?"

Now, that was something I couldn't say no to.

At Burger Lounge we found a quiet outdoor table. I dipped a french fry into the watery ketchup. "The shelter closes at five," I reminded her.

"You know how hard it is for me to say no to you." Mom sipped her iced tea. "What's wrong with the fries?"

I found a ketchup-free fry and nibbled on it. "She's going to die if we don't do something."

"We already have a dog, Rae. I'm sorry. I just have too much on my plate."

I threw the half-eaten fry on my plate. Ketchup splattered on the table. "Georgina's going to die. And it's going to be your fault!" I stood up.

Mom jumped to her feet too, quickly checking her jacket for stains. Then she started wrapping the food to go. Her phone rang, and she ignored it. "You have such a huge heart. I wish I could help you save every dog."

"I'd settle for one," I seethed. "Georgina."

We walked back to the car, and Mom greeted people along the way—mostly folks who recognized her from city council.

After a few minutes, Mom tried again. "Let's talk about the theater production. I was hoping you would invite your father."

"Nope." As if I wasn't furious enough over her refusing to save a dog, now she wanted me to deal with Dad. "Why do you want to suck up to him after he's been such a jerk?"

Mom flinched. "We all make mistakes. You can't punish him for the rest of his life."

Boy, was she wrong about that.

"It's just . . . I think it would be good for you, too . . . ." Mom's voice trailed off. When I looked over, she was staring down at my hip. My sweatshirt had ridden up with the seatbelt. I quickly pulled it back down, but it was too late. She'd seen my *T-Rex* tattoo.

"Why didn't you ask me before you did that?" There was an edge to her voice. Her phone rang again. She muted it.

"Duh. I knew you'd say no."

She leaned in to take a closer look. "Where'd it come from?"

"Black Diamond Tattoo in Venice. Five stars on Yelp. I took the Metro."

Mom's shoulders sagged.

"The tattoo artist talked about how values don't change, so if it's the right tattoo, it'll never go out of style."

"Did you discuss this with Jill?"

I pushed my sunglasses back on top of my head. "Theoretically." My therapist would understand that I wanted to make my own decisions.

Mom just shook her head.

When we finally got home, she changed into workout clothes. Gym time always improved her mood.

"Mommy?" I stopped her at the front door and handed her the Save Our School flyer. "You might want to see this."

She frowned as she read it. "Please tell me you're not in this . . . this . . . club."

I snorted. "Give me a little credit."

Mom set her gym bag on the floor. "Rae. Hear me out. I want us to have a serious talk about residential boarding schools."

"Not again," I sighed.

We had the money. My grandparents on Mom's side had owned a coin-operated laundry chain. When they died, it all went to Mom because she's an only child. All that money paid for the house, my therapy, my mom's Tesla. Mom had an economics degree from UCLA, but she quit her studio job when I was three years old—about five minutes after my autism spectrum disorder diagnosis.

"Wait," I said. "Is this because of the tattoo?"

"You went behind my back," Mom said sternly. "You betrayed my trust."

"Mom, I have impulse control issues."

She took a deep breath. "I know this is difficult to hear, honey. But we must make a change."

I loved the way she said *we*—as if I had any say in the matter.

5

BRADEN

Sports and emotions go together like spaghetti and meatballs. That's what Dad liked to say. And anyone who tells you *It's just a game* is full of shit.

I thought about this bit of wisdom during lunch period in the journalism room, as I chewed on a PB&J. Beside me, Lucas read aloud from my latest *Neon Vikings* piece, "Parents and Coaches— No Love Connection":

> Although crazy parents are found everywhere, youth sports attract them like nothing else. The most common parent complaint: "Coach isn't being fair to my child!" closely followed by "Coach criticizes my child!" and "Coach plays favorites!"
>
> But as Coach Sanchez says, "It's not my job to make parents happy. If I cared about everyone liking me, I would've been the ice cream man."

Lucas snorted, attracting the attention of the *Neon Vikings* news editor, Naomi. She beckoned to us from her perch on the prized, faded couch in the back of the room, where she huddled around a tablet alongside Shanice, the features editor, and Alicia, the photographer.

"Madame President," I said, saluting her.

Naomi adjusted her wire-rimmed glasses. "Here." She passed me the tablet, and Lucas and I sat on the arm of the couch.

It was a YouTube video titled "Saving Our School." Andy Jennings, in a wrinkle-free, button-down shirt, was giving an enthusiastic school tour of runaway weeds, backed-up toilets, and busted lockers while explaining how funds from the nearby recommissioned oil and gas tower could fix . . . well, everything.

Alicia—whose eyelashes were so long, I thought she'd stab herself with a viewfinder—asked, "Are his dress shirts supposed to symbolize credibility? Social status?"

Naomi cleaned the lenses of her glasses. "Maybe it was a two-for-one sale."

I wasn't surprised by their disdain. I mean, one hundred percent sure, the school needed attention. But Pac Crest was no slum. Plus, on our apathetic campus, I didn't see much of a future for a Save Our School club.

"Aside from his style . . . ." Shanice brushed her braids aside. "Kids lobbying to ramp up an oil and gas rig? Really?"

Lucas yawned. "Can we go back to—"

I filled in the blank. "Procrasturbating?"

Naomi frowned. "*Bisho'ur!*"

"What'd you call me?" I asked.

Naomi could swear in four languages. "Idiot. In Farsi. But I meant it in an endearing way."

"Thank god, we're on sports," Lucas muttered.

The passing bell rang, and everyone started to clear out while I stood motionless. Just one more period—Spanish—and I would be done for the day. Normally, after seventh period, I'd head down to the locker room and change into my practice gear for basketball. Since I'd swapped basketball to add Life Skills in third period, though, technically I would be done for the day.

Did I enjoy being unburdened? Of course not.

I'd been rash yesterday. I hadn't factored in the unknown reality: that after dropping the team, I'd be expected to care for special needs kids—something I knew nothing about. How was *I* supposed to be responsible for other human beings? I could barely manage my own life.

A wave of dizziness washed over me.

Lucas picked something out of his teeth. "Folks are out of town."

"Again?" I replied. The Cruzes did business in the Philippines—exporting technology or importing supplements or something. I could never remember.

Lucas nodded. "Swing by after practice?"

I hadn't told him yet—about being a quitter. My lungs shrank at the thought, and I coughed.

Lucas looked alarmed. "Dude! Try not to die."

I coughed again. Perhaps it wasn't just the thought of being a quitter, but a life-threatening allergic reaction that impaired breathing. Perhaps the strawberry jelly on my PB&J was causing anaphylaxis.

I cleared my throat, then forced a smile. "All good!" I croaked.

Lucas's family lived in an apartment one mile south and five million dollars shy of the Starline celebrity bus route. Our school was like that: filled with rich kids and poor kids and everything in between.

Lucas had recklessly left the front door ajar. Inside, I kicked cat toys out of the way and followed the sound of chewing. I found

Lucas in the kitchen, eating onion rings from a fast-food cup. Surprised to see me, he asked, "Practice end early?"

Whatever energy I had left, all seemed to drain out. I sagged into the seat beside him. "Actually, I quit basketball."

"For real?"

I nodded.

Neither of us said much for a minute. Finally, Lucas peered at me through those thick glass lenses and said, "You never really liked it, huh?"

I shook my head. Was it that obvious? Lucas was being so chill about the whole thing, I instantly brightened.

"Then you made a good move," he said, taking a covered plastic plate out of the refrigerator.

I wanted to hug him. Which would've been weird.

Stuck to the refrigerator was a photograph of a water buffalo that seemed to be staring at me. Above it was a to-do list:

Change bathroom bulb

Buy apples

Call manager—freezer not cold

"Why the buffalo?" I asked.

"It's a carabao, the Philippine national animal," Lucas answered. "My sister thinks they're cute."

My eyes flicked up. Lucas's older sister, Sally, rarely spoke to me. As usual, her bedroom door was closed. I only knew two things about her, from what Lucas had told me: She liked to get wasted, and she was her parents' favorite.

The microwave dinged, and Lucas removed the plastic plate.

"I don't think you're supposed to microwave plastic."

"Maybe not," he said, folding leftover chow fun into a slice of pizza. "But I'm conserving water by not washing dishes." He held up his food. "Want some?"

"Nah, I'm good."

A claws-on-cloth sound got my attention. Lucas's cat, Masulta, had jumped onto the sofa and was using it as a scratching post. The cushions looked like string cheese.

In between bites, Lucas commented on the Dodgers, and I complained about another Spurs defeat. As soon as Lucas finished his food, he struck a match and lit a cigarette.

"Seriously? Do you want to kill yourself?" I remarked.

"I don't think so."

"And what about secondhand smoke? You want to kill *me?*" I opened the kitchen window for fresh air, and a piece of peeling paint fell to the sill. "Oh, sorry!" I picked up the paint chip and attempted to stick it back on the window frame.

"The lead in that paint is more dangerous than nicotine," Lucas murmured between puffs. "It effs up your nervous system."

"Oh, god!" I flicked the chip. It struck Lucas in the chest. "Can we just finish the page layout before I'm Code Blue?"

"Chill, Braden. Unless you eat the paint, or crush it and inhale the dust, you're safe!"

Dust? This place had dust everywhere—the floors, the glass windows, even the refrigerator. I stared at the carabao photo, knowing I'd never see a real one because my nervous system was disintegrating, cell by cell.

Lucas tamped his cigarette into a coffee cup and opened his laptop. "Observe." He entered his student ID number and his grades appeared onscreen: A in Advanced Journalism, the rest B's and C's.

I clapped him on the back. "Congratulations, you win Slacker of the Year. Done amusing yourself?"

Lucas clicked more keys. His grades morphed to straight A's. "I'm sort of proud of this." He didn't mean the fabricated grades. His specialty was stupid stuff like commandeering the sound system at Baja's Tacos so he could change the play list from mariachi to rap. School servers were a new and disturbing target.

"Change it back, hacker boy. Before you're expelled."

His thick fingers pushed keys and—poof!—his real grades reappeared. "Grades don't guarantee a happy life." He blew a smoke ring. "I want to have some fun before I die. And just like you, I want to be rich."

"When did I say that?" I waved my hand around in a feeble attempt to clear the air.

"If I do get rich, I want to fly in a private jet and own the Packers."

"I'll never understand your fascination with Green Bay."

The conversation turned to the *Neon Vikings* sports page, and for a while we focused on our layout for the next issue. When we were satisfied, I packed up. I was just preparing to head home when Sally's bedroom door opened.

The skunky smell of weed invaded the air. Sally slinked out, wearing short shorts as she usually did, seven days a week. Not that I had a problem with that.

"Hey," I said, wondering if my nervous system breakdown was visible to outsiders yet.

"Hey." She brushed past me and squeezed Lucas's shoulder. "Can I get a ride to Starbucks?" He nodded, and she retreated to the bedroom, softly closing the door.

"She just dropped out of school," Lucas said, sounding uncharacteristically down. That really threw me. I had never met a college dropout. "Without a student visa, she could lose her green card."

I stared at Sally's closed door. "What's up with that? She in a hurry to fly back to Manila to do laps in the Pasig River?"

Lucas's shoulders relaxed, and he cracked a smile.

I motioned to his computer. "And by the way, hacker boy, you shouldn't be taking any chances yourself."

6
RAE

My 504 plan—which is how federally funded public schools, teachers, and parents guarantee certain accommodations for students—gave me perks: Extra time for tests. A laptop for taking notes. Preferential seating at the front of the class. That might have worked in fourth grade. Now I sat in the last row, next to a shy girl named Souraya, putting as much distance as possible between me and Ms. Sauer, the English teacher. Ms. Sauer thought I was a mental case. I thought she was a bitch.

Some problems don't have 504 plans.

That didn't deter me from trying in English, and I tried everything: I tried sleeping through class, cutting class . . . I even tried reading dog training manuals in class. Those weren't on the syllabus, so it didn't work out.

Logic dictated that reading actual assignments might please Ms. Sauer. I had to admit, *Educated* was an excellent memoir. It was interesting to read someone's personal history and see how they felt about their own life. I'd often thought about writing a blog on how I felt about my life as an autistic person.

"Tara Westover didn't attend school until she was seventeen, the age most of you are now," Ms. Sauer lectured. "With no money and limited resources, how does her journey fit into the concept of the American dream?"

My hand shot up in the air, and I started talking before Ms. Sauer called on anyone. This happens a lot. My brain works faster than my mouth, so the second an idea pops into my mind, I have to express it.

Ms. Sauer ignored me and called on Andrew Jennings, who sat in the row to my right. No matter how many times that happened, it was still so embarrassing.

"She had hope?" Andrew guessed.

Ms. Sauer nodded her approval.

I stretched my hand up again, desperate to get her attention.

She called on the girl beside me, wearing a cheerleader's uniform—the same girl who, weeks earlier, had taped a *Kick Me* note to my back. "Even though it seemed impossible," the cheerleader said, "Tara was fearless in pursing the American dream."

Pursing. I sighed heavily.

Ms. Sauer gestured to me. "Rae?"

Finally. I turned to the cheerleader. "I think you mean 'pursuing.' I make those mistakes too."

The cheerleader gave me a dark look as the other kids snickered.

I started to talk about Tara's isolation. Her shame. These were familiar to me. "Her determination to *pursue* a different path is pretty incredible since Tara's parents accused her of being a liar. But I question the whole American dream thing—"

"Your tone matters, Rae," Ms. Sauer interrupted me. "How you say things matters."

I frowned. "I thought if we could back up our points, then—"

"Stop!" she snapped.

The silence in the room told me the class was holding its collective breath, waiting for the inevitable showdown. After Mom's threat about boarding school, I didn't need a fight.

I shrank into my jean jacket and drew my legs up, hugging them to my chest to avoid the feeling of my legs hanging in front of the chair—normal for most people, but unnatural to me. I stared at the stupid laptop, which the 504 plan had promised would make my life better.

Andrew raised his hand again. "The American dream is making something from nothing. It's seeing an opportunity and grabbing it by the . . . whatever you grab when you see an opportunity." He moved his eyebrows up and down, which made the other boys hoot.

Ms. Sauer narrowed her eyes but remained silent. My "tone" had to be shut down, yet it was okay for other students to whistle and holler.

Andrew held up his hands. "Sorry! Dumb joke. But Tara moved out, got several degrees, and hit the bestseller list. *That's* the American dream."

"Getting diplomas isn't equivalent to achieving your dream," I blurted out. "She didn't fit in for a long time. She had to work at multiple jobs. She suffered."

"Maybe it's hard for you to get this, Rae, but she was *happy!*" Andrew said it like unhappiness was the only thing I could understand.

"Easy for you to say!" I snapped. "You're rich!"

Ms. Sauer tried interrupting me. "Rae—"

I wouldn't have it. "And powerful! You're the son of a politician."

"Says the daughter of a councilwoman who lives in a mansion," Andrew replied coolly.

The teacher stepped up to the lectern. "Our classroom community is based on respect. At the beginning of the year, everyone signed the Student Handbook Agreement."

My bra chafed my left shoulder blade, and I wanted to rip it off. Why was Ms. Sauer staring at me?

"And in it," Ms. Sauer droned on, "all of us agreed to foster an environment that encourages lively and *friendly* discourse. We park our attitudes at the door. Today, Rae, you didn't abide by the agreement. Unfortunately, I must ask that you please step outside to the vice principals' office." She looked at the ceiling for a moment and sighed. "All of us, and I do mean all, have some days that simply get away from us."

Her voice went right through me and made my teeth hurt. Andrew stared at me. The cheerleader glared. Only shy Souraya gave me a sympathetic look.

Ms. Sauer uncapped a dry erase pen and began scribbling the next day's assignment on the board. "Take time to reflect, Rae. I'm positive that when you return, you'll better monitor your tone to avoid making things unfriendly."

I had been dismissed.

My hands curled into fists. Ms. Sauer had no idea how unfriendly I felt at that moment.

The noxious odor from the pen drifted to my desk. The overhead lights pulsed. It was all getting to be dangerously too much. In times like this, I couldn't distinguish my personal issues from the situation around me. Tears stung my eyes, and I tried blinking them back. I didn't trust myself. I was a puzzle with pieces missing.

As I rushed to gather my books, my pen fell to the floor. Souraya picked it up and handed it to me. Her small act of kindness almost made me weep.

My mind was a whirlwind. I slunk out the door and dodged into the girls' bathroom, my secret sanctuary. How ticked would Mom be about me getting kicked out of class again? Would she dump me in Manhattan Beach at Dad's house? Or send me to a residential school?

I shrugged out of my jacket and reached inside my tank top to unclasp my bra. Then I slid it right off and stuffed it into my backpack along with my jacket. Immediately, I felt better. Not ready-to-face-the-vice-principal better, but the tears had dried up.

In the front pocket of my backpack, I found pomegranate lip balm and slathered it on my chapped lips. Then I uncapped a purple Sharpie and scribbled on the stall door:

MY BRAIN HAS TOO MANY TABS OPEN

7

BRADEN

had officially flip-flopped.

During homeroom, I nervously cracked my knuckles, earning me an *Eeewwww!* from Taylor—one of the popular girls from ASB, the associated student body. Her friend Kennedy, sitting behind me, gave my ear a sharp flick. First period, I could barely focus on the US History lecture as the minutes ticked down. After second-period Chemistry, I'd have to show up at Life Skills. But I didn't belong there. I had nothing to offer those kids.

When the passing bell rang, I decided to visit Ms. Nguyen in the vice principals' office, hoping she'd get me a hall pass for being late to Chem—twice in one week. Stepping through the doorway, I caught a flash of blue hair. There sat Rae in a corner, legs tucked beneath her, reading a book and nibbling from a bag of popcorn.

Just my luck. I hadn't noticed the girl all year, and now I was running into her more often than a striker pulls a hamstring. I searched the waiting area for a seat, praying she wouldn't ask what I was doing there.

"What are you doing here?" she asked between bites.

I had no time to concoct an excuse for my soon-to-be disappearance from Life Skills, so I casually pulled a test prep pamphlet from the receptionist's desk. "Debating SAT or ACT." I'd already taken the ACT. My scores were meh. None of this needed to be put out there. "You?"

"Got kicked out of class and sent to the vice principal."

The only time I'd been kicked out of class was in Hebrew school when I got caught playing FIFA on my phone. And that wasn't even like real school. "What happened?"

Rae thought about it a minute. "Ms. Sauer has it out for me."

"I have her fourth period. She's the worst!"

Rae shrugged and started reading again. She looked different somehow. Without the bulky black sweatshirt, I could see the smooth, bare skin of her arms and neck. Beneath her thin cotton tank top, I thought I detected the outline of a bare boob.

I quickly looked away, but Rae was already observing me, possibly trying to determine whether I was a certified pervert. I cleared my throat. "What are you reading?"

"*Until Tuesday.*" She held up the book so I could see the cover: a photo of a golden retriever holding military dog tags in its mouth. "It's by a retired Army vet, Luis Carlos Montalván. He had PTSD—post-traumatic stress disorder. One in five veterans has it. Symptoms can range from flashbacks to nausea to sweating to intense feelings of anxiety . . . ."

I had heard of PTSD, of course, but I didn't interrupt. I liked hearing her talk about it. She could've been describing me during midterms. Or whenever I reflected on my friend in heaven and the fact that he should not have died.

". . . and his service dog, Tuesday, saved his life." As Rae talked about Montalván and his service dog, her eyes lit up like before, when I'd first met her. She went on explaining how the dogs were trained and how she'd watched documentaries on wounded veterans. By the time she got to the part about how vets were matched with their dogs, I began to relax.

I set the test prep guide aside on a nearby table and lowered myself into the seat next to her. She leaned in closer, still talking. I could smell her body lotion, or maybe it was just her. Whatever it was, it made me a little crazy. I felt drunk.

"Service dogs aren't pets," she continued. "They've been trained to do certain things for people with disabilities . . . ."

My brain vaporized into clouds. I found it harder and harder to focus on what she was saying.

". . . so the dogs are taught to recognize when a vet is having a nightmare. They climb onto the bed and wake them up to comfort them . . . ."

I pulled myself together and started to ask how, but she didn't give me the chance. She was a motor-mouth, but I didn't mind.

". . . and they can even open drawers if a soldier's hands are blown off by an IED . . . ."

On second thought, maybe I did mind.

She ran her own hands almost lovingly over the book cover. "When I turn eighteen, I'm going to get certified so I can become a trainer."

Rae was smart. She was pretty. She had a hole in her pajama pants. When she paused to take a breath, I asked, "Can I borrow the book when you're done?"

"Oh, I've read it three times." She handed me the book. "Take it."

"Wow! Thank you." I flipped through the pages. "Listen. I'm sorry about before . . . if I was being a jackass . . . ."

Rae looked totally confused.

"In Life Skills." I felt my face flush. "I didn't realize about the . . . how you were . . . I mean, are . . . on the spectrum. God, I sound like an idiot."

"Not at all," she said. "You didn't know. Now you do. It's what I am and how I think. Basically, it's how my brain works. It's everything that happens to me, from walking to peeing."

I didn't know what to say to that.

"Even my own mom doesn't totally get it." Rae repositioned her feet and stared at the floor. "She thinks I should tell people I'm twice-exceptional instead of calling myself autistic. She thinks people will judge me."

I had to agree with her mom, but I kept my trap shut. Plenty of jerks at school would look down their snooty noses at me for simply talking to Rae. At that moment, I couldn't have cared less.

She held out her bag of popcorn. "Want some?"

"Uh, thanks." I chewed thoughtfully, not knowing what to say but not wanting the conversation to stall out.

"Arman says I'm an oversharer."

"Arman?" I asked, feeling jealous and disappointed at the same time. "Is he, like, your boyfriend?"

"Arman's gay." She unzipped her backpack and pulled out a jean jacket. "We're in Drama Lab, and he's my best friend. I don't have a boyfriend. Zach broke up with me over spring break."

I reached for another handful of popcorn, suddenly feeling much, much better. "Zach Gotleib? Baller with the big ego?"

Rae nodded and busied herself pulling on her jacket.

Zach was team captain, point guard, presumed scholar-athlete of the year. And didn't we all know it. He went through girls like baseball players went through a bag of sunflower seeds: He'd chew on them a while and then spit out the shells when he got bored.

I reached for more popcorn. "Well, you should know something about Zach. He's a prime example of the penis inversion theory."

That got her attention. She quit tugging the jacket tighter around her body.

"It goes something like this: The bigger the ego, the smaller the penis."

Rae broke into the most gorgeous smile, and all I wanted to do was think of things to say so she'd do it again. Except I didn't have the chance.

Ms. Nguyen popped her head out of her office. "Hi, Braden! Come on in."

Rae picked up the test prep guide I'd forgotten all about and handed it to me. "Good luck with testing."

"See you at Life Skills!" I waved.

And just like that, I had flip-flopped again.

I didn't bother to sit down in Ms. Nguyen's office. "Just saying thanks for helping me with my schedule. I think being a student aide is going to work out."

Ms. Nguyen made a big deal out of it as she wrote me the pass back to second period, but I barely heard a word she said. On my way out the door, I saw a poster on her wall that said: *Keep going! You might almost be there.*

Being superstitious, I thought it was a good sign.

8

Whenever Mom was right, it made me angry. Because if she was right, then that meant I must have been wrong. When she was wrong, it also made me angry. She was my mom, so she should know better.

When she was half right, I was furious.

She'd been half right about Life Skills class. "You'd be the only girl," she had warned me. "And those boys aren't in mainstream classes. I just don't understand why you want to be there. It's not the right fit." She had talked to the counselors at school and conferred with my educational consultant. It didn't matter. I wanted to be in that classroom.

Mom still bit her tongue every time the subject came up. She was forever choking back the word *high-functioning*. But whatever I'd hoped for—self-understanding, learning to trust myself, becoming an adult—this class wasn't making it happen. Instead, I basically helped Ms. Hinojosa (who I adored) and dealt with odd noises and strange smells (which I abhorred).

So there I was again, hiding out in the supply room. Not

fitting in at Life Skills class, just like Mom predicted. I could have screamed in frustration. Other than Arman, I didn't fit in with neurotypicals either.

Through the supply room door, I heard muffled voices: Ms. Hinojosa and Braden, talking by her desk. I knew I should get out there, but I really didn't have the bandwidth to deal with it.

My therapist Jill told me to write things down when I was feeling overwhelmed. So I sat on a stepstool, pulled out my spiral notebook and my trusty purple Sharpie, and began to write:

Here is my theory about why auties and neurotypicals don't get along.

You (a neurotypical) ask me, "What's up?"

I think you're asking me to explain whatever it is I'm doing, like reading a particular book. I offer tons of details, like who the author is and why the subject is of interest to me.

What you're actually asking me is: "Can I hang out with you?"

But I miss that social cue.

Yes, correct—I use the appropriate terms because I've done a lot of research on autism. Since I was a little kid, I've been in therapy to help me deal with existing in a world that doesn't get me.

Anyway, while I think I'm answering your question— "What's up?"—you're thinking: Rae doesn't like me.

Pretty messed up, right? Here I am, thinking I'm being polite by responding to your actual question, when all you hear is: Rae doesn't want to be friends.

So you neurotypicals think I'm cold and odd. IT'S ALL A MISERABLE MISCOMMUNICATION!

Most of you spend a lot of time talking about frivolous

things. I think 90 percent of your conversations can be translated as: Can we be friends?

Meanwhile, I'm still learning to give you the chance to ask questions and weigh in on what I've said. I get this wrong. All the time. And when you back away, I get super angry.

At you, mostly. Maybe that's not fair, but because you've moved on before I even have the chance to figure out what I did wrong, much less fix it, I get frustrated. I wish you would just say what you mean so I didn't have to read your mind!

And society thinks autistic people are the mentally ill ones.

Your awesome AutieFreak,

Rae Wolf

I'd been thinking that someday I could use my notes for a blog. I even had a name: AutieFreak.com.

Jill was right this time. Feeling better, I ventured out of the supply room.

"Guys, guys!" Ms. Hinojosa moved in front of the other Life Skills students to get their attention and handed me and Braden some recycled paper. "Today we are going to do a very cool art project."

Braden and I started placing paper at each spot at the table. He smiled at me, but I pretended I didn't notice. He seemed sweet, but Zach had been charming too. Now, whenever Zach passed me in the hallway, I felt humiliated. How stupid I'd been! I mean, the guy gives me a ride home a few times, and I let him put his hand down my pants? Half the time, I didn't know why I did the things I did. That's why I didn't trust myself now.

A voice jolted me. "Captain America!" Simon screamed, jumping up and down for Braden's attention. "Captain America!"

"Stop!" I snapped, my teeth on edge. If only I'd had two pillows, one to clamp over each ear.

Braden lifted a pretend TV remote and aimed it at Simon. "Volume control," he said with a lopsided smile.

Simon grinned, then whispered, "Captain America."

Grrrr!

I didn't want to like Braden. He slouched when he walked and used too much hand sanitizer. Then again, he loved pit bulls.

The boys followed Ms. Hinojosa to the center table. As she demonstrated the art project, I inched closer to Braden.

"Do you have a girlfriend?" I asked.

He paused. "Nope. Do you? Have a boyfriend, I mean."

"Nope," I said. "And I don't want one! Or a girlfriend!"

"Um, okay." Braden scratched his ear. "So, uh, why'd you ask if I had one?"

"Arman says I'm a defensive dater."

Braden leaned in too close, as though he was about to say something.

I cringed. "I have a thing about personal space." He backed off, and I relaxed. "Anyway, because of Zach, I need to better understand myself. No way I'm going to have any kind of serious relationship."

Braden rubbed his chin. "How about a not-serious one? Like, all we do when we see each other is tell dirty jokes and show each other funny dog memes?"

My stomach felt fluttery, and I couldn't possibly look Braden in the eye. I wasn't sure if he was serious or joking.

9

BRADEN

The boys in Life Skills were so excited to shred old papers, you'd have thought they had floor seats at a Lakers game. After Rae and I helped them with the recycled paper art project, Simon surprised me with his finished product: a card that said *To Captain America.*

"This is a keeper. Thank you!" I threw my backpack over my shoulder and smiled at Rae. "See you tomorrow?"

"Class doesn't meet tomorrow," she reminded me. She and the boys sometimes left campus for a job where they earned money serving food. "But they always argue over who does what job. I hate it there!"

"You don't *have* to go—"

"You don't understand," she snapped. "These guys are my tribe."

"Am *I* part of your tribe?" I joked, trying to get her to smile.

Her blank expression threw me. "Jerome and Simon and I have brains that are wired differently from yours. Like the way our amygdalas underperform."

"Don't think I don't know what you're doing." I waggled a finger. "You're throwing big words around to scare me away from being in your tribe."

The corner of her mouth twitched like she was holding back a smile. "You are so weird."

Fun fact: The amygdala, as it turns out, is an almond-shaped mass of gray matter that regulates emotions. And I needed to know that . . . why? Because it had to do with Rae, and I suddenly wanted to know everything about her, even her brain.

We hung out with Jerome the rest of class, which was interesting. He communicated through a special app on his iPad, where he moved photos, audio, and text around to make sentences, like *I+want+see+whales*. The app also had preloaded stories like "Waiting My Turn," but what Jerome loved was whales. Because of him, I decided to follow a few Instagram pages on humpbacks and orcas. Now I could stop wasting time on my main feed, comparing my life to other kids with hot girlfriends/killer quads/fill in the blank.

At the end of class, Ms. Hinojosa took me aside. "The kids really look up to you, Braden," she said. "You have such a good feel for people. How would you like to help out with the Special Olympics in Rosemead this Friday? I know it's last-minute, and you'd have to miss your morning classes."

"Are you doing it?" I asked Rae. She nodded, and I turned back to the teacher. "Count me in!"

Friday morning, I texted Rae the thought cloud and runner emojis. I got nothing back, not that I was too surprised. But when the bus to Rosemead arrived, the Life Skills boys, Ms. Hinojosa, and three aides—me included—boarded it without her.

"Um, should we be worried about Rae?" I asked Ms. Hinojosa again as we got on the freeway.

"The attendance office just confirmed that she came to school late. Kids oversleep. It happens." Ms. Hinojosa's words didn't comfort me. It meant Rae wasn't sick—just sick of me, probably.

As the bus drove along the freeway, the boys were nervous and excited, talking too loudly and snapping photos nonstop. No matter how many times Noah and I reminded them, they kept popping out of their seats.

At the sports complex, I texted Rae a few more times in between events. Nothing back.

On the ride home, the guys had mellowed out, but Rae still hadn't responded to my texts. With me being me, my mind went to the worst place: I got the distinct feeling that I had made up the entire thing about her liking me.

I knew Connor would give it to me straight, so once we got back to school, I met him at his usual lunch spot on the cafeteria patio. By the look of his Starbucks coffee cup, he'd already snuck off campus.

I got to the point. "She's somewhere on campus. Maybe eating lunch in the auditorium before Drama Lab?" I complained. "Which means she's avoiding me on purpose."

"If you really want to know my opinion," Connor replied, "I don't think this has anything to do with you."

"You don't know that!" I checked my phone. Still nothing.

"Awfulist! Can you stop?" Connor begged. "Stop chasing her."

I pocketed my phone. "Sorry! It just doesn't make sense. These boys are her tribe."

Connor stopped sipping his coffee. "Did you just say 'tribe'?"

I opened my sack lunch, which had spent the morning getting

smushed in the bottom of my backpack. The turkey sandwich now resembled a large, multicolored turd. I shot it into a nearby trash can.

"Look, I hate to tell you this, but you may never know why she didn't go," Connor said. "She's a girl. She probably had cramps. Or tickets to Stagecoach."

"I wanted to talk to her about this book she lent me," I whined. "And I was going to ask her out."

"Okay." Connor peeled the lid off his coffee. "That could still definitely happen."

Could. And the US *could* qualify for the World Cup. And climate change *could* be fake science.

Connor tried changing the subject. "Just want to say, I think it's really cool what you're doing with the special needs kids."

"It's no big deal." I shrugged. "Anyone could do it."

He wiped steamed foam off the side of his mouth. "I doubt that." He pressed something on his phone and handed me his earbuds. "New song. Want to hear it?"

My cousin barely kept track of his own class schedule, yet he could write amazing electronic music on some gizmo he'd bought online. This new song had a hypnotic quality. My mind began to float. It flashed on bodysurfing with Connor in Malibu. Riding my bike in Franklin Canyon. Practicing free throws with Hojun.

The song ended and I opened my eyes. "Amazing, as usual!"

Connor grinned.

"You still think much about Hojun?" I asked.

"Yeah. But I try not to because, like, it still bums me out."

"Does that work?"

"Not really."

When the bell rang, we wandered through the cafeteria, down the stairs, and outside to the front lawn, chatting about nothing.

Then Connor hooked an arm around my neck and steered me across the walkway, into the arts building.

"Wai—wai—wait." I dug my heels in. "What if she hates me for some reason?"

"Awfulist," he muttered.

We turned down a hallway plastered with posters for the upcoming spring musical, *The Drowsy Chaperone*. In the auditorium, drama kids were seated at various spots around the stage. The lights were dim, and it took me a second to see what was what and who was sitting on whose lap.

Pairs of students were reading lines to each other. A girl in flowery tights and combat boots stood up and began singing a duet with a boy with spiky blond hair. Two or three stage crew guys walked in the background, tweaking lights and checking the set. I caught eyes with one of them.

Andy Jennings—the YouTube sensation, Mr. Save Our School himself.

Unlike the other stage crew guys in their graphic T-shirts and baggy shorts, he wore a lavender button-down with sleeves rolled halfway up his forearms and a brown leather belt with a brass buckle shaped like a dollar sign. This was his kingdom, apparently, and he directed his stage crew subjects where to move the set pieces.

We nodded to each other the way you greet someone you've known for years but were never really friends with.

Finally, I found Rae.

I did a double take. She had changed her hair color from blue to black. She and a golden-skinned boy, wearing jeans so tight you could practically tell his religion, were leaning against the stage wall. I figured this was the "best friend," Arman. Rae said he was gay, but their legs were touching. Hey, maybe he'd changed his mind.

As we got closer, I tried for casual. "Hey, Rae."

Rae mumbled, "Hi." To me, I think. Hard to say since she seemed to be studying a small tear in her black Converse.

"Basketball Braden?" her friend asked. His voice was soft and breathy.

"Not anymore," I said, straightening my shoulders.

"*Neon Vikings*?" He snapped his fingers. "That's it. Journalism, right?"

I nodded. Now Rae was observing the set, the rows of seats—anything but me.

Her friend, on the other hand, was very animated. "I loved that last thing you wrote about the baseball team! It was so funny!"

The article, with the headline "How to Make Your High School Baseball Team," had included some helpful hints: *Show up. Keep your uniform clean. Memorize Coach's favorite coffee order.* Pac Crest hadn't posted a winning score all year.

Connor spoke up. "Braden's a funny guy. It runs in the family. I'm Connor, his cousin."

The corner of Rae's mouth twitched as she finally glanced at me and then Connor. "Braden played some of your songs for me."

"Oh, yeah?" Connor shifted his backpack from one shoulder to another, waiting for a compliment. It never came.

"Braden! Connor!" Arman offered his hand. "I'm Arman." We took turns shaking hands with him.

After an awkward silence, I turned to Rae. "What happened this morning? Did you forget the Special Olympics?" I cleared my throat. "Did you see my texts?"

Her eyes briefly shifted in my direction. "That's three questions."

I exhaled in pure frustration. "Did you forget the Special Olympics?"

"No."

Blammo! She was not into me. I nodded knowingly to Connor.

Rae shrugged. "I ditched."

"Of course, you did." Connor elbowed me in the ribs. "It's like, why should we spend the first eighteen years of our lives stuck in jail . . . I mean, school?"

Rae said nothing.

"And you probably don't catch any crap for it either. You're lucky your mom's on the city council." He did a half smile that most girls fell for.

Rae wasn't most girls. "I wouldn't call it lucky having to share your mom with thirty-five thousand people." Her voice had an edge.

Connor sputtered, "I just meant, you know, the Get Out of Jail Free card."

Rae stared at him like he was speaking Swahili.

Arman smiled good-naturedly. "It's complicated."

I just wanted things to go back to the way they'd been. I took a step forward.

Rae cringed. She actually *cringed*!

Instinctively, I took a half step back. I wanted to slap myself for forgetting about her personal space. "Do you think we can talk for a sec? In private?" I asked her.

"Nice meeting you." Connor bowed to Rae and Arman before nodding to me on his way out.

"Do you need me, love?" Arman asked Rae.

She took so long to respond, it went into extra innings. Finally, she shook her head. Arman waded off into a group of kids.

"You left me there alone," I said.

"Where?"

I rolled my eyes. "The Special Olympics!"

"That's not true. Coach Grant and Ms. Hinojosa were there." She reached over her shoulder and tugged on the back collar of her T-shirt.

"You don't do that to a friend. The boys kept asking for you. Plus, I was worried. Where were you, anyway?"

"Starbucks."

"I am on a bus bound for Rosemead. There's a space on the seat next to me. Simon wants to sit there. I tell him, no. That seat is saved for Rae. He's bummed, but I tell him I'll make it up to him. Then you don't show up." I swallowed hard. "Why can't you see this?"

Rae blinked.

"I'm thinking to myself, *Does Rae have appendicitis? An impacted wisdom tooth?*" I tried for charming. "'Does she still like me at all?'"

Rae tugged the tag on her shirt until it finally gave with a rip, leaving a hole the size of a quarter. "Mind-blindness."

"Excuse me?"

"It's impaired moral judgment associated with distinct neural systems."

I exhaled, trying to understand. And failing.

"Basically, I have a hard time imagining what another person feels." She said each word slowly and deliberately.

I crossed my arms, not sure what to think.

"I didn't understand that I would be letting you down." She touched my hand. She'd never done that before.

Her new hair color made her blue eyes stand out even more than usual. She held my gaze, something I knew was super diffi-cult for her.

I sighed. "Just . . . text me next time?"

"Next time?"

"I mean, if you have to cancel something."

She stared at me, uncomprehending.

"Something we have planned. Like the Special Olympics or in Life Skills."

"I dropped Life Skills," she said.

"What?" I couldn't hide my disappointment.

"I don't need that kind of support. It took me a while to process what I do need. I'm still figuring it out."

I suddenly hated life. "I finished *Until Tuesday*," I said, sounding pitiful.

"Great, right?"

"Yeah, the book was great. But I thought the dog saved his life."

Rae frowned, like I'd completely missed the point. "PTSD is unimaginably hard. For him to open up and share his story . . . it helps me put my own struggles in perspective. I understand how he felt: the hopelessness, the loneliness. The anger."

But the dog got left behind! I wanted to shout, even though the last thing I wanted to do was piss her off. I rubbed my eyes, trying to think of something intelligent to say. Turns out, I didn't have to. Rae was in full-on chatterpillar mode.

"Some people questioned why Montalván needed a support dog in the first place since he looked normal, or not disabled enough to warrant having one," she went on. "Do you know how many times I get asked if I'm really autistic? At one of my IEPs, an administrator wanted to cut back my services because I wasn't throwing tantrums."

"IEP?" I asked, barely able to keep up with the information overload. Not much penetrated my skull. I was still digesting the part about Rae dropping the one class we had had together.

"Individualized Education Program. It's a special educational plan for students with disabilities. I had one until I got my 504 plan—that was freshmen year." She uncapped a purple Sharpie and made a note in her spiral notebook. "Montalván's book really inspired me. I'm starting a blog." Her voice had changed. I could hear the excitement.

"That's great." I tried to sound enthusiastic. I had to take a chance, or she would write me off for good. "Maybe we can hang out sometime? I could read your stuff. You could read mine."

"Just as friends, though," she added quickly. Too quickly, in my opinion.

Before I could figure out my next move, the drama teacher summoned the class, and it was time for me to move on.

Rae's soft voice stopped me. "We *are* still friends, aren't we?"

I smiled at her. "You're not getting rid of me that easily."

Her mouth twitched as she tried to hold back a smile, and then she skipped away.

Feeling encouraged, I sidestepped around the corner and almost collided with Andy, who'd been standing in the shadows. He glared over my shoulder, looking like someone had killed his pet rat or stolen his duct tape.

It took me a moment to realize he was staring at Rae.

10

RAE

"**Y**ou're right." Arman nodded. "They do kind of look like sheep."

We were sitting on top of a table outside the cafeteria, where other students stood in clusters on the grass. Both Arman and I wore dark sunglasses because a) we looked cool, b) we could observe our fellow students undetected, and c) the glasses cut back on glare, which kept life a little less sensory-intensive for me.

"Except it's a diss to sheep," I insisted. "Sheep have to follow each other for safety. The ones that stand out will be attacked by wolves." Watching our classmates graze—I mean, mill around—I counted seven girls with the same pink designer handbag. "What's *their* excuse?"

Arman laughed softly. "Fear of attack by Rae *Wolf?*"

I smirked, fairly confident I got the joke this time. I could always count on Arman. Having him beside me was a little like wearing armor, if the armor were cushy and fluffy and purple.

As the sun rose higher in the sky, Arman and I lost the shade we'd been enjoying. The heat penetrated the black cotton of the

Grateful Dead T-shirt I'd swiped from my mom's drawer. Arman smoothed back his wavy hair and lifted his face to the sun.

"I'm happy for you," he said, pushing his sunglasses back on his head and closing his eyes. "Braden seems very nice."

The picnic table was hard, and I shifted my weight to one side to ease the pressure. "I told you, it's strictly platonic."

"That'll only make him want you more."

"That makes no sense." I pressed pomegranate lip balm across my lips. "I'm sticking to my No Boyfriend status. My therapist and I talked about how people who don't set boundaries don't value themselves."

Arman opened his eyes and gave me a quick kiss on the cheek. "There's a Persian saying: Only from the heart can you touch the sky."

"What does that mean?" I pictured a human heart, slick with blood, sailing through the clouds, raining red droplets.

"When you fall crazy-full-on-in-love, you know it because your ordinary life suddenly feels like a fairytale."

The first time Zach had kissed me, it didn't feel like a fairytale. For starters, I didn't like the texture of his tongue. He didn't get offended, and that was a ginormous relief. Alone in his room, he called me "boo"—which, looking back, was kind of cliché. Zach would ask: *Can I take off your bra? Can you get on top of me? Can I touch you down there?* I totally trusted him—a mistake. I got used to saying yes—another mistake. In fairytales, they live happily ever after. Here in the real world, not so much.

"There's something I've been meaning to tell you," Arman said, his voice soft and far away. "Rae?"

"Hmmm?" I wasn't paying close attention. My mind was a camera: one minute focused on how I missed running my fingers through Zach's hair, the next minute focused on a tall boy at another table who looked like Braden. It wasn't him. I sort of wished it were.

"Rae?"

I heard my name, more urgently now, and pulled my head from the fog.

Arman pointed to himself. "This is what a distraught teenager looks like. I'm giving you emotional clues here. I'm sort of having a day, and it'd be great if you were actually listening to me."

I nodded and gave what I hoped was a super-compassionate friend face. I'd learned this expression from studying Emma Stone movies. Pulling it off still took a lot of energy.

"You know I've been crushing on Spencer since . . . well, the dawn of time," Arman continued. "Saturday night we went to see a movie and then he invited me over. His parents have a pool, you know? With a pool house." Arman gazed off into the distance. "Spencer said he had a headache, so . . . I offered to give him a massage."

I shifted on the picnic table again. The wood felt like it was bull-dozing into my butt cheek.

Arman sighed. "One thing led to another, and . . . ." I waited for him to explain. He rubbed his eyes and pulled his sunglasses back down on his face. "And . . . I got it wrong. I thought it was the beginning of something deeper. Something personal, you know?"

I'd learned that in these situations, sometimes it was better not to say anything. Usually, the person would just keep talking and assume I was following everything they'd been saying.

"Now it's like it never happened," Arman continued. "Spencer won't look at me. He won't talk to me. He's already gotten back together with his ex-girlfriend."

"Why would he do that?" I asked. "I mean, if Spencer likes you—"

"God, Rae!" Arman shook his head. "Spencer doesn't want any-one to know that he's gay!"

"And everyone thinks people on the spectrum are weird," I complained.

"Honey, this isn't about you or being on the spectrum."

Ouch. That was mean. I was only trying to help. Seeing life through this prism was all I could do.

Arman sighed and rested his head on my shoulder. "My heart hurts," he said.

So does your head, I thought. His skull was surprisingly bony and heavy. I squirmed, and Arman sat up—that felt much better. But when he gave me a look and inched away, creating a space between us, I knew I'd missed something. "You don't need to . . ." I started to say.

Arman stared straight ahead and crossed his arms. I expected him to talk more about Spencer, but he didn't.

Before I could sort it out, a pack of stage crew dudes drifted toward our table. One of them had frizzy hair, and another had crooked teeth. The third was Andrew Jennings.

When they stopped in front of us, the one who needed orthodontics pulled a tiny box of matches from his pocket and slid it open. "If I toss this box in the air," he asked, "are you gonna, like, instantly count the matches that fall?"

"No," I answered.

"Then what's your special talent?"

I took that to mean that because I was on the spectrum, he assumed I possessed super abilities. "For most of us, it doesn't work like that."

"No talent. She's just a freak," Andrew said, pushing his friend to move along. We watched them walk away. They were laughing. At me.

Arman pulled his glasses lower on his face for a better look at them. "We should report them."

If we did, then the vice principal would call my mom. Who could say how I'd rate? Would Mom get it? Or would she lock me away in a residential treatment facility?

"It'd only make things worse," I replied.

But before I knew it, I had pushed off the table and bolted after Andrew, stubbing my pinky toe along the way.

"Excuse me!" I said loudly. "Excuse me!"

Andrew spun around.

"This can't be about English class, I hope. Remember, *I'm* the one who got sent to the vice principal's office." I was a little breathless from running after him. "I don't dislike you or anything."

"Get away from me, psycho!" Andrew hissed.

My mouth fell open.

Arman rushed to my side. "What the hell is your problem?" He leveled a fixed stare at Andrew.

Andrew rubbed his chin, like he was giving the question thought. "Ever ask yourself if there's a psycho gene? 'Cuz I think it runs in Rae's family." Then he locked his eyes on mine. "Only way your mom got elected is because she donated money to fix the gym. And the auditorium. And the library. Rich bitches get what they want."

I started shaking. "Are you calling my mother a 'rich bitch'?"

Nobody *ever* said a bad word about my mom. People constantly stopped her on the street to thank her for looking out for them. Gratitude Café named a quinoa salad after her.

My head felt like a spinner on one of the board games from Life Skills: pointing to my attackers . . . pointing to my pinky toe, swelling in my old Converse . . . then a blur as the pointer spun again, landing on myself as a preschooler.

Mom had dropped me off at my first playdate. I didn't understand that she'd be leaving. That my friend's mom would pressure me to drink milk and eat raisins, both of which I detested. That they'd leave the television on the whole time, blaring noise at me. That my friend didn't want to look at dinosaur videos. That the carpet smelled weird. I did the only thing I could think of: I locked myself in the bathroom.

They knocked and pounded. At some point, a kind police officer spoke calmly to me through the door. He told me he was about to break the lock, and I didn't need to be scared. When he opened the door, he looked as friendly as his voice sounded.

It would have been really nice if the next day, when I saw the preschool teachers, the other kids, and the parents, they had looked like the police officer. But they didn't. Instead, they walked around me like I was a leper. And the Andrews of the world had tried to tear me down ever since.

Andrew's voice ripped me from the past. He gestured toward the oil well across the street. "We're sitting on a pot of gold, and your mom does not get it. Maybe you should take off your stupid sunglasses once in a while and take a good look at our school."

His two minions nodded enthusiastically.

"Math wing looks like someone took a big dump on it," snorted Frizzy Hair.

Lopsided Teeth waved a hand in front of his nose. "Are you sure it's the building that smells right now?"

The three of them busted up laughing.

I was so shocked, hurt, and embarrassed, I couldn't speak. I knew other people at school avoided me—I'd told Jill about it in a recent therapy session. Other than in Drama Lab, people just did not like me.

"Rae." Arman touched my shoulder. "We don't need to give them an audience." He pushed off the picnic table, and I started to follow him even as I registered nearby kids migrating toward us. Behind me, I could still hear Andrew talking to them.

"Councilwoman Elizabeth Wolf is against the new oil well company and the guaranteed money to the schools," Andrew exclaimed. "She's against us!"

My mind went into overdrive, and I whirled around, the words spilling out. "No one even knows if it's safe! Do you want to see Pac Crest explode into a fireball?"

Andrew leaned in, totally invading my personal space, and whispered, "Boom."

Without thinking, I sprang at him and shoved both hands against his chest. He wasn't expecting it, and he tripped over his own feet, landing hard on his tailbone. Kids started talking louder, pressing in on us.

Arman reached down to help Andrew get up.

Andrew waved him off. "Save yourself, man. She's a crazy bitch." The two stage crew friends lifted Andrew to his feet. He made a big deal out of testing his weight on his ankle.

All around me, I saw a blur of faces—a mob, staring at me, like the day I went back to preschool after my disastrous playdate.

The day everyone decided I was untouchable.

11

BRADEN

Why can't pizza *fight infection? Or combat free radicals?* I wondered, listlessly peeling a tangerine while sitting at our usual table in the center of the sunny cafeteria courtyard. I tried to be content with absorbing my daily allotment of vitamin D and consuming a menu designed to boost my T cells. There was no point discussing my uneasiness—or my immune system—with my journalism buddies.

Shanice sat across from me, bent over her laptop, her brow furrowed as she worked on her next feature. She'd drawn her braids together and wrapped them in a little bun on top of her head. Beside her, a sophomore shared his opinion of the Save Our School club and its dedication to pumping fossil fuels, basically on school property. He was on the fence.

I had a deadline too—an article about the school's star pole vaulter, due at the end of the day. Lamenting my lack of focus, I sloshed the water in my thermos, wondering if it contained heavy metals. Some days, I hardly noticed my anxiety at all. Other times, it weighed as heavily on me as a dentist's lead apron.

Next to me, Lucas also had his mind on other things. Girls, mostly. He stared across the patio and brought my attention to Rae. I'd caught a glimpse of her earlier in the lunch period, but she'd been in some sort of intense conversation with a few other drama kids—Andy Jennings and the stage crew guys.

"Didn't she used to have blue hair?" Lucas asked.

"Yeah," I said, smashing my brown paper lunch bag into a ball and wondering how I was going to get us—Rae and me—back on track. "And tomorrow it could be green. Her name's Rae. Met her in my new Life Skills elective."

Lucas half smiled at me. "You like her!"

I shrugged. "She wants to be friends."

"Oh." Lucas frowned over the top edge of his glasses. "Then you're doomed."

Lucas and I crossed campus to the athletic department, where I was supposed to meet Coach Gillman for an interview. As we entered the building, Lucas asked, "Got five bucks I could borrow?"

Didn't I always? I handed him a bill, and he veered away to buy snacks at a vending machine. Heading toward Coach Gillman's office, I passed two baseball players who were giving me the Death Stare. One of them had monstrous biceps.

"Hey!" he called out. "You do *Neon Vikings*, right?"

"Yeah." This guy didn't seem the type to appreciate journalistic prose. I threw a tense look at Lucas, who was meandering my way while fishing in a bag for jalapeño chips, not a care in the world.

"You the one talking smack? About how to make the baseball team?" He looked poised to hurl his full Gatorade bottle at my nose.

"Nah, that was Cooper," I said, hoping it sounded nonchalant. Cooper had graduated the prior year, but that was beside the point.

"Tell Cooper he's hilarious," the baseball player said, taking a swig of his drink.

I brightened. "In that case, I wrote it."

The players laughed loudly, and I began to feel my worries retreat a smidge.

Inside the athletics office, the secretary brought us right into Coach Gillman's room, promising, "He'll be here soon."

We sat on chairs in front of the coach's desk. On one wall, a big corkboard was pinned with photos of Coach Gillman alongside the track and field and cross-country teams. Mixed in were shots of Coach with his buddies and one with his arm around an attractive, tanned woman.

Lucas finished the chips. "Coach Gillman gave me a C last semester in PE for not suiting up."

"That's nothing," I replied. "Every time he sees me, he calls me Brett."

Minutes ticked by. I bit a hangnail on my thumb, trying to calculate how much time I'd need to study for the upcoming AP US History exam.

"Where the hell is he?"

"You know what your problem is?" Lucas stood up and stretched. "Seminal fluid backup. You don't"—he made a jerking motion with his hand—"enough."

"Wow. Just, wow." I made a mental note to ignore him like I always did. Lucas announced these sorts of things as casually as if he were commenting on the weather.

"Don't take my word for it." Lucas stood up to inspect Coach Gillman's corkboard. "Check WebMD."

My parents had banned me from WebMD after I mistook a clump of hair in the shower drain for a sign of deadly thyroid disease. "Worry about your own seminal backup, why don't you?"

Lucas sat down in the coach's chair and started pecking around on the keyboard. He swiveled the monitor in my direction. On the desktop in an open file were photos of the tanned woman, this time in a lace bra and panties.

"What are those doing on his school computer?" I was unable to look away. "How'd you do that?"

"Combination of carelessness, cunning, and boredom."

Footsteps sounded in the hallway. I shoved the monitor, almost tipping it over. "Jesus!"

Lucas stood up, pecked at the keyboard, and plunged back into the seat next to me.

"Hello, Brett." Coach Gillman walked around us and sat at his desk.

"Hello, Coach!" Sweat beaded on my upper lip. My chest thumped so hard, the thought crossed my mind that I could be one of those students who has a sudden heart attack, just crumples and dies without warning.

"Lucas. Still bench-pressing ninety-five?" Coach asked.

"Good memory! But no," Lucas said, somehow having a regular calmversation.

What if the sexy photos popped up on Coach Gillman's monitor? Lucas, of course, would find a way to talk himself out of it, while I'd be expelled. The event would go on my school record. No college would accept me because I'd have to register as a sex offender.

"How can I help you?" Coach Gillman's voice tore me out of my nightmare.

"Uh, I'm doing this article on Amanda Stansbury?" I sounded nervous, like maybe I was hiding the fact I'd just seen his girlfriend's boobs.

"Amanda is driven," Coach Gillman said. "When she makes a mistake, she doesn't dwell on it. Athletes can get very emotional when they underperform. Amanda shakes off disappointment."

I scribbled notes dutifully.

"Would you say she's the best female pole vaulter in school history?" Lucas asked.

Coach sat back in his seat. "If she remains on this trajectory, yes, she could be the best."

My eyes darted up from my notepad, and I made a mental note to leave that part out—about how Amanda *could* be the best. I was a firm believer in the Cosmic Fucker-Up Theory: You didn't talk about a great thing until it had already happened. You didn't want to be the reason Amanda fell on her pole and broke her back.

Then I knocked on the wood leg of my chair for luck and protection. You just never knew how this superstition stuff worked.

After getting the quotes we needed, I stood up to go. But Coach stopped me before I could escape. "Brett, I heard about basketball," he said. "You're a good athlete. I know Coach Sanchez would love to see you come back."

There it was. My shoulders tightened. "I can't."

"Can't?"

Our school's culture was competitive, and I didn't expect Coach Gillman to understand that I had to step back. When I looked around at my high-achieving peers, who seemed to be handling the same workload and sports with grace, I just felt like a failure.

I glanced at the corkboard, then turned back to Coach. "It's just that, uh, I have other stuff I like to do better. Thanks for the meeting."

Coach Gillman grunted and turned his attention to his computer.
Walking out of the athletics office, I punched Lucas in the arm.
"Don't do that anymore. Hacking into school computers. Not okay."

Lucas rubbed his bicep. "For the sake of my health and our
friendship, I promise. No more messing with school computers."

Back in the journalism room, I fanned myself with my binder and
somehow knocked out the puff piece on Amanda Stansbury. That
sense of unease I'd felt since lunch had ramped up into something
bigger and scarier. I took a break to check Instagram, thinking I
could find a new superhero meme to share with Simon or a cool
whale post for Jerome.

As I scrolled through my main feed, I was surprised to find a
post with Rae's photo, from someone going by "Jack Meoff." It was
obviously posted without her permission. It had been viewed 203
times.

In the photo, Rae's expression looked blank. She wore a
loose-fitting tank top, where you could see the side of her left
boob and part of the nipple. Written beneath the photo—*Missing:
Over-the-Shoulder Boulder Holder*.

I wondered who had posted the photo. I wondered whose neck I
could snap. And mostly I wondered how upset Rae would be when
she saw it. I had a sinking feeling that she wouldn't be like Amanda
Stansbury. Some disappointments weren't so easy to shake off.

12

RAE

Of course, Mom was late again—today of all days. Waiting on campus was more torture than I could handle. I sat on the low brick wall as usual, unable to stop myself from fidgeting.

I debated internally whether to tell Mom about shoving Andrew, until a dull pulsing in my temples signaled an oncoming migraine—or worse. To stave it off, I listened to one of my "safe" playlists: a compilation of soothing music that I had on repeat. Over and over, I listened to handpicked songs by some of my favorite artists: Kacey Musgraves and Taylor Swift, of course. For me, it was a form of stimming. These playlists helped me regulate.

A small, unathletic girl named Laura plopped down next to me on the brick wall. In PE class, when we had to team up, she was always chosen second-to-last. That's how I recognized her—the order was Laura, then me. "You seem normal to me," she said now. Her voice was unfamiliar, because she had never, ever spoken to me before. "I don't think you're autistic. You're just a really mean person."

For the second time that day, I was gobsmacked. Hurt. Unmoored. *Is this what people secretly think about me?* I wondered.

Still no sign of Mom, so I fled from Laura.

In the distance, the oil well looked just like a giant giving me the middle finger. Mom cared more about her city council duties than her own daughter, and that said a lot about our relationship.

All in all, it had been a horrible day. I suddenly realized that no one knew the real me. Not Braden. Not Arman. Not even Mom.

Walking home, I smeared snot on my Ray-Bans in a failed attempt to avoid crying. Then I turned up the volume on my playlist and clamped the headphones onto my ears so tight, I thought I might crack my skull. Did I bring all this pain on myself? Was it autism, or was it just me being defensive of my defective personality? Who could say?

I was just pushing open the front door when Mom drove up.

"Where were you?" she asked, getting out of the car.

"Same place as usual," I seethed, stepping inside. "Waiting."

Mom followed me through the house. "We need to talk."

"Not now!"

Her phone rang, and I wanted to scream. She quickly muted it. "It's like every day there's a new crisis with you. I can't keep up! I can't help you if you don't let me."

I turned to face her, but when I looked out at the world, I saw nothing but mucus.

Mom reached for the smudged sunglasses. "Here. Let me clean those for you."

I recoiled. "Leave me alone. I don't want your help. Just go back to studying your oil recovery reports and big data. Pacific Crest needs to be saved! I don't."

Her eyes went wide. She opened her mouth to say something, but I ran upstairs before she could begin.

When she followed me into my bathroom, I spun around and shouted, "You like to talk about boundaries! Well, here's one: I need privacy. Go away! Please, please, just leave."

Mom slowly backed up, talking quietly to me. "When you're ready to talk—"

I closed the door before she could finish and locked myself in. Then I tore off my clothes and dug under the sink for a new bar of lavender soap. Standing back up, I caught a glimpse of myself in the mirror. Eyes bloodshot. Cheeks wet with tears. Nostrils red.

I raised my phone and took a selfie from the neck up. The image summed it all up: how the constant insults and misunderstandings chipped away at me and left me depressed and depleted.

The landline rang. I padded over to the bathroom door, hoping to overhear. "Hello?" When Mom spoke next, she sounded scared. "She did what?"

Obnoxious Andrew. He'd ratted on me!

"Was he hurt?" I heard her ask.

There was a long pause. I strained to hear through the door. "Yes, of course. I'm terribly sorry. I'll talk to her. I'm sure we can get to the bottom of it." A moment later, there was a soft knock on the bathroom door.

Ignoring it, I turned the shower on full blast and grabbed a washcloth off the countertop. As the hot water cascaded over me and tears mixed with the water, I bit down on the towel as hard as I possibly could. My jaw ached, and the pain radiated through my face and down my neck, but it was a good kind of pain. Somehow, the physical pain released some of the mental anguish I felt.

When I finally stepped over the edge of the tub, I was shaky. I barely had the energy to wrap myself in a towel before crumpling to the cold tile floor.

A little while passed. Mom tapped lightly on the door and offered me a cup of pureed vegetable soup—my favorite comfort food.

"No! Thank you!" I wasn't ready to forgive her for being late on one of the worst days of my life. I closed my eyes. I think I fell asleep.

Sometime later, I heard my phone bleep. Arman and Braden had both been texting me. I checked the time: past midnight. I'd never been so tired. My muscles ached, my bones hurt, and holding up my own head took so much energy that I could barely keep my neck straight.

I read Braden's texts first:

> People suck.

> I'll be up for a while . . .

My phone *binged* again. And again.
Arman's texts were next:

> DO NOT CHECK INSTAGRAM WITHOUT ME.

> CALL ME!

I opened Instagram on my phone. My ugly face stared back at me. My too-large breasts did too, one of them practically pouring out the side of my tank top, with a full-on display of nipple.

Who would take secret body shame photos of me? Who hated me that much? I tried so hard to stay away from people. Why couldn't they just leave me alone? How could I go back to school? How could I face seeing Mom?

Right there on the bathroom floor, I opened the Notes app and wrote:

> ## TEN Ways to Identify an Autie Girl, by Rae Wolf
>
> - Vacant stare with mouth hanging open. Gently teased by friends, mercilessly mocked by foes.
> - Soulful eyes that either can't focus on you or focus too intensely—in either case, causing discomfort to both parties.
> - Second-guesses herself. All. Day. Long.
> - Never comfortable in her own body unless talking about something of interest (e.g., dogs, Drama Lab, autism).
> - Has a lot of opinions but is often invisible.
> - Gets angry easily. Emotional overload can lead to loss of control—a meltdown.
> - Trusts too easily.
> - Deeply reflective and desperate for alone time to recharge.
> - Can inspire others. Can infuriate them just as easily.
> - Will fold up and dive inward when life becomes too much—a shutdown.

Once I'd finished, I wasn't sure how I could possibly get up and crawl to bed. So there I sat, curled up in the corner, with no idea how I'd ever move again.

13

BRADEN

Rae didn't come to school for two days. I kept texting her—I couldn't help myself—and she kept not responding.

How was she taking the post? Was it binge-eating-pints-of-Ben-&-Jerry's bad? Or was it pack-up-a-duffle-bag-and-hitchhike-to-Alaska bad? The dial on my daily anxiety doubled, and the mean post hadn't even been about me. I was so worried about Rae, I could think of little else. As I brushed my teeth or took notes in class, I felt an undercurrent to everything I did. The me below the me. The real me.

At lunch on the second day, I ended up sitting on the front lawn with Connor and his Scout troop buddies, Alex, Jeremy, and Joe. I wondered if they could see the change in me.

Jeremy nodded his head in time with the beat to Connor's new song. "No lie. My dad said, 'No Eagle, no license.'"

Alex snorted. "Harsh!"

"At least your project's been approved," Joe complained. "I can't even get the Scoutmaster to sign off on my Eagle proposal."

Connor sipped coffee from a tall disposable cup. "What's your idea?"

"Cleaning the poop out of the duck pond in Franklin Canyon."

Connor almost spit his coffee, and then he burst out laughing.

I was just about to explain all the health risks of wading into duck fecal material when I saw Zach approaching our table.

He was a physical guy, not afraid to foul you or get in your face on the basketball court. He spent every spare minute in the gym, maxing out, and his favorite catchphrase was *Do you even lift?* He'd openly cried when we lost to Miramar in last year's finals—and if anything, he became more popular.

I had a grudging respect for the guy, but I didn't particularly like him. Especially now that I knew he was Rae's ex, and he hadn't been very nice to her. I figured I could do better.

But first I had to know if Rae was okay. This was not me being an awfulist. I just really, seriously cared.

As he walked past, Zach lifted his chin. I lifted mine back. That's how dudes roll.

Before lunch period was even over, I rushed downstairs to the auditorium, where I found the drama kids eating lunch on the floor of the stage.

"Hello, hello!" Arman greeted me.

I got straight to the point. "Have you talked to Rae?"

"No. Not since . . . ." He moved out of earshot of his friends. "Have you?"

I shook my head. "Has she done this before?"

"Totally." Arman nodded. "Don't take it personally. When Rae gets overwhelmed, she has a meltdown. At least I *hope* it's a melt-down and not a shutdown."

"Uh, what's the difference?"

"Meltdown is when she's full of rage. Shutdown is when she's so stressed and overwhelmed, she can't even see anyone, except her mom maybe. She goes into a very dark place and gets really depressed. Like, scary depressed."

Hearing this, I felt protective and furious and worried all at once. "Any idea who created the post?"

"You know Andrew Jennings?"

"Andy. Andrew. Yeah."

Arman looked to his left and cocked his head. "The other day at lunch, he majorly messed with Rae."

I glanced at Andy and his stage crew minions. He looked harm-less in his pink pressed button-down. "He like her or something?"

"It's more to do with their parents being on the city council and having some kind of beef."

I pushed out my lower lip thinking. "So, are you going to stop by her house?"

Arman shook his head. "No, no, no. She *hates* that! You just have to leave her alone."

"Thanks for the advice," I replied, heading for the door.

There was no effing way I was leaving her alone.

After school, I played detective on my phone and found Rae's address within seconds. I also found out that her grandparents had been Holocaust survivors, and that her name was really Rachel. I could've kept researching, but a wave of fear pulled at me so hard, I could almost hear it buzzing in my brain.

Not long after I steered the old Ford SUV out of the student parking lot and onto the street, some jackass ran a red. I slammed the brakes. My breath was shaky, and I started sweating. It brought me back to that night.

We were freshman nobodies at a huge graduation party we weren't supposed to be at. People were making out in the pool, micro-dosing, driving high. I didn't even want to stay, but Hojun saw the best in everyone and everything. The older girls thought he was hot, and he didn't want to go home. One second, I'm laughing with my best friend. The next, he's gone for good.

Still sweating behind the wheel of the Ford, I managed to keep it together, but the traffic sucked even more than usual, and I was catching every red light. Maybe it was all a sign that going to Rae's was a bad idea.

When the next light changed to green, a car up ahead signaled before pulling out of a space as big as the Grand Canyon, right in front of Carly's Cupcakes. Another sign? I liked this one a lot better.

I blew through a week's worth of allowance, having no idea what flavor Rae liked. But at least I'd stopped sweating.

Outside the white Spanish two-story home where Rae lived, a team of gardeners was tending to the flowers and trees. A massive fountain gurgled in the courtyard. It seemed like kind of a big place for two people.

Each step closer to the front door made my heart race a little faster. I didn't even know if Rae liked cupcakes. Or me, for that matter. Finally, I pushed myself to press the doorbell. I'm not sure who I expected to answer, but a woman with the same heart-shaped face as Rae's swung open the door.

If Rae's mom is home in the middle of the day, I thought, *things must be really bad.*

"Hi." I forced a grin. "I'm Braden. A friend of Rae's. Um, is she home by any chance?"

Her mom glanced at the cupcake box and back up at me. Her face opened up into a smile. "Come in! I'm Elizabeth." She opened the door wider. Upstairs, a housekeeper wiped down the windows from a wood balcony. "Is she expecting you?"

"Err, not—not exactly," I stammered. I stepped inside, holding the box of cupcakes like a shield. The faint sound of a TV drifted from another room.

"Are you in Drama Lab too?" She closed the door behind me.

Rae obviously hadn't told her mom about me. "No. Actually, we met in Life Skills." I cleared my throat. "I'm a student aide."

Elizabeth nodded thoughtfully. "That is truly a beautiful thing. Pac Crest offers a plethora of electives. That you do something for others . . . . Well, it says a lot about you."

I shifted my weight from one foot to the other.

"One second. I'll let her know you're here." Elizabeth's heels clicked against the big tiles as she sped down the hallway and turned into a room, out of sight.

I distinctly heard Rae saying, "No! That's a *hard* no!"

My mouth went dry. Arman hadn't mentioned what a meltdown looked like, and I wasn't sure I wanted to find out.

Elizabeth poked her head out and beckoned me.

"If this isn't a good time . . ." I started.

She beckoned harder, nodding her head.

Okay then, I thought. *We're doing this.*

When I walked into the living room, I found Rae curled up on a deep, white sofa, watching a cooking show. She had a cashmere blanket slung over one shoulder. Her eyes flicked over to me for a millisecond. She wore a stretched-out T-shirt with a big smiley face and faded jeans rolled up at the ankles.

She had really cute feet.

"Rae's been resting, but I'm sure she's thrilled to have company," her mom said. The two of them exchanged a tense look. "She'll be back at school tomorrow. And frankly, who doesn't love cupcakes?" She took the cupcake box from me and set it beside stacks of expensive-looking books on the thick glass coffee table.

It was strange—her doing all the talking, and Rae letting her.

"I can come back later," I suggested. *Or never.*

"Rae!" Elizabeth urged. "Please turn off the TV."

"You're talking to me like I'm nine years old. I told you I don't want to see anyone. I'm not ready." She started to turn up the volume on the cooking show.

"That's rude," Elizabeth said. "And it isn't okay."

Rae huffed and turned it back down. "Sorry!"

Elizabeth turned to me. "A pleasure meeting you, Braden." She gave me a quick hug and smiled. "I'm a hugger."

After she left, a white fluffball shimmied over to me, tail wagging, and I kneeled to greet him. I scratched behind his ears. "I think your dog likes me. Noodle, right?"

"He's like that with everyone," Rae said, her voice monotone.

Alrighty then. Arman knew how to handle Rae's quirks. Me? Not so much.

On the TV, some celebrity chef had tricked a contestant into trying to pull a tablecloth from under a bunch of glasses and plates. Like in a cartoon, everything went flying.

"Um. I didn't know what flavors you like so, yeah, I got banana, chocolate, and red velvet. Those are my favorites."

Rae pulled her blanket tighter around her. "I'm on a gluten-free diet."

I opened the lid of the box and pointed to one of the cupcakes. "This one *is* gluten-free."

Rae plucked the cupcake from the box. "Thanks." She didn't sound particularly grateful. She sounded like she wanted me to hit the highway.

"Oh, yeah, this one is for Noodle." I pointed at a mini cupcake with a dog bone decoration.

Rae sat up. "Really?"

She pinched off bite-sized pieces and hand-fed Noodle. This seemed to make her happy, and I relaxed a bit.

"I wanted to rescue this red nose pit bull from the San Pedro shelter," Rae said. "She's probably dead by now."

"That's so sad." I sat down beside her, but not too close.

"Mom didn't want another dog." Rae sank into the couch, and I could see she was trying not to cry. I tried not to read too much into it. Jenji once cried when Dad cut the pizza wrong and her slice ended up containing a microscopic piece of pepperoni.

"I'm volunteering at a dog adoption this weekend," I reminded her. "I don't do a whole helluva lot." The truth was, my responsibilities mostly consisted of filling water bowls, waving posters at adoption events, and cleaning poop.

Rae wiped her eyes and sat up. "Do you think I could come with you sometime?"

"Yeah!" I was flooded with relief. Rae wanted to see me. "That would be great."

It was a small victory, and I rewarded myself with a red velvet. As I chewed, I checked out the room. Soaring beamed ceilings. Priceless-looking art. A grand piano.

"This is a really nice house," I said. "Do you have any brothers or sisters?"

"A half brother. He's going to be nine in August." She looked me in the eye and paused, as if she'd just remembered it was her turn to ask me a question. "What about you?"

"A little sister. She's eleven. Jenji. She's gluten-free too."

"Is she on the spectrum?"

"No. Why?" I asked, wondering what flour had to do with autism.

"Never mind." Rae took a bite of her cupcake, and we watched the cooking show.

"So, it's just you and your mom?"

"Yep. My dad's remarried. He lives in Manhattan Beach." Rae fiddled with Noodle's collar. "We don't get along." While I tried to think of something mature and sensitive to say, Rae tilted her head and looked out the window. "That your car?"

"Yeah."

"Ugly color."

I laughed. "Looks better when it's clean. Cars are overrated, though, don't you think? Traffic . . . the cost of gas . . . ."

The side of her mouth twitched where she'd tried to hold back a smile. "You're weird."

"And that's a bad thing?" I edged an inch closer to Rae. Close enough to see the faint bluish-green veins on her chest. Close enough to see her bloodshot eyes. "So, uh, they took it down," I told her, hoping that would give her some relief. "The post."

She stiffened.

We watched chefs scuttling about a kitchen on TV. In his British accent, the celebrity chef called someone a horse's arse. In a fake English accent, I asked, "Did you report the horse's ass to the principal?"

She shook her head and studied her fingernails, and I couldn't get a read on her.

"What happened to your blue hair?"

Rae visibly relaxed. "I change my hair color all the time."

"I like the old color. And the new one." Her face lit up, and I could see her pretty, straight teeth. "I'm really glad you're coming back to school tomorrow. I've missed you."

Rae petted Noodle and didn't make eye contact. Still, I caught a glimmer of a smile. As I stood up to leave, I gave her a brief kiss on the cheek.

Her face flushed and her lips parted. She seemed startled, and I started to apologize, but she held up a hand, stopping me. "Thank you for the cupcakes."

On the drive home, I cruised down Sunset, listening to Motown and feeling much better. The worried me beneath the me was still there, but not as intense. I made a mental note to find out what time the dog adoption event was happening on Saturday.

A sharp thump startled me. I'd driven over something.

In the rearview mirror, I thought I glimpsed a branch, or it could've been a box in the road. The car directly behind me drove over whatever it was I'd hit. But as the blocks slipped by, the me beneath the me grew louder.

What if it hadn't been a box?

What if the thump had been me hitting a dog?

Or a person?

By the time I pulled into my driveway, the object was a person. A dead person. Like Hojun. This time, it was someone *I'd* killed. My blood felt like ice in my veins. I couldn't stop thinking about what I did/might have done.

Bracing for the very worst, I turned around and drove back down Sunset, trying to find the area where the thump had taken place. I took my best guess and slowed once I got there. There was nothing unusual in the road. Unsatisfied, I parked on a side street and back-tracked on foot.

Cars zoomed past me. I felt like an idiot, side-stepping along the gutter and getting gunk on my sneakers. My inspection yielded wet leaves, a discarded battery, and a water bottle filled with yellow fluid that definitely wasn't water.

A normal person would let it go. Something within me would not.

I checked the Nextdoor app for accidents. Nothing. I called the police department to find out if they had received a report on Sunset in the last hour. Again, nothing.

When I finally walked in through the kitchen door, I found Mom serenely sipping her tea. Setting down the newspaper on the table, she said, "You look like you've seen a ghost."

14

My therapist Jill always reminded me to make small, attainable goals and decide on an action plan to achieve them. Dwelling on who created the body-shaming post—Andrew? Zach? Random cheerleader?—threatened to throw my already fragile self into a very dark place. After forty-eight hours in meltdown mode, I didn't totally trust myself.

My goal was to avoid a fight. My action plan was to say next to nothing my first day back at school. As I went about my day, I avoided raising my hand in class and making eye contact with people around me. Until I got to Drama Lab, of course.

Arman and I spent most of the period jumping around the stage with other kids in the ensemble, rehearsing our role as monkeys. I pretended to groom Arman's hair, and everyone thought it was a hilarious bit. At least the drama kids still seemed to like me.

When the passing bell rang, the stage crew flooded the auditorium with the house lights, which made me feel exposed. I squinted up at the bleachers, wondering if Andrew and his henchmen were discussing the size of my boobs. All in all, though, I thought I'd been successful in my goal to avoid confrontation.

Arman and I walked out of the auditorium and cut through the lobby, where the Red Cross had set up for the annual blood drive. We hopped in line, followed by three girls in matching *Neon Vikings* hoodies. Behind a screen, a guy was lying back in a reclining chair, a bright red tube extending from his arm to a shelf below him.

"Do you have an appointment?" asked a girl with a pen tucked into her bun. The junior class president—I recognized her from the spirit assemblies.

"Not yet. How old do you need to be to give blood?" Arman asked.

"You're gay, right?"

Big duh. What was her point?

She pulled the pen from her bun and started tapping it against her clipboard. "Well, if you've had multiple partners or had anal sex in the past three months, you're not eligible," she announced.

Arman's golden skin turned ashen.

I gritted my teeth. "That's *not* what he asked."

"Eighteen," she answered curtly.

Arman stood still while I desperately tried to find something comforting to say. *Think! Think!* I ran my hands through my hair, and my T-shirt started riding up.

The girl stared at my hip. "Was that tattoo applied in a state-regulated parlor? You may not be eligible to donate, either."

"Technically, we're too young to give blood," I corrected her.

The girl walked away, past boxes of prepackaged cookies.

"And technically, I've never had sex," Arman added glumly.

Behind us in line, the *Neon Vikings* girl with long braids muttered, "God help us if these idiots are in charge of running the blood drive."

The one with round, gold-rimmed glasses stepped toward Arman. She wore a white lace button-down under a pin-striped vest, and a big Western belt. Very '70s and very cool. "I'm Naomi, and that's Shanice and Alicia. Would you mind if I interview you?"

"Am I going to be in the paper?" Arman asked.

"Yes, if we have anything to say about it." Naomi looked at Shanice and Alicia. They all nodded, like they were equally in charge.

Arman's warm complexion returned.

Naomi held her phone close to Arman as she recorded his answers, squinting like she didn't want to miss a single word out of his mouth. She smiled easily and seemed to assume that a) she was likeable and worth talking to, and b) she was exactly where she should be. I couldn't remember ever feeling that way. For a split second, I wished I could trade places with her. Or that she was my friend.

"I hate needles," Arman explained. "It took a lot for me to even show up for the Red Cross today. Last thing I expected was homophobia!"

He turned to me for approval. Or was I supposed to chime in? It was hard for me to read the cues.

"Some people still think our school is divided," Arman continued. "Gay, straight. White, Brown. Rich, poor. But it comes down to this: We all have the same blood in our veins."

I was so proud of Arman. If only I could be that cool, that well-spoken, Mom wouldn't have been pushing for boarding school.

Arman's and Naomi's voices faded to nothingness as memories of my recent meltdown—and past meltdowns—flooded my brain. Arman knew how I sometimes bit down on a washcloth until the ache in my jaw obliterated my mental anguish. I'd even told him how, when I was eight years old, I used to bang my head against the wall when I was overwhelmed. I had to stop the cycle of negative thoughts, or I was sure I'd die.

My dad never understood any of it, though. And I couldn't explain it properly, other than to insist I had to keep doing it. "I refuse to stand back and watch you hurt yourself," he'd said, kneeling in front of me. "If you can't stop harming yourself, Rae, we're going to have to send you to a facility. To live."

I'd never been so scared in my life. If I didn't quit banging my head, my parents were going to send me away to an institution.

Eventually, Mom found Jill, who helped me figure out that chomping down on a towel would give me the relief I needed. Now, all these years later, not much had changed. If I didn't make things work at school, Mom would send me away.

A shiver ran through me, and I rubbed my arms.

Arman's comforting voice gently brought me back to the present. "We're all connected."

Then Naomi shoved her phone too close to my face, and I flinched. "What do you think of all this?" she wanted to know. She adjusted her vintage glasses and patiently waited for me to tune back into the conversation.

"Personally? I think we're *dis*connected from each other," I answered. "And from ourselves."

"Any thoughts on how we could change it? So someone at a blood donation site wouldn't be so insensitive?"

I took a step back, away from Naomi and her phone. "I have no idea."

"Yeah, changing behavior is a bitch." Then she winked at me. "If you think of something you want to add, private message me on Instagram."

Instagram.

A chill went up my spine. Had Naomi seen the body-shaming post about me? I crossed my arms tightly in front of my breasts. Like that would make me any less recognizable.

When the final bell rang, Arman and I headed outside and down the grass hill, toward the street. A boy in soccer clothes sat in my usual place on the low brick wall, so I moved closer to the bike rack. I found an open space where the noisy kids were putting their bikes in and pulling them out.

Arman settled beside me and gently bumped his thigh against mine. "I don't mean to bring up a sore subject, but the last time you had a meltdown, it took a really long time for you to feel . . . okay. Happy. Yourself."

The last time, over spring break, was a stay-in-my-room, be-alone-for-days, think-negative-thoughts meltdown. Zach had come to my house and asked me to take a walk. I'd grabbed the leash and Noodle, and off we went. By the time we'd returned, Zach had dumped me, and I was in full meltdown. So, by comparison, this recent episode hadn't come close to that one.

"I actually felt somewhat better when Braden stopped by," I told Arman.

Arman looked confused. "Braden visited you? In person?"

I nodded. "With cupcakes."

"Rae! I'm happy for you, but what the . . . ? You didn't answer my calls and texts."

"Excuse me!" I exclaimed. "I didn't hear from you for days when you and Spencer had your thing going on!"

"Please! Keep it down!" Arman looked around, suddenly paranoid. "It's not the same. You aren't *with* Braden."

What a hypocrite. Like my friendship with Braden wasn't as cool or as deep as Arman's with Spencer? "We *are* talking about the same Spencer who dropped you and then got back together with his ex-girlfriend, aren't we?"

Arman's mouth curled down at the corners. "You *so* don't get it." He turned his back on me and left.

A chill went through me. He'd never done that before.

A horn tooted. Mom. Before she even found a spot, I ran between parked cars, threw my backpack through the window, and got in.

"How's it going?" Mom asked, smiling.

I slumped in my seat. "You ask as if it could possibly be going well."

15
BRADEN

During Advanced Journalism on Friday, I sat between Lucas and Shanice on the coveted sofa, pretending to work on my March Madness bracket. No one seemed to detect my ever-present fear about whatever I'd hit with the car. What if I'd hurt someone? What if I had to go to prison? What if I never graduated?

"Can you proof this?" Shanice asked me, sliding her laptop toward me.

"Sure." I was relieved to have any distraction. She'd written an article on Andy Jennings's Save Our School club. Apparently, they were planning a demonstration in front of Bex's Bagel.

"What do you think?"

"I recommend the everything bagel."

"I meant the club," Shanice said, rolling her eyes.

"Isn't it obvious? Andy Jennings is the president. His dad is trying to get the school improvement project passed through the city council. End of story."

Shanice arched one eyebrow. "Bernstein! And I thought your area of expertise was athlete's foot and jock itch."

"Who said it isn't? They're both caused by a fungus that can travel from feet to—err, groin. Or from a dirty towel or even your hands."

"TMI!" she squeaked.

I raised my hands up. "Sorry! Sorry!"

Lucas made a face. "What's with your fingers?"

My hangnails had been picked raw. "Midterms."

"Not a good look," he said. "Those nasty fingers prove school is toxic."

"Speaking of school," I said, changing the subject, "whatever happened with your sister's immigration thing?"

"Thank god, Sally met with her DSO."

"Her *what?*"

"Designated school official. If she registers for community college classes like she promised, there shouldn't be any problems with her student visa."

My phone dinged with a text from Rae—the cupcake emoji and a smiley face with the tongue sticking out, followed by:

> Thanks again. I think Mom likes you. Possibly
> more than I like you.

"Want to check out the Mint tomorrow night?" Lucas asked. "Southern Tier's playing."

I reluctantly looked up from my phone. "You know I'm not into country music."

"Just 'cause the lead wears a cowboy hat doesn't mean . . . ."

My phone dinged again:

> Can I go to the dog adoption with you?

For a brief moment, I forgot about self-destruction. My mind went quiet. I recognized all my *What if?* questions as borderline insane. Levitating away from my real life and suspended in that safety bubble, I still had a chance with Rae.

I responded to her text:

> Totally. Pick you up tomorrow at ten.

Once again, I became aware of the journalism room, of Lucas's faint yet stale odor of cigarette smoke.

"You have a very goofy look on your face, you know that?" Lucas asked.

I put the phone away and smiled. "I'll take that as a compliment."

Saturday morning, I trudged into the kitchen and found my little sis slurping her smoothie, being careful not to stain her tae kwon do uniform. At the stove, Mom sprinkled cinnamon on bowls of oatmeal. Weekdays were hectic, so Mom strove for quality family time and home-cooked meals on weekends.

"Mommy? What kind of protein powder did you use?" Deep down, all Jenji really cared about was that no animals were harmed in the making of her smoothie.

"Plant Warrior," Mom replied. "The one you told me to get."

Mom limited her lawyer work to depositions so she could manage her hours and do mom-like tasks like buying an obscure protein powder for her conscientious daughter. Her specialty was labor law, which meant asking questions like *Did you play video games on your work computer in front of coworkers?* and *Did you clock out for required breaks?* Some lawyers got boxes at the Staples Center. To Mom, the big perk of her job was the ability to be home by three o'clock for Jenji and me.

Sitting at the kitchen table, I pushed the oatmeal around with my spoon. I had no appetite. Spark sat by my feet, waiting in vain for scraps. The worries about running someone over had started replaying in the middle of the night, and I hadn't slept well.

Dad swept in and poured himself a cup of coffee before sitting down with his tablet. The deep wrinkle forming between his brows told me he was probably reviewing cases. He was a partner at Valencia and Bernstein, specializing in family law—which was a funny name for it, since Dad mostly handled divorces. It was a toss-up as to who was more stressed: Dad or his clients.

Before I could think too much about the consequences, I decided to mention my predicament. "Dad. I may have, uh, had some sort of car accident."

Dad's eyes narrowed. Questions were taking shape in his legal brain, and this time I was the one about to be deposed.

"Burton." Mom waved a spatula, warning him. "It's nothing."

"Shannon," Dad said, waving a spoon, trying for funny and not quite pulling it off. "What happened?"

Mom set the oatmeal pot down too hard, scaring the dog out of the kitchen. "There's no damage to the car. No one was hurt. But Braden being Braden . . . ." Her voice trailed off.

"That's one way to put it," I said, unable to keep the skepticism out of my tone.

Dad folded the newspaper before speaking again. "What happened?"

"Two nights ago, I drove over something and it made this . . . noise."

"Why am I just hearing about it now?" He looked at me, clearly annoyed.

"I told Mom, and she didn't think there was anything to worry about."

Dad set the paper down. "What kind of noise?"

"I don't know! A noise. You're missing the point!" I raised my voice.

Dad looked at Mom, who gave a subtle headshake. Then he turned back to me. "You put so much pressure on yourself, Braden. I guess you got that from me. We're glass half empty people, always looking for what can go wrong."

What my parents didn't understand was that my worry was a physical thing, like a weight on my chest. I knew Dad was trying, but he didn't get what was going on. For that matter, neither did I.

"Try to have a little fun," he continued. "And I'd like to make it to your next home game."

Just when I thought the day couldn't get any worse. Dad still didn't know I'd quit the team. "About that . . . ."

Jenji took one last slurp on her straw. "Why is everybody fighting?"

Mom gave a gentle order. "Go brush your teeth, Jenji." My sister scrambled out of the kitchen.

I picked up my bowl and started to scrape the oatmeal into the trash can. My spoon circling the rim of the bowl reminded me of a whirlpool, only it was me going in circles, being drawn down into a dark place. I spun deeper and deeper, sinking far beneath the waves until I was on the ocean floor, and I couldn't push off and get to the surface. I had no control. My lungs filled with water. I couldn't breathe.

Am I dying?

I slumped into my chair. No, I wasn't dying. I thought of my life, all those years unfolding ahead of me—a future of heavy thoughts that wouldn't leave me alone, of fears that would not stop no matter what I did.

Dad looked at his watch. He had things to do. I was a burden. "I think you spend too much time at home, Braden. Shy doesn't work. You need to push yourself to get out there more."

"Most parents would be happy to have their child spending time at home!" I responded irritably.

My parents looked at each other, and the room got very quiet. Then Jenji bounced into the kitchen, her tae kwon do uniform spotless and her pink backpack slung over her shoulder. "Ready!"

Dad stood up and pawed through the key basket by the door. Before he and Jenji walked out, he clapped me on the shoulder. "We'll talk later. For now, put this in a box."

Did that really work for anyone? The me beneath the me had been hijacked by some really disturbing thoughts, and they weren't going anywhere. Especially not into a box.

Once Mom and I were alone, she took a sip of coffee and sat at the table beside me. "I'll find a therapist."

I gave her what I hoped was a look of complete disgust. "The last time we did this was when Hojun died, and that therapist was *not* the right guy." A huge understatement. I'd actually tried to nap on his office couch rather than pretend to pay attention to him. It didn't work, of course. Nothing about that situation did.

It was nearly ten o'clock. Mom walked me to the Ford and leaned in the window. "I know you're not feeling . . . yourself. You okay to drive? I'm happy to give you and Rae a lift."

"That's okay." A guy had to have some pride.

I turned on the radio and hummed along to an old Marvin Gaye song. Rae was waiting for me to pick her up, and that was all I wanted to think about.

16

RAE

Mom barged into my room. She was having a moment. "I've been monitoring your time on the computer. You said thirty minutes, Rae. Thirty. It's been an hour and a half. Once again, you've gone down the rabbit hole."

"Rabbit hole," I repeated, looking up from my laptop. That's how she saw my passion for posting on social media and emailing dog rescues. "Explain to me how saving fur babies' lives is not an excellent use of my time?"

Mom put her hands on her hips. "Being online is no substitute for the real thing. It's important to cultivate friends you can see and touch. Animal advocacy will be even more meaningful and worthwhile in person."

What she didn't know was that when I was online, talking to others on the spectrum or dog rescue peeps, we exchanged useful information—in as few words as possible. That's what made it both meaningful and worthwhile.

That's how I met Brenda. She lived in Louisville and loved

dogs and horses and was really into animation. She'd even sent me a drawing that showed how she pictured her anxiety: a girl's face sketched into the shape of an iceberg. As Brenda explained, an iceberg is mostly submerged. Everyone sees the top. People don't realize what's swirling below—that feeling when you tell the truth, and people freak out and make you feel crazy.

"Sorry if I don't constantly hug my friends and go on morning hikes with them, like you do with Nicki and Cheyenne and Olivia," I said sharply, shutting down my computer. "But the people I talk to online still qualify as friends." For me, social chatting and small talk seemed like a huge waste of energy and time. I could do it, but it took as much effort as doing algebra, and I sucked at math. It drained me, and I was always happy to be done with it.

Mom took a deep breath. "It's just hard for me to understand. When I'm going through a tough time, it's such solace to be able to—"

"Okay, Mom." I'd heard it all a million times. "Well, you'll be happy to know that today I'm going out with Braden. We're volunteering at a dog adoption."

"You are? Really!" Mom sat on my bed, her excitement overflowing. "That sounds like so much fun."

I got up to stretch. "Uh-huh."

"Are you going out like that?" Mom asked.

"Hmm?" I absent-mindedly checked myself out in the full-length mirror: freshly colored pink hair, black yoga pants, and a gray tank top that had been through the wash hundreds of times. I reached into my closet and layered on an oversized plaid flannel shirt—my favorite.

"It's such a gorgeous day out." Mom was choosing her words carefully. "I don't know, maybe you could wear your new jeans and the teal tank top?"

"To impress who? The dogs are color-blind. They don't care what I'm wearing."

Mom nodded to herself. "That's true. What you wear should make you feel good."

"If we keep talking about it, obviously I won't feel quite as good," I snapped. The sunlight glaring through my windows bothered me. I put on my sunglasses.

Mom stood up and straightened the comforter. "Last thing, just so we're clear. Please don't fall in love with a dog today. We can't get another one."

I'd had enough. I darted downstairs and stationed myself by the window, waiting for Braden. It was probably too late to cancel, but suddenly I really wanted to lock myself in my room and read my latest book: Robert Crais's novel *Suspect*, about a cop and his partner, a retired Marine dog. I felt the faintest pulse behind my right eye, which may or may not have been an oncoming migraine.

The main problem was that Mom was one of my triggers, and sometimes she really set me off. My other problem—actually, this might be the main problem—was that I was breaking a promise to myself: I'd sworn off guys for at least three months. After Zach, that had seemed like a perfectly reasonable goal. Jill wholeheartedly agreed with me. "Small, attainable goals," she'd said.

Yet here I was, coloring my hair bubblegum pink and wishing my head would just shut up. I seriously wanted to hang out with Braden. Well, that was a lie. Hanging out is what I did with Arman: eating Chipotle, playing video games, talking about our favorite TV shows. This felt completely different. I didn't just want to hang out. I wanted Braden to kiss me.

But what if cupcakes were just effing cupcakes? And hadn't I been the one to invite myself to the dog adoption? What if I had completely misread the situation?

Arman would know. I totally relied on him when my negative self-talk got out of control. Who needs haters when you have a mirror? Unfortunately, Arman and I weren't talking. We'd had some kind of misunderstanding at the blood drive, and now there was residual weirdness.

Reaching in my pocket, I found my pomegranate lip balm and carefully applied it. If by some miracle Braden did like me, I wanted soft, pillowy lips.

His car finally pulled up to the curb. I ran out of the house and flung open the passenger door.

"Good morning!" Braden cracked a smile. "Ready to save some dogs?"

That did it. My whole body felt energized. All the negative crap, the arguing with Mom—*poof!*—Braden made it vaporize. He turned the key in the ignition and the radio came on. Springsteen. Perfect!

I expected him to pull out of the driveway, but he was still in park. When I turned to him, he was staring at me.

Self-conscious, I touched my hair. "What? Do I have dandruff?"

"No!" Braden shook his head. "I like the new pink hair."

"Ohhh, thanks."

The butterflies in my belly went berserk. I had to look away, turn my attention to my sneakers, out the front windshield. Anywhere other than his soft eyes. Otherwise, he'd see me, all exposed.

Sometimes, when I'm in a situation with strangers, I forget that they don't know me. To them, I'm a new face. Only *I* carry the weight of what I know about me—my autism—on my shoulders. Neurodiverse versus neurotypical.

This was one of those times.

Everyone had a task to do at the dog adoption, and mine was to follow Braden around. I could think of worse things to do. During the tour, Braden touched my upper arm three times and brushed his hand against mine once, although that may have been unintentional.

The rescue setup had been organized in a parking lot behind the Pacific Palisades Pet Pavilion. I was relieved that it was outdoors. With twenty-eight dogs, volunteers constantly coming and going, and all kinds of yo-yos wandering about, it could get loud. Crowds were always tough for me.

Each dog crate had a description of the animal, along with their name: *Khaleesi. Arya. Sansa.* This cracked me up. Who from the rescue group was the *Game of Thrones* freak? Adult volunteers stationed by each crate walked the dogs, gave them treats, and answered potential adopters' questions.

Kids like us were assigned to patrol the sidewalk while waving posters advertising the adoption. The smell of diesel and the constant traffic noise grated on me. After about an hour, I started to get agitated. I hadn't eaten much for breakfast, and the bottled water they gave us tasted like metal.

"Is it okay for us to take a little break?" I asked Braden. "Or I could take one by myself?" Lately, Jill and I had been discussing self-care. I was proud of myself for actually remembering to do it.

"A break sounds pretty good right about now," he said.

Braden and I escaped to the residential streets with their shade and peaceful buffer from all the action.

"You're quiet," I said.

"Just tired, I guess," he replied.

"Big plans last night?"

He forced a smile. "Party all night, every night."

We got to the end of the block and turned a corner. I studied

Braden out of the corner of my eye. His shoulders seemed more slumped than usual. His gaze was focused low on the sidewalk. Then he sighed. Something was bothering him—not that I could identify the cause.

"Look," I finally said, "you've seen me post-meltdown, practically at my very worst. You can talk to me. If you feel like it."

He took my hand and gave it a squeeze. My stomach clenched, and a bolt of electricity traveled from my hand to the center of my body. "I want to, Rae," he said. "Not here, though, okay?"

"Is it—is it . . . me?" I stammered.

"God, no." But before I knew it, he'd let go of my hand, and I saw him wipe his palm against his jeans.

"I don't have cooties," I said, feeling stung and ridiculously vulnerable.

Braden's face and neck turned pink. "Of course, you don't. It's me! I get sweaty palms." He held up his hands, and I saw a slight sheen and immediately relaxed. *He* was the one being vulnerable. It made me want to not only hold his hand but wrap both of my arms around him.

"Like I care," I said softly.

He took hold of my hand again, and we walked a few more minutes. The electric heat returned, only it radiated even deeper than before. If only we could've continued like that for hours, in companionable silence, I'd have been delirious with happiness.

Back at the parking lot, Braden introduced me to Caryn Espinoza, founder of the Sage Foundation—a woman around my mom's age with a long blond braid down her back, who was ripping open a packet of dog treats with her manicured red nails. "Caryn, this is my friend Rae. She's the biggest dog lover on the planet—aside from you, of course."

"You're with Braden?" Caryn looked at me for a millisecond. "Great. We love Braden."

"How do you coordinate everything with all the fosters?" I asked, totally in awe of her.

"That's Yasmine's department. We have the best volunteers," Caryn said, already walking away.

I followed her. "How do you find your volunteers?"

"Word of mouth, mostly." She made an adjustment on one of the dog's collars, then waved a guy over and directed him to refill another dog's water bowl before walking swiftly to another area.

I stayed on her heels. "How many dogs have you saved?"

"Hundreds."

Hundreds. That astounded me. "How did you get your start?"

An elderly woman drove up and waved to Caryn, who directed a volunteer to heft a heavy bag of donated dog food from the trunk of the car. As soon as Caryn had thanked the woman, she turned to me. "I don't have time to talk about all this. I'm sure you can see that I'm really busy at the moment!"

"Okay, maybe later," I said, watching her march off to talk to another volunteer.

I went back to where Braden was hanging out, under a shade tent with a handful of other volunteers. Luckily, some other kids had taken over on poster duty, so we got to spend time with the dogs.

I was so proud to be part of this community. "How does she do it?" I asked.

Braden shook his head. "I have no idea."

"Thank you so much for this." I held up my arms. "It's amazing!"

We visited each crate. My favorite dog was a small white pit with a brown patch over one eye, appropriately named Patch. She keyed into me right away, her round eyes following my every move. Her coat was silky to the touch, but you could see her ribs too easily. She hadn't been fed enough before, but soon she would be in a caring home with people who loved her.

And there I was, right next to Braden, doing what mattered most to me. For once in my life, I was exactly where I was supposed to be.

17

BRADEN

Around the dogs, Rae was different. I could see how much more relaxed and self-assured she was. She pressed her hand against Patch's crate and let the dog lick her fingers through the bars. They were already bonding.

"She hates it in there," Rae said. "Do you think she'll be adopted today?"

"Not sure," I replied. "But at least she isn't in danger of being put down. And I've met some of the fosters. They're really nice."

Rae cooed to Patch, "I wish *I* could be your foster!"

When she kneeled closer to the dog, Rae's yoga pants slid lower on her hips. The black letters of her tattoo stood out against her creamy skin. I resisted assuming the worst about getting tattoos: hepatitis B or staph infection. Okay, that was still in the back of my mind—way back, though. Somewhere after the fear of never losing my virginity and being sentenced to vehicular manslaughter.

Rae took a photo of Patch. "Have you noticed when she gets excited, one ear goes up and the other stays down?" She held the screen up so I could see.

"Yeah. I have the same problem," I said with a straight face.

"You're so weird."

"You keep saying that like it's a bad thing. Now, how about a selfie of us?"

She looked down at her phone and scowled like I'd offered her a bacon-wrapped tadpole.

"With Patch," I added, a bit defensive.

"I hate having my picture taken. I always have that vacant autie stare."

"Not to me."

Rae turned her gaze from her phone to me. Our eyes locked, then she looked away like it didn't mean a thing. But then she met my eye again. Oh, hell—of course it meant something! My knees were rubbery, and my body felt like some basketball player on a fast break had slammed right into me.

Before I could figure out exactly *what* it meant, one of the pups whined, setting off the inevitable chain reaction of all the other dogs barking. We shushed the animals and distracted them with treats until they settled down.

"Did I say something wrong?" I asked her once it got quiet again.

"Instagram," Rae said, tugging her flannel shirt around her. "I guess I'm sensitive about pictures right now."

"Listen, if I knew who did that, I'd punch their lights out."

"Really?" She perked up. "Have you ever hit anyone?"

"Plenty of times," I confessed. "But it was Connor, and we were fake fighting."

A dark expression crossed her face. "I've thought about hitting people."

I rubbed the back of my neck, thoughtfully. "I wish you'd report the post to the vice principal."

"What for?"

"For starters, they might stop bullying you."

She shook her head, unconvinced.

"And at least the administration might finally realize nobody listens to those useless anti-bullying assemblies."

Patch let out a whine, getting Rae's full attention. "Can I walk her? Please?"

I didn't want to disappoint her. "I'll find out. They're kind of strict, though."

"I'm *positive* I know more about dogs than ninety-five percent of the people here."

"Well, well, well. Aren't we Ms. Dog Whisperer?" I teased before I wandered over to Yasmine.

"She's not eighteen, right? Did a parent sign the release form?" Yasmine asked, glancing past me at Rae.

"No, but she has a lot of experience with dogs."

Yasmine pulled a release form from her stack of papers and handed it to me. "No walks without this." Then she handed me two posters. "Until then, I need you back on poster duty."

Rae scoffed when I showed her the form.

"It's a pain, but maybe one of your parents could swing by here and sign it?"

"My *parents*?" she asked, raising her eyebrows. "Yeah, right. Mom's superglued to her desk. And my *dad*? He has a new family. He doesn't care about me."

"That sucks. I'm sorry."

"Don't be. *He's* the one who owes me an apology."

"Listen, I hate to do this, but we need to get back on poster duty."

Rae stood up and whispered to Patch, "Bye sweet girl."

Back on the sidewalk with our posters, Rae looked over her shoulder once or twice, as if checking whether Patch was still watching.

Her fingertips barely gripped the corners of the poster, which kept slipping from her grasp.

I made an attempt to coax her smile out of retirement. "Hey, I'm really glad you came here today."

Rae pointed back at the parking lot. "Look! Someone's interested in Patch!"

In the distance, Yasmine had Patch out of the crate on a leash, playing with some people.

"Maybe we can help," Rae said, moving away.

"H—help?" I mumbled.

Rae strode through the parking lot, and I scrambled after her.

By the time I caught up to her, she was motormouthing it, her hands gesturing all over the place. "You've never owned a dog before? Dogs need consistent training and a serious time commitment. Also, don't worry about their jaws. There's no such thing as 'locking jaws'! But you do need to be careful about the kinds of toys you buy for them."

Watching her, I felt a pit in my stomach.

The guy who'd seemed interested in Patch had on a flashy watch, and as Rae continued blabbering, he kept checking it. His girlfriend, in a pale pink sundress, frowned. At one point, she whispered something in her boyfriend's ear.

The worst part was that Rae was totally oblivious. "If a dog swallows a piece of rubber or plastic, it can be life-threatening!"

Yasmine interrupted her. "Um, Braden's friend, yes?"

"Yes," I answered for Rae. "We're actually over there today. On poster duty." I dropped the not-so-subtle hint, but Rae didn't pick up on it. "C'mon. We've gotta go."

Rae reluctantly stepped away with me. "Can't you see I'm trying to help?"

"I get that. Still, I think they expect us to kind of be in the support role," I said quietly.

I could still hear the sundress woman talking. "We want to start a family soon, and we thought we should start with a dog first. You know, get used to the idea of being responsible?"

Rae shook her head, disgusted. "Do you believe her?" She stared daggers at the woman, who was petting Patch under the chin.

Suddenly, Patch jumped up playfully on the woman, and she shrieked in surprise. Two black paw smears ran down the front of her sundress. Yasmine was already on it, securing Patch in the crate and offering a clean rag and water bottle to the woman.

Rae charged back to Patch's crate. "This dog is not for you."

Yasmine's jaw dropped. Mine fell off and hit the pavement.

Confused, the woman stopped scrubbing the stains and turned to the man.

"Excuse me?" he said, glaring at Rae.

"You're not dog people," Rae said matter-of-factly. "Owning a dog is a huge responsibility. You don't look or act like you're interested in that kind of work."

Yasmine stepped between Rae and the couple. "Listen, I know you're new and everything, and I don't mean to sound harsh, but you should probably go."

Rae's face flushed as red as if someone had dumped a gallon of cherry Gatorade on it.

"What a mouth on her!" the woman said. "How old are you?"

"Seventeen," Rae answered glumly.

"A shame no one ever taught you manners." The couple hurried away toward the parking lot.

Rae looked at me, and I could see her eyes watering up. I had no idea what to say.

Then Caryn appeared. The thing about Caryn was, she loved

dogs, but when it came to people—even shlubs like me who worked for nothing—she could be extremely harsh. "What's going on?" she snapped.

Yasmine folded a rag and slapped it against her thigh. "Well, in *her* expert opinion, those people were not fit to own a dog."

Rae straightened up proudly. I realized she was painfully unaware of the sarcasm in Yasmine's voice.

Caryn's eyes flashed. "What?"

Yasmine nodded. "Oh, yeah. Maybe we need to turn over the entire operation to—I'm sorry, I didn't catch your name?"

"Rae." She blinked a few times. "Those people weren't right for Patch."

"Outrageous!" Caryn exclaimed. "You're not even a volunteer here."

Rae's shoulders drooped. She looked like one of the abused rescue dogs, expecting to be kicked any second.

I stepped in. "It's on me. She was just trying to help."

"Yes, Braden. You are responsible for your guests," Caryn snapped.

"I am so sorry." I tried to explain. "She really did mean well."

"Will you stop talking about me as if I weren't standing right here?" Rae's volume rose.

Caryn raised an eyebrow. "You overstepped."

"You are not going to bully me!" Rae boomed.

Caryn and Yasmine shared a look.

I touched her arm. "Please, Rae. Calm down."

Rae recoiled. "It doesn't help when you say 'calm down'!"

"Okay. Fine. Whatever. Let's just go," I said, giving Caryn and Yasmine what I hoped was an apologetic look.

Rae slid on her sunglasses, ignoring me as we walked back to the car. "Hey," I said quietly. "Are you going to look at me or what?"

She was on the verge of tears. "It's neurological! It's not emotional. It's my brain!"

We drove home in silence, with Rae sitting all the way over, practically glued to the passenger door. When I pulled into her driveway, I turned off the engine. But she blew out before I had the chance to walk her to the door.

To be honest, it was a relief.

18

RAE

Apparently, I'd done something wrong. Again. And for the past twenty-four hours, I'd been tirelessly trying to figure out what.

Animals don't have voices. They need humans to protect them, and that's what I did for Patch. So why had Caryn attacked me?

Braden hadn't stuck up for me, either. Not really. Then again, hadn't I been expecting this to happen all along? I had this dark, doomed feeling in my gut. What I did or said had upset Braden. But I had done the right thing, protecting a dog. Hadn't I?

I sank to the floor of my bedroom, onto the cushy faux sheepskin rug Mom and I had picked out over spring break. That memory seemed to belong to some other girl. Now everything sucked.

Soon I was second-guessing myself about the dog adoption. Did I take things too far? Did Braden think I was a freak?

Freak. It had to be the most damning word anyone could say in high school, and I'd been called it so many times—that was my claim to fame. No one understood me. No one probably ever would.

I desperately needed to share all this with my best friend, but Arman had shut me out. It was unacceptable.

I broke down and texted him:

> I MISS YOU! I don't know what I did. Do you realize this is the longest we've gone without talking since you had your tonsils removed?

My cream-colored bookshelf was within reaching distance. I slid out my trusty copy of *The Mindful Path to Self-Compassion: Freeing Yourself from Destructive Thoughts and Emotions* by Christopher Germer, randomly flipped to page twenty-five, and read: "The challenge is to turn toward our difficulties with nonjudgmental awareness and compassion."

My instinct was to do the exact opposite: flee memories of the dog adoption gone wrong and embrace negative self-talk. Thoughts swirled inside my head, of Zach and Braden and Arman and all the friends I'd ever had and lost. My eyes kept filling up with tears, so I replaced the book on its shelf. It was hopeless. You could treat symptoms and sensory processing disorders. You could prescribe pills for anxiety and depression. But at the end of the day, there was no cure for autism.

I knew my parents wished there were one. Seriously, what parent would want an autistic child? Everyone's lives would be easier if I were normal. Dating wouldn't disappoint me. Car deodorizers wouldn't derail me. My parents might still be married.

Mom denied all that. She claimed the world needed people on the spectrum, who can be incredibly introspective and analytical. I mean, I analyzed myself *all the time*! And since neurodiverse people are expert self-analyzers, Mom believed they were also amazing at analyzing other things, like climate change, political movements, and yeah, dog rescue. She swore we brought a unique understanding to the world.

I knew she was right, and even as low as I felt in times like these, I wouldn't really want to be "normal." But still . . . .

A dull throbbing behind my left eye warned me to pay attention to self-care. Options included over-the-counter Tylenol, which rarely touched the stress-induced migraines I suffered once or twice a month, or the heavy-duty prescription Zomig, which made me want to catch some z's. Or I could simply meditate.

Meditation often worked pretty well for me. I closed my eyes and did a mental scan of my body: throbbing behind my left eye, tight neck, stiff shoulders. My heart was beating, but all it was doing was keeping a dead person alive.

I focused on my breathing, but the unwanted negative thoughts still came streaming in: *You just need to try harder. You lack self-discipline. Something in your environment is holding you back. Somewhere along the line, you stopped believing in yourself.*

I heard a knock on my door and became aware of Mom's voice in a distant way: "Dinner's ready! You know, I have a special council meeting tonight."

Actually, I didn't know. I'd forgotten that the oil well had officially become the Big Thing at school. If you were against it, you were "narrow-minded" and "old-fashioned." If you supported it, you were "greedy" and "reckless."

I pried my eyes open and forced myself back to reality, where I felt nothing but raw. Everything hurt. My legs felt shaky as I stood up from the sheepskin rug. My energy reserves were long gone.

"Coming," I said, trying not to let my voice give me away. Now was not the time to pop up on Mom's worry radar.

She had ordered Thai food, usually my favorite. I'm not what you'd call an adventurous eater. Pad Thai, spring rolls, rice, and chicken satay—I had this same meal two to three times a week. Tonight, though, the food smelled rotten.

Sitting down in the breakfast room, I tried mouth breathing to escape the odor and busied myself by checking my phone for texts from Braden or Arman. There were none.

Mom nodded at my phone. "Not at the table, okay?" In between bites, her jaw made a cracking sound.

"Ugh. Stop. That sound . . . ."

"Sorry. I need to get a mouth guard. Think it's TMJ."

"What the heck is TMJ? I'd look it up on my phone," I said, pausing dramatically, "*except you won't let me.*"

"It has something to do with the joints connecting your jaw to your skull. While I sleep, I've been grinding my teeth." One of the kitchen lights shuttered on and off, and the refrigerator hummed, and Mom dug into the noodles. *Click. Click. Click.*

Anger stirred within me.

Mom wiped her mouth with a napkin. "Tell me about the adoption with Braden?" She bit down on a spring roll. *Click. Click. Click.*

"It was nothing special." The fury roiled through me.

Oblivious, she sipped her water. "I don't know what's been going on with you lately: locked doors, ditching school, pushing another student to the ground. It's very upsetting to me."

I stopped chewing and spat a mouthful of food into my napkin. "The chicken tastes different."

"It's the same chicken we always order."

"There's too much salt. It tastes like teeth." I pushed my plate away.

Mom sighed. "This. What you're doing. It's a pattern."

"What do you want me to say? It's not edible."

"Fine. Don't eat it," she said, obviously annoyed. "But you owe Jill an apology. And I expect you to reschedule the appointment."

It wasn't like Mom to get exasperated this quickly. Believe me—I'd tried many times to provoke her. I got up from the table and found a bag of popcorn in the pantry.

Mom wiped her mouth again. "Rae, I'm going to ask you to consider something. I've found a school in Ojai. I think you'd be a lot happier there than you are at Pac Crest. Imagine being around other 2es all the time."

I yawned. The boarding school option was designed for 2es like me—short for *twice exceptional*, a catch-all label for kids who were gifted but also had special needs—when we weren't thriving in a traditional learning environment. If this place were anything like the others Mom had trotted out in the past, they'd have a ratio of three staff members to every student. My classes would be customized. And if Mom tried to ship me there, I would rather have died.

Mom ignored my complete disinterest. "You'd have friends who are more compassionate and understanding. You'd have more in common—"

"So, you want to get rid of me." I slumped in my seat, chewing popcorn. "Because I'm a problem child and you can't date while I'm around."

Mom set down her fork. "That's outrageous, Rae."

"When's the last time you went out on a date? Try never."

"My private life isn't really any of your business." Mom studied me. "You're scared. It's new. Change is hard."

"Did you read that off a fortune cookie?"

She closed her eyes for a second. "Trust me, the prospect of us living apart is the most frightening thing I've ever faced."

"I'm glad we agree this is completely unnecessary." I threw down the popcorn bag and pressed on my temples. It was too late for the migraine medicine. I should've taken it hours ago. Instead, I got up from the table and dimmed the kitchen lights.

Mom got up from the table and set the teapot on the burner. "I've come to the realization that nothing I do has been improving your situation at school. At Meadow Ranch School, you'd have a team of professionals around you to find solutions that work for you. You'd have interesting classes and friends who inspire you. There, bullies don't exist."

"Hell, no. I am not going."

Mom sounded desperate. "I *need* you to have an open mind."

"I want to stay here! In my *home*." I stood in front of her and tried to force down a bite of chicken to demonstrate my commitment. Then I started to gag and spat it back into my hand.

Mom exhaled. "I've given this a lot of thought, Rae."

I threw the chicken in the trash can and then realized I felt a little hungry after all. "Can you make me scrambled eggs? Please?"

Mom looked at all the to-go containers still sitting on the table. "They'll even make your favorite recipe from home once a month."

"Give me a break, already." I snatched up the popcorn bag again and dug around in it.

"Of course, you won't find any tattoo parlors on campus," she said, letting out a little laugh.

Hot fury flared in me. I dropped the popcorn, balled my hand into a fist, and slugged my mother in the face.

She screamed, and her hand flung up to her cheek as she staggered backward into a chair.

I was filled with instant regret. What had I done? "Mommy! I'm sorry. Oh, my god. I'm so sorry!"

But then a small voice deep within reminded me of the times when Mom didn't understand what I'd been going through or appreciate how hard I tried, and how in my darkest moments, I'd wanted to hurt her.

Mom sat still, rubbing her jaw.

I had never felt so ashamed in my life. "I didn't mean to do that! You were laughing at me and I . . . I lost control!"

The teakettle whistled. Mom calmly got to her feet and turned off the flame. Strangely mute, she rummaged for a bag of frozen peas in the freezer and held it against her jaw.

"Does it hurt, Mommy? I . . . I am never going to forgive myself for that."

What if *she* could never forgive me? I literally could not imagine being alone in the world without her love and support. A new level of desperation threatened to rise within me, a feeling that I might be incapable of going on.

I didn't want to live if Mom wasn't with me.

She finally spoke. "Set your alarm. Tomorrow you're going to school. No arguments." Then she walked out of the kitchen, and I started tugging violently at my hair.

Mom returned a few minutes later, holding her messenger bag.

"Where are you going?" I said, pulling a lock of hair out of my head.

"The special meeting on the oil and gas development." Mom had combed her hair so it covered the spot I'd punched.

"Can't you cancel it?"

"No. And to be honest, I'd like to take my mind off of . . . ." Her voice cracked, and she couldn't finish her sentence. She took a deep breath and hoisted her messenger bag up on her shoulder. Then she left and closed the door behind her.

I went berserk, smacking my head against the wall.

The dog scrambled away from me.

I finally stumbled to the bathroom and bit down on a washcloth until I thought my head would explode with pain. Next thing I knew, I was on the floor, unable to move.

Then something else happened.

My peripheral vision quit, and it was like looking through a telescope—only the viewfinder kept getting smaller until all I could see was a teensy dot of light. Just as that light winked out, so did my hearing.

I was alone in that nightmarish darkness.

The next morning, my alarm went off at seven. I quickly shut it off. I couldn't lift myself from the bed, let alone face school. Mom came in and tried to pull the covers off. "Let's go!"

I hadn't seen her again the previous night, even after I came out of the shutdown a few hours later and crawled on all fours to my room. Autistic people need time to heal from a shutdown. We need to be away from bright lights and loud noises. We need understanding.

I pulled the covers back over my head. "I'm sick."

"Take two Tylenol. You are not missing school again."

"Okay!" I said, my head already plopping back on the pillow.

A minute later, or it could've been fifteen, I heard purposeful knocking on my door. I knew it wasn't Mom, because she would've just come on in and opened the blinds.

A man's deep voice startled me. "Good morning, Rae. My name is Detective Figueroa of the PCPD, and I'm here with Officer Stanten."

WTF! I sat up, in complete shock.

"We'd like to talk with you for a couple minutes. Are you dressed?" a female voice asked.

Beyond scared, I pulled on the first thing I found in my closet: a black sweatshirt and worn-in jeans.

The woman spoke again. "May we come in?"

Opening my door, I looked straight into the eyes of a Pacific

Crest police officer. She was younger than Mom and about my height. Behind her stood a tall, older officer with black-framed glasses and a kind smile.

"Good morning!" he said, cheerfully.

My mind whirled. It was inconceivable that Mom had left me alone with two strangers. Maybe she'd suffered a concussion and was in the hospital. Maybe she had died. "What's going on? Where's Mom? How'd you get in here?"

"Actually, your mother let us in," Officer Stanten said.

It took a minute for that to sink in: *Mom called the cops. Mom called the cops* on me.

Detective Figueroa's eyes quickly scanned my room and then returned to focusing on me. He might have been curious. Or suspicious. I had trouble telling the two expressions apart. "She did the right thing, too, by calling us. Families need support, and sometimes it's easier to talk to us."

I ran past them and rushed downstairs to the kitchen. My mom was still there, sipping coffee, her face sporting an apricot-sized bruise. I was mortified. "Why are they here?" I looked over my shoulder at the cops, who had followed me downstairs.

"Refusing to go to school is not okay with me. It's also illegal."

My heart pounded. "What did you tell them?"

"It's your choice, Rae," she said loudly, avoiding my question.

"Okay, okay. Let me get on my shoes."

"And the day after tomorrow is the Meadow Ranch School tour."

I froze. She was locking me up.

Mom set her coffee cup in the sink. "Your shoes?" she said expectantly, looking at me as if my entire world hadn't just imploded.

19

BRADEN

My alarm clock jarred me out of a deep sleep. The tightness in my chest was there before I'd even slipped on my lucky four-leaf clover boxers. It could've been nerves over the history midterm that day, or maybe a cardiac event. I still couldn't rule out the fact that I'd sent a girl—a girl I *finally* liked—running.

The scene at the dog adoption had caught me off guard. I knew that Rae had the best interest of the dogs in mind. Should I have stuck up more for her? Then again, she'd totally sounded off about something that wasn't even remotely her call. That thing I adored about Rae—her unfiltered, no-bullshit, sheer honesty—was also the thing that embarrassed me.

In the kitchen, Mom set some breakfast in front of me: a mug of green tea and a yogurt bowl filled with granola and berries. My focus was all over the place; one minute I was reviewing flash cards, the next I was staring off into space, wondering if I would see Rae at school.

As I brought the mug to my lips, Dad walked in and made himself a cup of coffee. "I ran into Ellis Mackay at the gym. I love finding out from *him* that my son quit the basketball team."

By the tone of his voice, you'd think I was selling meth to toddlers. *Quit* was a dirty word that didn't mesh with my dad's Never Give Up philosophy.

"I don't understand." He took a sip from the *World's Greatest Dad* mug, the one I'd ordered four years earlier when he'd coached my travel basketball team and we'd won the championship. "Why wouldn't you run this by me?"

I started packing up my stacks of flash cards. "I was going to tell you. I switched into another elective—Life Skills. I'm helping kids with special needs."

Dad threw an annoyed glance at Mom, who calmly finished tucking Jenji's stray strands behind her ears. "Correct me if I'm mistaken. For as long as I can remember, your mom and I have been carpooling you to basketball practices and games, paying for sports camps, and supporting your dream of being an athlete. What happened?"

Homelessness? World hunger? Please! We have a crisis on our hands, people! Braden is no longer a member of varsity basketball! Never mind that he's struggling to keep his shit together. The fate of civilization hangs in the balance!

"Can we not talk about this right now?" I pointed out the mountain of flash cards next to my untouched breakfast.

Dad firmly set his coffee mug down on the table. "You kept this from me for weeks. You can give me five minutes."

Avoiding his intense stare, I bit into a strawberry. It promptly lodged in my throat. Coughing and gasping, I saw my obituary clear as day: death by fruit. An unwelcome whack to my back sent the fruit from throat to mouth. Eyes watering, I spit into my napkin, lucky to be alive.

Not yet able to speak, I tried to read Dad's expression. Concern for my health? Reverence to the almighty that his only son was breathing?

"Keeping this from me," he said, shaking his head. "So disappointing."

"Jesus, Dad," I rasped. "Playing high school basketball is not what you think it is, okay?" I could see Dad forming the words, starting some lawyerly argument I wouldn't be able to win. "And I'm done with it."

"We could've talked through this."

"No, Dad," I said, taking a micro-sip of tea. "You're wrong."

Mom played referee. "He's making a difference, Burton."

"You can't help but love these kids, Dad. Especially Simon. He's got Down syndrome, and he's a superhero freak, and he has this giggle—when he starts, you can't help cracking up too. And Jerome is passionate about whales—"

"Braden." Dad sat beside me. "You're a tutor. I respect that . . . ."

Aide. Friend. Not tutor.

". . . but it doesn't take away from the fact that you walked away from a rare opportunity that could've been equally worthwhile. Perhaps you could do both."

I gritted my teeth. It didn't matter what I said. He'd never get it. Dad couldn't compete in high school sports because he'd skipped two grades and was physically too small to make the team. Meanwhile, I was six feet tall and had some talent. Dad would never understand me walking off the court.

"You don't even know what you don't know!" he insisted. "You never gave yourself the chance to see how the season could develop. How you might have grown as a person and a player." He stopped talking and I foolishly thought he was done. "I know things don't come easy to a Bernstein."

Ah, there it was: the We're Bernsteins philosophy, a companion lecture to the Never Give Up sermon. I'd rather have contracted pink eye than take one more minute of it. "I don't want to talk about this anymore."

"Son, what happened?" Dad asked, impatient.

My throat went dry. "I can't really explain . . . ." It came out as a croak. My chest felt like someone had cinched a band around it. And Dad would not shut up.

Jenji got off the kitchen stool and stood next to me, holding my hand. Mom smoothed her bangs and said, "Go brush your teeth." But Jenji just held tighter.

"I'm okay, Jenji." I cleared my throat and made myself sound chipper. "Promise." She slowly let go of my hand.

Mom lifted a piece of waffle off Jenji's plate and popped it into her mouth. "At the end of the day, it's your life," she said, still chewing. "If helping others makes you happy and competition does not, then you're discovering who you are."

It wasn't the first time I'd appreciated Mom's special way of effortlessly normalizing tense moments.

Dad wrapped both hands around his mug and stared at it, as if it were a crystal ball. "What else haven't you told us?"

I have a goddamned midterm! my brain shouted.

"Time to go," Mom said in a sing-song voice, a reminder to Jenji. To Dad and me, she said, "This isn't working, and we need to fix it."

Then she swung two lunch sacks and held them out, urging us toward the door.

"I've been on the hunt, and I'm happy to report that I found a highly recommended therapist and, wait for it . . . she takes our insurance," she continued. Going off my look of utter disgust, she added, "Apparently she's amazing, but if she's not for you, there are plenty of others."

Digging my eye out with a spork seemed less painful and more promising. A quick glance at Dad told me that when it came to this one thing, we were finally on the same page.

Locker doors clanged shut and kids laughed too loud and all the while, I tried to keep my head screwed on and get to my first-period class. After recklessly touching the door handle to the History classroom, I thought I detected a tingling in my right thumb.

In my hurry to escape my disappointed dad, I had picked at a new hangnail until it bled. In my hurry to escape my well-meaning mom, I had forgotten to smear antibiotic ointment on my bloody fingertip. Death wish? Of course. What else would you call it when I'd left myself wide open to contracting a lethal infection in the high school cesspool?

Stepping into the classroom, I inspected my swollen, self-inflicted wound and worried that invisible, furry MRSA superbugs had already burrowed into my tissue. *Antibiotics are useless against methicillin-resistant staphylococcus aureus*, I recalled as I shakily dropped into my front-row seat, holding my deck of flash cards like a castaway clasps to a floating log.

I had gotten in the habit of preparing in advance. Way in advance. Basically, I studied until my eyes drooped from their sockets. Memorizing hundreds of 3×5's lent order to my life and flipping my flash cards gave me a sense of control. Only today it wasn't working. Midterms and MRSA and what if that something thumped over by that car was really a somebody? Now a new worry loomed: What if I royally screwed up my chances with Rae?

I stared down at the exam. Words ran together. A distant alarm sounded in my guts. My mind went blank. Beads of sweat hovered above my lip. My hands trembled. My pen slipped through my fingertips, clattering to the desk.

Looking around, I caught eyes with the teacher. Did Mr. Rose think I was trying to cheat? To get a look at my neighbor's answers? I anticipated the horror as he hauled me out of my seat and sent me to the vice principal's office. My chest thumped. My stomach clenched. It had been almost two years since Hojun died, but I knew the signs: I was having a full-blown panic attack.

I was suffocating in my seat. I had to get out . . . or die. I must've looked like hell because when I stood up to bolt from the room, Mr. Rose didn't stop me.

When I pushed the bathroom door, it flung open and banged against the wall, reverberating off the tile. I tottered to the toilet. My stomach contracted, and I fell to my knees. Helpless, I dry-heaved over the bowl.

It took a few minutes for life to trickle back into me. Though I was completely wrung out, I forced myself to go back to class and complete the history exam.

As I went through the motions the rest of the day, one thing became painfully clear: As much as I dreaded therapy, it was probably my only hope.

> *In the past four weeks, have you thought you were losing your mind?*
>
> *Do you believe that genetics, environment, or brain structure has caused your mental illness?*
>
> *Do you have something seriously wrong with you?*
>
> *Have you ever really been happy?*

That's what the survey from Mimi Kim, the therapist Mom found, seemed to be asking me. But what the survey actually said was:

In the past four weeks, have you had any emotional problems that interfere with your daily life, such as sadness, anxiety, or depression?

Overall, how would you rate your mental health? How often has your mental health affected your various relationships?

Have you ever been diagnosed with a mental disorder?

How often do you feel positive about your life?

Mimi herself oozed confidence and seemed to really care. Diplomas dotted the walls of her office. But my expectations about therapy were low. The last time I'd tried, when Hojun died, had been an epic fail.

After the requisite introductions, Mom went out to the waiting room and Mimi asked me to tell her a little about myself.

"I'm a junior at Pacific Crest High. Um, yeah. I'm a sports editor in journalism."

"You're into sports," Mimi said. "Which ones?"

"Basketball, soccer. I'll pretty much watch anything."

"Do you also *play* sports?"

My shoulders tightened. "For fun."

We soon got into the real reasons for the visit: the panic attacks, the worry thoughts that were multiplying daily. Mimi told me to buy *The Worry Cure* by Robert Leahy and gave me the game plan. "We'll go chapter by chapter at our sessions. There'll be some little assignments along the way. You'll see that many people are going through the same things."

She made it sound so straightforward, like we'd be reading *Macbeth*, and at the end of the semester I'd be a Shakespeare expert. I wasn't so sure it worked that way with learning to be normal and happy.

Then Mimi invited Mom back into the room and mentioned that she worked in partnership with a psychiatrist, Dr. LaViolet. "Research backs this up," she explained. "Therapy results come faster when the client takes certain medication."

Mom rubbed her chin. "Aren't there side effects of antianxiety medications? Unintended consequences?"

Mimi urged us to talk to Dr. LaViolet about this and ask questions to find out more. But a new worry had already sprouted in my head: unintended consequences.

20

RAE

ate last night, after two hours staring at the blank screen, two hours of torrential typing, and four hours of executive dysfunction, I finally finished drafting my first blog post. It was right there on the screen, ready to go, under Brenda's sketch of the girl with the iceberg face. She'd given me permission to use it as a banner on the home page if I ever decided to publish the blog.

AUTIEFREAK.COM:
Unfiltered Views from Your Average Awesome Autistic

OUT OF THE COMFORT ZONE

If I hadn't hit rock bottom, I would've never gotten around to blogging. No way! I'd be online, researching and rescuing dogs, and snacking on popcorn. Or I'd be holding hands with the cute boy that I (*still*) really like or practicing scenes for Drama Lab with my sweet (*former*) BFF.

Look at me now! I'm all about free WordPress accounts and figuring out how to embed hyperlinks. I'm all about laboring at my laptop trying to figure out: *How did I get here?*

Before I get into that, here is my pros/cons list on blogging:

Cons:

- Bloggers open themselves up to trolls.

- Bloggers share personal details of their lives in the mistaken belief that they're contributing something useful to the world.

- Bloggers can't resist sharing their opinions about everything, usually in a boring, overly simplistic way.

  Woops. I think I'm already boring you by oversimplifying.

Pros:

- Bloggers* help others feel less unhappy.

- Bloggers* connect to like-minded people.

  *Insert "may" here.

About me:

My name is Rae, short for Rachel—which no one ever calls me because the classic biblical name doesn't fit. For one thing, I'm an atheist. Also, in Hebrew, Rachel means "ewe," or female sheep. Sheep stay with the flock. They fit in. They wear the right outfits. They tend to play it safe.

That's not me.

I do not play it safe. I have impulse control issues. I spontaneously decide to get tattoos. I blurt things out. I have been known to throw a punch.

It's not uncommon to have impulse control issues when you're on the spectrum. When I was in preschool, I was diagnosed with autism spectrum disorder.

I'm a seventeen-year-old junior at a public high school in Southern California. My hair is pink. Last week it was black. Before that, it was blue. And I've been a dog freak for as long as I can remember.

Current status: I feel like I don't have a friend in the world.

There! Now that the hard part is out of the way, I promise not to throw a pity party. Hey, maybe *we'll* even become friends.

My best friend, to be fair, is my mom. She's a house dancer, a fan of Queen and the Eagles and pretty much anything '80s, and pretty enough to be one of those hipster-mom models you see in Anthropologie catalogs. No matter what, she will fight for me. I would not be doing well in school or anything else without her here to guide me and support me. Without her, I don't want to be on this planet.

At the same time, she bugs the living crap out of me.

Right now, Mom's seriously considering sending me away to boarding school. She believes this would be the best thing for me, and I can't blame her. Lately, I've been an epic turd. (Spoiler alert: It's possible my next post will be written from teenage autie lockdown in beautiful Ojai, California!)

Since middle school, I've been called all sorts of things: *misfit, odd, slut, freak.* Granted, my social skills suck. I get depressed. I hate life sometimes. I don't like me very much. Millions of memes target teen angst, but don't be fooled into thinking we're the same as other teens. There are major differences between neurotypicals and us spectrumites.

For example, I *know* I get bullied more than most "normal" kids. Even *adults* have unintentionally bullied me with unhelpful advice such as: *Get out of your comfort zone.* It's ironic, because trying to act normal *is* out of my comfort zone. Thanks to years of acting camp, social skills classes, and being in Drama Lab, I know how to do it—and I do it all the time. I modulate my voice and mimic the body language of a neurotypical until I am so exhausted by the whole effort that I crash.

Sometimes it's hard to know how much of my struggle is my diagnosis and how much is just who I am. And here's where you, the reader, come in: Do you think all of us teens grapple with finding and keeping friends? Do we all have trouble communicating with other people? Are we all just fighting to make it through the day?

As I proofread the post, I started to get excited—really excited. I uploaded my favorite photo of me holding Noodle on the About Me page. I couldn't wait to get it out there. I felt stronger than I had in days, maybe years.

Then it was time to press *Publish*, and fear drowned the excitement. Publish? How could I? By publishing, I'd be publicly confirming that I was stupid, ugly, and unlikeable. My blog would be like an open mic night for negative self-talk. Trolls would find my site, and they'd bait me and single me out. It would be even worse than the mean post on Instagram. This time, they'd crush my soul.

The noise in my head reached an unbearable volume.

Suddenly, I was back at my preschool playdate, with the police officer opening the door to the bathroom where I'd locked myself in. Then came overlapping thoughts of an equally terrifying future me: alone in a sterile-looking room, staring out the window at the golden hills of Ojai.

In the back of my mind, a tiny treasure shimmered: Braden's promise. He'd offered to read my stuff. A semblance of sanity filtered through the madness.

During lunch on Tuesday, I didn't see Braden in the cafeteria, so I slinked out, hoping to find him in the journalism room. Stepping in, I was struck by the laid-back feel of the classroom: old trophy cases, stacks of yearbooks on filing cabinets, chairs askew. Along the back wall, four kids were crammed onto a faded couch, the kind you generally see discarded on the sidewalk. They took turns tasting what looked like colorful cream-filled hockey pucks. I could hear snippets of their debate: *Are Japanese desserts just a fad or here to stay?*

More students clustered around a long, rectangular table. I saw that stocky Filipino guy, Braden's friend, sipping from a glass bottle of Coke. When he noticed me, he hoisted the bottle, like he was making a toast.

I looked away, my boldness faltering. Where was Braden?

From across the room, I caught eyes with Naomi, sitting with the other two journalism girls I'd met with Arman at the blood drive—Alicia and Shanice. They sat on their desktops, as if that were the most natural way to hang out in a classroom. Naomi adjusted her gold-rimmed glasses and waved. Then she and Alicia slid off the desks and stopped me before I could escape.

"Rae, right?" Naomi said. "What brings you here to our little dungeon?"

"I'm looking for Braden."

Naomi nodded to the back corner of the room. "He should be done soon."

Inside a glass-walled office cubicle, Braden and a stooped, gray-haired man leaned over a desk, deep in conversation.

"How is Arman?" Naomi asked.

"Right. He's fine," I said, not knowing if he was fine or in a coma. "I'll come back later."

Alicia stopped me before I could bolt. "I almost didn't recognize you," she said. "Wasn't your hair black the other day?"

I looked at my feet, self-conscious.

"I love your style!" Alicia touched the ends of my bangs.

Boundaries! Wow! I had to consciously hold myself in place to avoid recoiling.

"Can I take your photo?" She'd already removed the lens cover from her camera.

"No!" I took a step back. "Absolutely not. I'm sensitive about having my picture taken."

Alicia lowered the camera and snapped the lens cover back on. "Can I ask why?"

"It's none of your business," I said, matter-of-factly. I wanted to look her in the eye, but instead my gaze flickered to the corner of the room, searching for Braden.

Alicia *tsked*. "I meant it as a compliment."

She seemed upset, but I didn't know why. I hadn't run *my* paws through *her* hair!

Naomi removed her glasses and cleaned them on her T-shirt. "Not everyone is obsessed with having their photo taken, Alicia."

The door to the teacher's cubicle opened, and Braden stepped through. When he saw me, he froze.

My chest felt like it caved in. This had all been a terrible mistake. I'd ruined everything. Of course I had. I did a nervous half turn and almost tripped on my own feet.

Braden rushed over and caught me, both hands on my waist, and steadied me. As soon as I was stable, he removed his hands. My skin tingled where he'd touched it.

"I can be really clumsy," I said under my breath.

"Inner ear problems can cause a lack of balance. Or nerve damage in your legs," he said.

Alicia rolled her eyes. "I don't know why you waste your talents on journalism, Braden."

"When you could be out there diagnosing all of us." Naomi flicked his ear.

"I should go," I said, still reeling from the feeling that Braden didn't want me there.

Braden blinked, confused. "Hold on a second. You just got here."

Maybe I'd missed the cues, because now it didn't seem like he wanted me to leave. "I finally got around to the blog."

Naomi looked closer at me. "Ooh! You're a blogger?"

I liked these girls, but I didn't trust them. I fidgeted with a thread hanging off my sleeve. I was *so* not ready to talk about AutieFreak.com.

"Aren't you guys on deadline?" Braden asked the girls.

Naomi gave Alicia a look, and they left, but not before inviting me back to the journalism room anytime and insisting I take one of the rice flour Japanese mochi they'd been sampling.

Licking powdered sugar off my fingers, I got right to the point. "You said you would read my stuff."

"I'd be honored! After how we left off the other day, I wasn't sure, if . . . . Well, you know what I mean."

Actually, I didn't. I waited for him to give me a context clue—or better yet not make me guess and just use his words instead. That didn't happen. But I still relaxed. Clearly, he wanted me to stick around. "Please don't tell anyone about this." I pulled my laptop from my backpack.

"Why? Is it illegal? Or dangerous?"

I couldn't tell if he was kidding, but I found myself cracking up. "No!"

Braden sat at the rectangular table with my open laptop and began to read.

"Oh, my god. Is it awful?" I asked. "You can tell me. I thrive on criticism."

"Let me read, woman!" he said in a mock deep voice.

I stood over him as he read. He had broad shoulders and a slight hunch. His nails were ridiculously short. If things had been different between us, I might have put my hands on his shoulders. I might have breathed in the clean pine scent of his skin.

"Now that you're a writer, I need to give you some hints. You ready?"

I braced myself for the worst. *Wait, did he just say* writer?

"One, no one thrives on criticism. And if they do, we hate those people. Two, you have a really unique voice. Three, you're missing a comma in the second paragraph."

In a small voice, I asked, "Do you like it?"

Braden tapped the seat beside him for me to sit down. I did. "And four, you have to keep writing. This is amazing!"

I felt my body float. This, it dawned on me, was pure happiness.

Braden understood what I wrote. Therefore, he understood me. And it stood to reason that he truly liked me. *More* than liked me. I desperately wanted to sit in his lap and throw my arms around him. I wanted to kiss him. He had a great mouth, big but not too big, with masculine, square teeth . . . .

"Rae?" he asked. "You look like you were somewhere else there for a second?"

I was so ridiculously grateful, I could barely form a sentence. "Thank you," I murmured, wiping my eyes.

"I just have to ask," Braden said, his cheeks flushing a little, "are you okay? I mean, boarding school? Ojai?"

That was three questions.

"Is there anything I can do to make you feel better?" he asked.

"Probably not," I said, truthfully. "But if you want to sit with me and not say much, that'd be okay."

He gave me a funny look.

"Sometimes the best thing you can do is just be available."

He nodded.

I slid the laptop closer and added in the missing comma. "About the other day at the dog adoption. Can we forget the whole thing ever happened?"

"God, I was hoping you'd say that!"

"When you're labeled 'high-functioning'—and you can see why I obviously hate that term—you're expected to get all the social cues. I'm supposed to know when to pause in a sentence. To get when it's time to stop doing whatever I'm doing and see to the needs of others. To wear the right clothes. To realize that when your friend invites you to a dog adoption, and you feel overwhelmed, you should recognize the warning signs of a meltdown."

Unexpectedly, Braden hugged me. I shrank back.

"I'm sorry!" he said, closing his eyes and putting his palm to his forehead. "I totally forgot you don't like hugs."

"*Sometimes* I like hugs. Depends on the situation. What I like least are surprises. It's better all-around if you ask me before you hug."

"You don't happen to want a hug right now, do you?" he asked.

"Actually, I kind of do." I went for it and hugged *him*.

It took Braden a second, but then I felt his arms reach around me for a gentle squeeze. He was so much taller than me that my head ended up against his chest and I could hear his heartbeat. It felt like love. But then, what did I know?

21

BRADEN

Across the journalism room, Lucas made sure I saw his tongue flick in and out of his mouth. Pretty freaking obscene, but I suppose I deserved it after keeping Rae a secret from him all that time. Plus, I had blown off his invite to the Mint on Saturday night, so there was that. The passing bell rang, signaling the end of lunch period.

I reluctantly released Rae from our first-ever hug. "Let's get out of here. I'll walk you to your next class."

Rae shot a glance at the teacher. "You mean, you walk out whenever you feel like it?"

"As long as we meet our deadlines and do a decent job, Mr. Hackbarth is totally chill."

Rae peered around our drab classroom like it was Disneyland. "You're so lucky."

Despite wearing my lucky boxers yesterday morning, I'd had a full-blown panic attack, which didn't seem so fortunate. Not that Rae needed to know this. "Why don't you submit your post to Mr. Hackbarth? If you want, I could help you adapt it." I grabbed my stuff, and we stepped outside into the deserted hallway. "Maybe you could be a staff writer."

As we walked, Rae adjusted her backpack, and her T-shirt rode up an inch or two. She absent-mindedly ran her hand over her hip, just above her tattoo. My attention shifted to her delicate fingers and the contrast between the shiny black nail polish against the paleness of her skin. I could've stared at those hands all day long.

"Look," Rae informed me, "on the outside, I'm badass. On the inside, I'm not self-confident. So, when you say, 'Hey, you can write for *Neon Vikings,*' I have to battle my negative self-talk, the monster voice."

Monster voice?

"I'm *super* sensitive about other people's negative reactions to me. And you should see me at home," Rae said. Her eyes got a faraway look. "I'm constantly apologizing to my mom when it feels like my autistic mind's taken control and the monster voice has gotten too loud."

Monster voice. When she said it the second time, my brain turned into WebMD: *Symptoms of schizophrenia and psychosis include hearing voices in your head.* Not good.

"It's like a voice reminding me every day that I'm wrong, that I'm not deserving of support. Growing up, a neurodiverse person gets thousands of negative dings compared to a neurotypical. I'm still working on getting the hang of not assuming I'll be rejected, like, every single time I put myself out there."

The matter-of-fact way Rae spilled her guts blew my mind. Who does that? I'd never met anyone as honest. Or naïve. No one I'd ever met confided in me the way she did.

I glanced over my shoulder at some kids chatting at their lockers nearby. "Listen, about that monster voice. You don't *actually* hear someone talking to you, err, in your head?"

The corner of her mouth twitched as she tried to suppress a smile. "You took me literally. Interesting. Literal interpretation is usually *my* default."

I relaxed.

Rae stared down the corridor. "Arman calls me an oversharer. Or at least, he used to." Her voice went flat. "There's a reason, though, why I keep bringing the subject back to me." She stopped and turned to me. "I'm sharing because I'm trying to reach out to you."

I thought that meant she liked me more than just a friend, which made me happy. Okay, *nervous* and happy. I still worried that people would judge me for hanging out with the weird girl. And Rae was unpredictable and complicated. Deep down, did I really want to work this hard over a girlfriend?

I could be a real asshole sometimes.

Rae stared up at me, blinking slowly. It became very clear that I should respond now, but she spoke first. "And I thought *I* was the one missing the conversation gene." And just like that, she took hold of my hand.

And just like that, my palms released enough moisture to make begonias bloom in the Mojave Desert. "Oh, geez. Sorry." I started to pull away.

She laced her fingers through mine. "Trust me, when something bugs me, you'll know!"

We walked down three flights like that. Just as we got to the auditorium lobby, she stumbled. I steadied her, saying, "Happens to everybody."

"But to me, happens a little more." Then she stopped in her tracks.

I followed her line of sight to Arman. He was near the stage, chatting with Taylor and Kennedy, who normally wouldn't spend three seconds of their fabulous lives on a "nobody" like Arman. The girls were modeling their T-shirts and having some sort of discussion about them.

Odd, I thought, as I observed Andy—resident stage crew boss and Accutane poster boy—fist-bumping Arman like they were bros.

Rae sagged out of her backpack. "I really don't want to be here right now."

"Arman and Andy? That's disturbing," I said, hoping that showed my support.

"It's nauseating."

"But once rehearsal starts, it'll be fun, right?"

If Rae heard me, I couldn't tell. As we made our way down the aisle, she seemed focused on a point near her feet. Approaching the stage, she accidentally bumped into Kennedy.

"Watch out!" Kennedy hissed, curling her fingers into claws. "Keep your hands and feet away from its mouth!"

Taylor chimed in. "It bites!"

Rae's face darkened.

Andy grinned, and the girls broke into laughter. Arman busied himself with his phone as Rae fled past him up the steps to the stage.

I joined their circle, startling them. "Hey, Kennedy? Taylor? Not cool." I sounded mildly threatening. I felt mildly threatening.

"It's called a joke, Braden," Taylor cooed.

From close-up, I could see that Kennedy's and Taylor's T-shirts matched. Each had a silkscreen design of a cheerful oil well and a slogan: *SAVE OUR SCHOOL!*

"Braaaden," Kennedy purred. "My eyes are up heeere."

I glanced back at her face. "Just . . . can you please quit messing with Rae?"

Andy carefully straightened the sleeve of his pressed button-down shirt. "Is that your attempt at chivalry? To get in Rae's pants?" He shook his head. "News flash, Braden! No need. It's easy—just ask your teammate Zach. Oh, wait! You're not on the basketball team anymore. My bad."

"Go to hell," I growled. I contemplated the idea of smacking the smirk off Andy's face.

Arman's soft voice stopped me. "Andrew, please. That's just so harsh."

Andy sighed and looked me over like I wasn't worth the effort. "Maybe you're right, Arman. I have to work on being more of a team player so we can close the oil well deal and get the funds to create a campus commitment to the LGBTQ community. Like I said, you deserve to be seen and heard." Then Andy held up his fist.

Arman hesitated. I was hoping he'd spit on the fist or at least walk away. Instead, he gave Andy a fist bump.

I searched for Rae onstage and found her standing in the wings next to the girl with the combat boots. The girl pointed to something in her script, but Rae stared off into nothingness. I wanted to smooth her unbrushed pink hair and tell her everything would be okay. Before I had the chance, Mr. Barsanti announced that everyone outside of the cast and stage crew had to leave the auditorium.

I pushed through the double doors, with Taylor and Kennedy right behind me. "What's with the T-shirts?" I asked.

"We're, like, a political action group? We're advocating to save our school," Taylor announced.

"Golly!" I raised my eyebrows. "I didn't realize our school needed to be saved."

Taylor sneered. "Andrew has insider info. Because of his dad being on the city council and everything? There'll be money for new cheerleader uniforms and new laptops for the language lab."

Kennedy perked up. "And an organic vegetable garden!"

"Right. Organic gardens and gas rigs. Always a winning combo," I said, with a sarcastic nod of approval.

Kennedy folded her arms in exaggerated defiance. "The oil well will solve so many problems, Braden. Budget deficits. Staffing shortages—"

"Don't forget world peace," I added.

Avoiding triggers was one thing. Avoiding the need to seek reassurance from my parents was another. Both were necessary, according to my new therapist, Mimi. She was adamant about me going alone to my appointment with Dr. Drug—I mean Dr. LaViolet. For seventeen years of my life, I had been getting my parents' advice, whether I wanted it or not. Now, when shit was getting real, I was supposed to fly solo and be happy with that.

At least there were no surveys and no assigned reading like I had with Mimi. Just a consent form so she had permission to discuss me with Dr. LaViolet.

In his Beverly Hills medical office, we did the getting-to-know-you chat, after which Dr. LaViolet pronounced, "You're a great kid!" and "You've got anxiety, okay?" Then came the moment of truth: He gave me a prescription for a pill to take at bedtime.

There could be side effects. Drowsiness. Nausea. Suicidal thoughts.

"We're going to monitor you very closely," Dr. LaViolet said. That sounded comforting and alarming at the same time.

Later that night, alone in the bathroom, I stared at the bottle. What if I became incapable of functioning without the pill? What if the chemicals screwed up my brain? What if the pill made me want to hang myself off our backyard basketball hoop and Dad found me swaying in the wind?

I gave myself a pep talk. "You can do this! Nothing's going to happen! You'll feel better!"

"Who you talking to?" My sister's voice outside the bathroom door startled me.

"Hey, Jenji, you wouldn't happen to have any snickerdoodles left . . . ?"

Her pride in her baking could not be underestimated. I heard her scampering away and finally got the nerve to swallow the tiny pill. As soon as it slid down my throat, I felt sick, like I was going to barf or faint, or barf while fainting.

I heard Jenji again, on the other side of the door. "Ready for cookies?"

22

RAE

'd looked up Meadow Ranch School and read their philosophy (inclusive!), modalities (clinically proven!), and testimonials (patently predictable!). None of it was encouraging. So while I packed the necessities for my unwanted visit—water, headphones, charger cord, popcorn—I also brought along my book bag in case I could convince Mom to forget the whole insane idea of boarding school and just drop me off at Pac Crest instead.

That didn't happen.

As we drove, Mom fielded calls on speakerphone. First, it was school board president Lisa Patel, babbling on about the oil well. "We've been running at a deficit for years, Elizabeth. Sometimes the easy thing is the right thing. With a good lawyer and the right contract—"

"Let me stop you, Lisa. I know enrollment is down, and that's not a good look for the city. Neither is an environmental catastrophe," Mom said firmly.

She'd barely hung up before someone named Ned from the Planning Commission called about—you guessed it—the oil well.

"The way they're spinning this," he said, "we've got our work cut out for us. Let's hope the EIR sheds some light."

"It has to," Mom replied. "When I see the data, I'll have a better idea. But my gut says this is a bad deal. Ned, you and I have been friends a long time. It's hard to not take this personally when they're bad-mouthing me. And now they've got kids at the high school lobbying for them."

BOR-ING.

After yet another phone call came in, I clamped on my noise-canceling headphones and listened to my handpicked playlists, designed to regulate me and bring me some peace for the rest of the drive. We exited the 101, took a series of turns onto smaller and smaller streets, and ended up on a bumpy dirt road.

I tugged off my headphones, feeling carsick. Mom had finally gotten off the phone and was singing along to Queen's *I Want to Break Free*. Ironic, considering its strong message of freedom and liberty. Sometimes I would sing with her, and maybe she was waiting for that. Not today. Maybe not ever.

"It's beautiful here," Mom commented, as if we were on a summer road trip admiring the scenery instead of journeying to my future jail.

"Can you not do that? The whole 'accentuate the positive' thing you do? We both know the real reason I'm here is because I . . . I hit you."

Mom studied the road and steered around a deep rut without further comment.

We pulled into the school parking lot—basically a dirt patch surrounded by boulders and tall grass. Scattered around a sizable main building with a tall, pitched roof were several one-story buildings. Mom had mentioned there were only fifty-eight students, in eighth through twelfth grades. Pac Crest High dwarfed this campus. It felt like I was going back to preschool, except in those good years, someone always arrived at the end of the day to pick me up.

The pleasant, nutty smell of hay drifted into the car, and I spied three horses grazing in a nearby pasture. Mom had tried to interest me in the school's equine therapy program. I stared out the window at the horses, wondering about how they needed to be "broken" so they'd learn the "right" behaviors to be around humans.

If I get stuck in this place, I vowed, *I'll learn to ride and then escape on one of the horses.*

"Let's go," Mom said as she gathered her bag.

I didn't budge. Nothing and no one could make me stay here, away from my precious Noodle. I would crawl seventy-seven miles on my belly all the way back to Pacific Crest if I had to, rather than be caged up like a prisoner away from my dog.

"How many times do I need to say this, Rae?" Mom rubbed her forehead. "It's just a forty-five-minute tour."

"What do you call it when your worst fears come true?" I asked her. "A nightmare? No, you eventually wake from those. A tragedy? Sounds much too literary, like a Shakespeare play full of epic characters in cool costumes, imparting wisdom—"

"Listen to you!" She sounded genuinely impressed. But she still got out of the car and waited—to see if I'd change my mind, I guess.

Don't think so, Mom.

"Okay. Have it your way." Mom strode toward the main building, leaving me behind in the car.

I was proud of myself for holding my ground. Even with the car door open, though, my brain seemed to be boiling. Soon I had trouble remembering what day it was, let alone coming up with an accurate description of my new impossible, horrid hell.

As the minutes ticked on, I sat in the Meadow Ranch parking lot, stubbornly glued to the passenger seat of Mom's Tesla, undies adhered to my butt cheeks while perspiration dampened my scalp and slid between my boobs. She could've left the car keys inside so I could enjoy air-conditioning, but obviously she didn't trust me. To be fair, I wasn't sure *I'd* trust me alone in the car with keys. Restraint didn't come naturally to me, and the temptation to bolt pulsed through my veins.

Maybe I'll pass out, I thought. *That'd be good.* Mom deserved to be punished for putting me through this.

For the zillionth time, I looked up at the doors to the main building where Mom had gone for her scheduled tour with the almighty director, Dr. Joanna Clark. A tall girl in a yellow tank top and jeans was walking past the doors with a freckle-faced boy wearing flip-flops and shorts. They didn't seem abused or overmedicated. In fact, their smiles appeared authentic. Evil Dr. Clark had probably given them an extra scoop of ice cream at lunch.

I scrolled on my phone for more information about Meadow Ranch. The website had an interview with Dr. Clark, who stressed the rigor of the college-prep coursework. "We're not looking for easy," she pronounced.

Among the video parent testimonials, one mother stood out. "More than academics, it is the culture here. My daughter felt accepted, and because she felt comfortable, she could settle in and become the person she needed to be." These were familiar arguments that Mom had tried to use on me. And maybe right now, Mom was inside not just touring but signing papers—papers that legally bound me to stay here.

Goodbye, Mom. Goodbye, Noodle. Goodbye, freedom.

As I pried my sticky thighs off the leather seat, I felt the rising panic, the desperate need to get out. Who could rescue me? Who had a car?

Dad? My mind whirled around, picking up memories of him. One day in seventh grade, he'd forced me to take a peanut butter and jelly sandwich on wheat bread to school after we ran out of water bagels, which were the only bread I liked. I cried half the day and had to be sent home. Then there was the time Dad had lost his temper when he signed up to coach soccer and I'd refused to get on the field. And after my tenth birthday, he had stormed into my room and thrown away my favorite blanket, the one I'd used to comfort myself when I needed to suck my thumb.

Next!

Braden? He seemed to really care about me. Plus, he had a car. I pictured him tearing into the parking lot, kicking up gravel and dust, and then me busting out of Mom's car and making my getaway. Then I remembered: Driving on the freeway made him anxious.

I checked my phone, and what do you know? I had a new text.

Braden: Where r u?

Me: Spell out "are" and "you." #PetPeeve

Braden: Where ARE YOU? Ditching and getting a cold brew? Get me one! Ms. Sauer is reading off her slides again. Death by PowerPoint!

Me: Ojai.

Three blinking dots pulsed in our text chain. He didn't know what to say. I had probably freaked him out. Well, if he was freaked out, imagine what *I* was going through! Then my phone *binged* at last:

Braden: Can I see you when you get home?

Before I could think of a response, the driver's-side door swung open. Mom took one look at me and then did a quick, nervous survey of the parking lot. "God, Rae."

My top was pulled up in my vain attempt to cool off. I tugged it back down.

"Do you need to use the bathroom before we head for home?"

I vigorously shook my head. *Home.* Hallelujah! Get us out of this hellhole. My eyes teared up. Mom blasted the AC, and I closed my eyes, relishing the cool air and my cherished freedom. "Did you really expect me to bunk with a total stranger?"

"If we do decide this is the way to go, it would be temporary," Mom explained.

Oh, shit. My eyes popped open. It wasn't over.

The bruise on Mom's jaw had shrunk to the size of a quarter, but it wasn't gone. Neither were the memories of my outburst and that unforgiveable punch.

"You think that I'm unfixable," I accused her, my voice thick with emotion, "that something is really wrong with me."

"You and I both know we can't go on like this, Rae. You're ditching class. You're not bonding with people. You're not eating or sleeping well."

"I punch my own mom."

Mom didn't skip a beat. "You're not coping well. Not yet." She checked the rearview mirror and backed out of the parking spot. "That boy you were seeing. Zach. I can't help thinking maybe you're not over him."

I fumed. "Please! You think you know more than you do." Mom could study city policy and provide her proclamations. What she couldn't do was study my entire romantic life, as pathetic as it was, and sum it up in fifteen words or less. That, I wouldn't accept.

We drove past a barn with more horses leaning out of their stalls, their long faces elegant and soulful. After a few minutes, Mom turned the AC down a bit. Traffic was moving, and she relaxed her hands on the wheel.

"There's a team, you know," she said as though we'd been speaking all along. "Teachers, coaches, consultants, therapists. They seemed kind. Professional."

"Did you memorize the brochure?"

Mom briefly gazed my way before turning her focus back to the road. "Everyone here is dealing with heavy stuff. Don't you want to be with people who understand you?"

"Sounds like the ninth ring of hell."

"Which one is that?"

"Treachery." My head throbbed. If my own mom, the only person in the whole world who supposedly understood me, wanted to send me away, then something was really wrong with me. I was broken beyond repair.

You're unlovable, my monster voice assured me, just before I drifted off to sleep.

I woke up as we were passing the mall near school. "What time is it?" I asked, rubbing my eyes.

"Noon," Mom replied. "Let's get you back for rehearsals."

Normally I would have welcomed those words. But Drama Lab—the only class I had genuinely liked, with people who had actually accepted me—now sucked. And I *still* didn't know why Arman had suddenly ended our friendship and would willingly hang out with Andrew.

Suddenly I wasn't so eager to get back there. "I have to pee."

We stopped at the closest Starbucks, and I rushed off to the bathroom before Mom had even stepped out of the car. After I relieved myself and thoroughly washed my hands, I met Mom in line. I bought a gluten-free bagel, a fruit-to-go, and two cold brew coffees—one for me, one for Braden, as I had to explain to my nosy mom.

When Mom finally pulled up to the curb by the front lawn at school, we noticed a huge paper banner affixed to a fence. Someone had painted an oil well surrounded by birds and trees with our school buildings in the background. In large green letters the slogan urged: *Save Our School.*

Mom squinted at the banner for a long time. Then she seemed to remember I was still there, sitting beside her. She cleared her throat. "Go try to have some fun, will ya?"

23

BRADEN

As I unlocked the kitchen door, it finally sank in: Rae had brought me coffee—me!—and now she was supposedly being shipped off to Ojai. I let my backpack slide off my shoulder and crash to the kitchen floor, mulling over my shitty luck.

Mom frowned from her usual post at this hour: the kitchen counter, where she was patting plant-based "meat" into patties. "Do you mind picking that up?" she asked, nodding at my pack. "Before someone trips on it."

"Sure thing," I said, reaching for the backpack. "Just make sure we don't die from salmonella."

She resumed her patting and lobbed a rhetorical question. "Do peas even carry bacteria?" That was followed by a loaded one. "How you feeling?"

Feeling about my first full day on the new medication? Feeling about Rae? "Fine."

She peered at me. "Don't you dare settle for 'fine.'"

My first therapy appointment with Mimi had felt promising, and today I hadn't freaked out as much. Maybe the medication was making a difference too. And even though she didn't realize it, Rae had a special way of making me feel important, worthy, enough. "Mom. I'm good."

She sighed in relief. "That's better." Underneath the table, you could hear Spark's tail thump against the wood floor, a reliable barometer of Mom's mood.

I decided to take our pup for a run. By mile two, the stress I'd bottled up began to loosen; I could breathe. The runner's high, or endorphins, or whatever that good feeling is after you go all out, hummed through me.

Minutes later, I stepped into the shower and let the warm water cascade over me. My eyes closed, and thoughts of Rae played in my mind's eye.

Then Jenji yelled through the door: "You're using up all the hot water!" She had the worst timing. Always.

Sitting at the desk in my bedroom, I ate half a bag of sourdough pretzels and read another chapter of *The Worry Cure*. Mimi had also given me therapy "homework": to track my worries. She'd instructed me to dedicate a time every day to worry. I wrote my worry thoughts and responses on a notepad that I kept buried in the bottom drawer of my desk. It was supposed to give me a sense of control. Weirdly enough, even after just two days, it was working:

Today I worried I contracted hepatitis A from the guy at Whole Foods who works at the fish counter. I don't have symptoms, but I did eat salmon last week.

During class, I worried Mr. Rose thought I was a cheater. He hasn't said anything to me yet. But what if he does? What if my transcripts are screwed, and no college will touch me?

*I worried at lunch that Connor drinks too much and that he's
becoming an alcoholic.*

*I shouldn't care, but I fear people will look down on me for
seeing Rae. And why won't she tell me why she might be sent
away? She doesn't have a problem telling me everything else.*

The hum of the air conditioner started to lull me to sleep, and I
returned the legal pad to its hiding place in my desk drawer before
kicking off my shoes and collapsing on top of my bed. The next time
I opened my eyes, it was dark outside.

Mom walked past my bedroom door. "Got time for a quick bite?
I made sweet potato fries to go along with your salmonella slider."

"Yum, pass the bacteria burgers and fries!"

I sat at the kitchen table with my parents, Jenji, and her friend
Felicity. Mom passed around a vegetable salad with tomatoes and
cucumbers from our own backyard—not that I liked tomatoes or
cucumbers. But Mom glanced at me, so I dutifully dumped a small
pile onto my plate.

The girls giggled the entire time, talking in some made-up language. "What's so funny?" Dad asked, prompting more laughter.

"I like this little impromptu family dinner," Mom said cheerfully.
"We should do this more often."

I didn't share Mom's zest for the family meal. Lately, it was trig-
gering. I chewed some fries and said, thoughtfully, "If I had my way,
we'd all eat takeout in separate rooms with our own laptops."

Dad pointedly ignored me. "Where do you kids see yourself in
five years?" Jenji wanted to be president of an animal rights club at
the high school. Felicity wanted to be the vice president.

"I'd like to live in a yurt and own the Lakers," I quipped.

The girls' conversation drifted to summer camp plans, and I used that break in the action to successfully hide most of my salad beneath a multigrain roll before scraping it all into the trash and putting my plate in the dishwasher.

Sitting on a cake plate was Jenji's latest baking project. I tugged on her ponytail. "That looks amazing, but what're *you* all having for dessert?"

Jenji and her BFF giggled again.

"No matter how hard we work, we must also eat," Mom said, returning to the previous conversation. "To sit down together to a good, nutritious meal nourishes body and soul. If our world is heartless, well, we've got to talk to each other! It's a start."

"Amen," Dad said, helping himself to a slice of cake and turning on the Yankees–Red Sox game.

After dinner, I walked up the block to Connor's house. Standing by the front door, I could already smell the weed. Connor let me in, and I found his Scout troop buddies draped over the furniture. Joe thumped on a bongo drum, his bloodshot eyes contrasting nicely with his green Celtics T-shirt. In his own world, Alex strummed the same two chords on a guitar. Jeremy recorded all of us with his phone.

"Colleges look at social media when they're reviewing applications," I reminded him.

Jeremy lowered his phone. "You don't trust me to not upload this to social media?"

I smiled sweetly. "I don't trust you to remember what you said ten seconds ago."

Connor settled on the piano bench, playing a moody tune. "I've been thinking about this, how we're the last generation before civilization goes south. You've got wildfires burning out of control and sea levels rising. Covid morphing. The disappearance of Venice."

"Venice Beach is gone?" Joe asked. "How did I not know that?"

I strode deeper into the room, hoping the skunky weed smell wouldn't cling to my clothes.

Connor waved a hand toward his parents' bar. "Help yourself."

Behind a six-pack of beer, I found a bottle of Pellegrino and plopped on the couch beside Joe. He slurped from a tall cup of something that looked like water and smelled like rubbing alcohol. I'd forgotten how incredibly boring it was to be the only sober guy in the room.

Last summer I'd gotten drunk for the first time at one of Connor's kickbacks and thrown up all over my Aunt Amy's rose bush. She was less than thrilled, but she still told us, "We'd rather have you guys safe at home than wandering who knows where or, god forbid, driving."

Aunt Amy and Uncle David were the cool parents with the go-to house. Honestly, I got the sense that they were living vicariously through us—that being an adult kind of sucked.

Alex set the guitar aside and pulled a vape pen from his pocket.

"Does it bother you?" I asked him. "Losing brain cells by the millions?"

Alex wiped his watery eyes. "That theory's been debunked. Alcohol and tobacco? *Those* destroy brain cells." Alex took all the hardest classes and got A's in them. Still.

"I read that the teenage brain can be adversely affected," I countered, "and weed can cause tachycardia and xerostomia."

"Meaning?" Alex picked up the guitar again.

"Meaning your brain is compromised, your heart beats a little fast, and you get dry mouth."

That set off a round of laughter. I gave my best courtesy smile and scrolled through my photo library until I found Rae at the dog adoption. I lingered on her.

"Time to leak the lizard," Connor announced, before tripping and going down on one knee. I helped him up and spotted him as he wobbled across the living room.

"You gonna hold it for him?" Joe teased.

"Only if he asks nicely," I said, steering Connor away from the corner.

Connor hugged me. "I love this guy." He took the last few steps to the bathroom, unassisted.

"Try not to destroy your liver before your twenty-first birthday, alright?"

Leaving the bathroom door open, Connor called out, "Speaking of cans, have you guys been to the boys' bathroom in the Science & Technology Building?"

Instead of sending a plumber, they'd sealed a bunch of busted toilets in black trash bags. Classy. I'd mentioned it to Naomi, thinking it would be a funny topic for *Neon Vikings*—even though it wasn't really funny that our school always seemed to be so cash-strapped.

"Why can't they friggin' *fix* 'em?" Jeremy slurred his words.

Like most of my classmates, I had a love-hate relationship with my school. Mr. Hackbarth was a character, but he knew his stuff. My freshman-year English teacher was incredible and kind and taught me more about writing than my sophomore- and junior-year teachers combined. Sauer and a few other teachers were awful—the ones who either couldn't stand us or didn't care at all and didn't belong within one hundred miles of a school.

"I know we're a public school and everything, but is it too much to expect to have working shitters?" Alex complained, dramatically plucking a string. "Geez, we're not asking for them to offer astronomy and oceanography classes like Campbell Hall!"

The tuition at Campbell and other private high schools cost almost as much as college, and my parents believed Pac Crest offered an equally good education. Then again, they hadn't taken a tour of the boys' bathroom lately.

Joe pumped his fist. "Save Our School! Drill baby, drill! We're going to finally get an entrepreneurship program!"

"Really?" I asked, thinking he had to be high.

"Hey, Andrew's dad is on the city council," Joe continued. "He oughta know."

I played with the cap on the water bottle, uncomfortable.

Alex said, "We're going to get the whole troop to sign up as Save Our School supporters."

I felt ice crystals form in my stomach. "Andy is not a good guy."

"Hey, I'm in it for the free T-shirt," Connor said, adjusting his zipper as he lurched out of the bathroom.

"I don't care if he's Attila the Hun," Joe said with a snort. "We've got an oil well sitting there. It's a no-brainer. We should monetize it!"

I don't know what bothered me more: Andy getting some kind of legitimacy in his quest for popularity or Joe using the word *monetize*.

This didn't feel like the right moment to remind the guys that the oil tower might be toxic, or that Andy had cyberbullied Rae and made her life hell at school. But I needed to get to Rae, to warn her that on top of wowing the ASB girls and stealing her best friend, Andy had succeeded in brainwashing Boy Scouts.

There had to be a law against that.

24

Once I got home from school, I took a hot, steamy shower and made myself comfy in my room, leaving the door ajar so Mom could see my attempt to catch up on homework. When she walked by, she gave me a thumbs-up. A wave of guilt hit me, like it did every time I saw the bruise on her face.

It was no use. Despite my repeated efforts to complete my algebra assignment, the math equations just swam on the page. I lacked the energy to focus on math. Instead, I navigated to a website with a link to a documentary called *To Be of Service*, about veterans with PTSD. They talked about losing faith and being scared just to leave the house. I knew what that was like.

Incredible trainers had taught golden retrievers to act as physical buffers to ease veterans' panic. Seeing the animals in action, quietly saving people's lives, relaxed me. Jill said that was because engaging in my special interests helped me regulate my emotions. It eased transitions and brought me joy.

The doorbell rang, jarring me from that budding sense of joy.

I peeked over the top of the stair railing, expecting to see one of Mom's besties. Instead, Mom had her arms around Braden. My mom the hugger—give her a glass of wine, and she'd tell you her life story. Give her two, and she'd serenade you with Stevie Wonder's "Master Blaster" while sashaying around the house. She was generous like that.

"I'm not sure she's up to seeing anyone right now," I heard Mom say when she finally released Braden. "Maybe tomorrow?"

My fluffy white robe made me look like a giant chrysalis: all head, thorax, and abdomen. I considered hiding, but Mom had to be muzzled. "Mom, stop! I can do my own schedule."

She and Braden stared up at me from the entryway.

"What're you doing here?" I snapped at Braden.

"I—I . . . Um . . ." he stuttered. Then he held up a bag of dog treats.

Mom winked at me. "Way to make a guy feel welcome!"

"At least I didn't try hugging him to death!" I snarled.

The way Braden peered about the entryway reminded me of someone searching for an emergency exit.

I squinted at the package in his hand. "Are those Behr Brothers Biscuits?"

Braden glanced at the bag in his hand. "Yeah."

"Come up," I said.

"Leave the door open," Mom commented before retreating to the den.

Shoot. Me. Now.

I stepped back into my bedroom. Braden appeared a moment later, lingering in my doorway. He handed me the dog treats.

From downstairs, the faint murmur of the TV filtered through the floor. I circled my hand, and Noodle did a barrel roll. I rewarded him with one of the new biscuits.

"Nice!" Braden casually braced himself against the doorframe. "Mind if I come in?"

"Yes." The last time I'd had a boy in my room, I'd let him under the covers.

From the doorway, Braden checked out my room, my pillow collection, my books. His eyes paused on *The Mindful Path to Self-Compassion.* I suddenly felt naked.

"I totally barged in," he said softly. "I should've called or texted."

"Exactly. I hate surprises. My life is filled with noise and inconveniences and sensory challenges. I strive for stability. I know that change is inevitably part of life. But whenever possible, I'd like that change to be gradual." I paused to pet Noodle. "And just as a reminder, the basolateral amygdala is the part of the brain that deals with emotions, and when mine's over-stimulated, like now, I get bitchy. It's an involuntary process caused by stress. I can't help it."

Braden looked genuinely pained. "I didn't think this could wait, Rae. Rumors are flying about the oil deal, and you shouldn't be taking heat for it at school."

"One more reason why Mom probably thinks it's a good idea for me to go to Ojai."

"Why *does* she want you to switch schools?" Braden asked quietly.

"I . . . I did something terrible." My voice came out too high. "You should go," I squeaked as I rushed past him. I could almost feel the tingling in my knuckles where I'd struck Mom's jaw. Halfway down the stairs, a sob escaped me.

"Rae?" Braden called out, following on my heels.

Shit. Shit. Shit. He'd heard me! I sped downstairs and almost tripped on the last step.

"Rae!" Braden repeated, louder this time.

I fled to the kitchen and grabbed a bag of popcorn. In my frantic state, while slicing open the bag with the kitchen scissors, I narrowly missed my index finger.

"Jesus, Rae," Braden said sharply, snatching the scissors from my hand.

I accidentally dropped the bag, and kernels spilled everywhere. Noodle scurried around, lapping them up.

Braden palmed a paper towel and got down on his hands and knees to sweep up the rest. "Screw Andrew! He can't bully you like that. We need to stop him and those bitchy girls."

We! Was Braden on my team? The sensation of sobbing subsided. Without thinking, I threw my arms around him.

Braden stiffened. "I don't know if this is a good idea."

I blinked. He didn't like me anymore. My heart contracted in confusion and pain. I took my hands off him and straightened my robe. I had gotten everything totally wrong. Again.

Braden leaned against the center island. "I mean, a few minutes ago, you wanted me to leave. And I'm . . . well, I'm trying to work on stuff, er, myself. I don't want to mess this up." His voice got thick. "You're too important to me."

I took in about every sixth word. "Do you like me or not?" I hated how small my voice sounded, how I couldn't look him in the face.

"Rae, I'm not the guy you think I am."

"So, no." My eyes burned with embarrassment.

"Are you kidding me?" he asked. "I can't stop thinking about you."

Wait. What? I wasn't processing right. It sounded like he *did* like me.

"You know, I've been seeing a therapist." He looked away. "I don't know why I'm telling you all this . . . . Terrible idea . . . . When you talk about yours, sounds so much cooler . . . . But as you can see, I don't entirely have my shit together."

"I always knew you were weird."

He smiled. "And by the way, you are the only one I've talked to about this."

The fact that he trusted me with his secret was about the biggest turn-on ever.

"I really, really want to give you a hug right now," he said, suddenly bashful.

I had to keep telling myself *Not now* because a) I was wearing a bathrobe and nothing more, b) I wouldn't put it past my mother to barge in on us, and c) I totally didn't trust myself to stop at the hugging part.

"Not that you necessarily want one," he went on, as adorable as I'd ever seen him. "From me, I mean."

At that point, I was a lost cause. I wrapped my arms around him. The rules about when I was supposed to let go eluded me, but since Braden hugged me back, I held tight.

Then he began stroking my hair, and I felt intensely safe and hoped a kiss would come next. But then a negative thought filtered through my happiness: *Will Braden change his mind about me like Zach did?*

Braden whispered, "Do I get to kiss you?"

"I think you'd better."

At once I felt his lips on my mouth and detected the faint pine scent of his skin. It wasn't cologne; it was just him. Amazingly, I forgot that Mom was in the next room, that everyone at school hated me, and that I was wearing a robe that made me look like a metamorphic insect. Braden's hands reached behind the small of my back, and when he pressed me against him, my mind went blissfully quiet.

Eyes closed, I pulled away and murmured, "I should warn you. I have impulse control issues."

"Meaning?"

"I think you should kiss me again."

He started to move in for another kiss, but then I heard Mom calling my name in the hallway, just seconds away from barging in on us.

Braden took two steps back and wedged his hands into his pockets.

"What's this about being bullied?" she asked, stepping into the kitchen.

"Mom! What is your problem?"

Braden's face turned three shades of red.

She waved one hand. "I overheard you. Before. About being bullied." She rinsed her wine glass at the sink. "Unpack this for me. Last semester went great! What changed?"

I straightened my robe and cinched it tighter. "People used to leave me alone. Until Andrew Jennings decided he hates me."

Braden's normal face color had started to return. "Andy and his Save Our School club members have it out for Rae."

"Why?" Mom turned away from the counter, light on her feet.

"Duh. I'm an easy target. Plus, he hates you because you're not on his dad's side about the oil rig."

Mom unwrapped a personal-sized pizza and slid it into the toaster oven. "Are they cyberbullying you, or is this happening at school?"

"Both," I said with a shrug, and I told Mom the whole story—what Andrew had said about her and how I'd shoved him and the mean Instagram post.

"Rae, I wish you'd said something!" Mom exclaimed.

"As if reporting Andrew or anyone else would change anything."

"But we're family, so we share these things with each other. Not to mention, instead of trying to make you apologize for toppling Andrew, I would've raised your allowance." Mom clapped a hand over her mouth. "I did not just say that!"

Braden and I laughed.

"It's no secret that Andrew's dad and I don't see eye to eye on the oil well project," Mom continued. "But there'll be more clarity for folks once we get the EIR."

"What's an EIR?" Braden asked.

"Environmental Impact Report. It's a detailed study on a potential project's ramifications. The effects on traffic, neighbors, the air quality, city services . . . ." Mom went on for a little while with details about the EIR and the history of Eclyra Energy Solutions. It was a huge company—contractors, engineers, operators—and they had been around for years. They used specialized equipment and were super well-funded.

It was a lot to take in.

Braden rubbed his chin, listening closely. "Kids at school think the well is a money-making machine. Is it?"

Mom shrugged. "The executives at Eclyra certainly hope so. They're offering a sizable percentage of the profit to the school district."

"But is it . . . safe?"

"Unclear." Mom rubbed her eyes. "This must be so boring to you guys."

Was it my turn to speak? I had lost track. "What're you going to do, Mom?"

"I'm going to ask Frank Jennings, in a very nice way, to have Andrew apologize for what he's done to bully you," she said.

"Screw Andrew's fauxpology!" I insisted. "That's not what I meant! How do we convince people that an active petroleum rig near our school is a terrible idea?"

Mom looked briefly at Braden and then at me. "Let's talk about this later, Rae."

"No, Mom, let's talk about it now." I wanted to get it over with. "Maybe *you* should worry about Mr. Jennings and let *me* worry about Andrew."

"Maybe I should go?" Braden asked.

I held his hand. "I don't want you to go."

He moved ever so slightly closer to me. After that, nothing else really mattered.

"I can help you deal with Andy—or do we have to call him Andrew now?" Braden said quietly. "I mean, if that's something you want. Or not . . . ."

Mom pulled the pizza out of the toaster, and we each took a slice. "If you're going to handle this your way, Rae, then you *cannot* fight me about going to school every day. And you absolutely cannot put your hands on another person."

"I won't," I said, blowing on my slice of hot pizza. "I swear."

Mom crossed her arms. "And you're going to have to communicate with me."

Saying yes to that meant . . . what? That I promised to check in with Mom daily? Every time someone called me a name? Whenever a teacher reprimanded me? Ugh.

I jumped a little when Braden gently elbowed me. "I'm in this too," he insisted. "That is, if you want me to be."

Mom looked from him to me and back.

"This thing with Andrew. It's not your fight—or your problem." I was just stating a fact.

"But I'd get to hang out with you." He gave me a goofy smile. "And if it's your fight, then it's my fight, too." His face and neck flushed pink again.

I let it really sink in. Braden was on my team. I snuck a look at him, thrilled and scared.

Breathe, I told myself. Were we a couple? *Breathe*.

"And maybe I'd get some free dog training advice along the way."

He raised his hands with a smile. "How could I go wrong?"

My knees buckled a little. *Breathe*.

Braden was most definitely on my team.

25

BRADEN

A couple days later, I walked Simon to the vending machine, but it had run out of SunChips. He cried. When we returned to the Life Skills room, we found Jerome stimming while he watched whale rescues on YouTube. Something new occurred to me: Rae and these boys were *exactly* who they appeared to be. Shouldn't that be the definition of "normal"?

I was starting to think that the neuromajority was what wasn't normal. Pretending you're okay when you're crippled by anxiety? Not normal. Acting like you aren't disappointed beyond belief when something goes wrong, like when your team loses? Not normal.

While eating lunch in the journalism room, I tried to explain this to Lucas. Until they lost in the finals, the Pac Crest girls' lacrosse had dominated all season. Between bites of my wrap, I read out loud, "Quote: 'This season has been so fun! I wouldn't trade a single minute of it!'"

I turned my laptop so Lucas could see the photo of the team captain, Brittany Chu, with her hands to her head, looking like her puppy had just died.

"People at school can be so full of shit," I continued, shaking my head. "Why can't they admit when something sucks? That losing can make you feel worthless? That winning can make you feel invincible?"

Lucas glanced at the photo of Brittany without any visible reaction. Then he pulled his thick glasses off his face and rubbed his eyes. "Ever eat your lunch, and your mind is somewhere else? So when you finish, you can't remember eating at all?"

I thought about it and then handed him half of my turkey and avocado. "So, you want another lunch?"

"Sure." Lucas slid his glasses back on and chewed. "What's on this?"

"Italian spices. Oil and vinegar."

"Do you realize how lucky you are to have your mom around to make you lunch?"

"Uh, I guess. Do you realize how lucky you are that no one nags you about eating kale?"

I started scrolling through X on my phone, catching updates from @LastWordOnSpurs. At times I hated myself for being a sports fan, wasting years of my life watching the teams I loved lose and listening to sports commentators weigh in on player trades, when I could have been learning how to tie a tie and what to do with girls.

Lucas finished the wrap and licked his fingers. Staring off into nothingness, he announced, "Tatiana broke up with me. By text. It's over."

Having never met her, I weighed my words carefully. "That sucks."

"Girls expect gifts and surprises," Lucas acknowledged. "I should've bought her roses and posted selfies on our three-month anniversary."

"I don't know. I think maybe couples that post photos of themselves on their anniversaries deserve a special place in hell," I joked.

Lucas didn't laugh. "I wouldn't call this the *best* day I've ever had," he said, brushing breadcrumbs off his belly.

I honestly wasn't prepared to see him care . . . about anything. I put away my phone. "Sorry, man, I didn't realize how much you liked her."

"There's more." Lucas grimaced. "I caught my dad in bed with some woman."

"Oh, my god!" I said, nearly choking on a slice of avocado. "That's . . . awkward. And embarrassing."

"I mean, the second I saw them, I took off. But he knows I know."

Here was Lucas, trusting me with the biggest secrets of his life. Meanwhile, I talked sports trivia. Hid my insecurities. Kept Rae a secret. "I'm such an idiot," I said. "I'm sorry I haven't been a better friend, Lucas."

"Shut up, Braden. You're one of the nicest people I know."

"Really? I don't know even what your parents do for a living. Or how you take care of yourself and your sister without them around."

"My parents work for a company that sells vitamin supplements here and in Manila."

"I should've known that. And a good friend would've asked you this stuff before."

"You're right." Lucas smirked. "Maybe you can make it up to me."

It was clear he had something in mind.

After seventh period, Lucas and I trotted downstairs toward student parking. His overnight city parking permit had expired, and with his car in the shop for something I'd never heard of, he needed a ride to Pacific Crest City Hall to pick up a new one.

As we passed the auditorium, we heard singing and poked our heads inside. Onstage, Rae and some other drama kids danced around in monkey costumes. I waved, and she smiled. Lucas didn't say a word about it as we drove to City Hall.

Vintage tiled murals decorated the interior walls of the City Hall lobby, giving it an old California vibe. We passed an ornate, brass-doored elevator and sat on a small bench near the cashier's desk. Stretched along the length of the opposite wall were two long counters identified with a sign that read *Planning Department*. Quite a few people seemed to be waiting there, carting around rolls of plans and clearly impatient for their turn to meet with the staff.

We took out our phones and waited for the parking cashier. Minutes passed. Without looking up, I asked, "Do you want to talk about—"

"No." Lucas paused. "You gonna tell me the story with the Girl in Black?"

Where should I begin? Autism blogger? Dog freak? Soft lips? "Her name's Rae. She's a cool girl. Definitely not the one calling in bomb threats."

He nodded, obviously waiting for more.

"Says what's on her mind. I don't have to guess. Different, you know?"

"Is that bro code for 'difficult'?" Lucas asked.

"I don't know. It's not like I've had a gazillion girlfriends to compare her to."

"She your girlfriend?"

"No, no. I mean—no."

"You're a smitten kitten!" Lucas softly punched my upper arm. "Let's see if we can't finally get you a girlfriend you like." Which meant that Lucas approved. That liking someone who wasn't neuro-typical was perfectly okay.

The bustling over at the Planning Department had dwindled, and no one was even at the desk when several people carrying briefcases walked out of the office. Over Lucas's shoulder I saw the unmistakable heart-shaped face that belonged to one of them: Elizabeth Wolf.

"There's her mom!" I whispered.

Lucas followed my sight line to the group as they strolled down the hall and stopped in front of the elevator. "Random."

"Not really. Her office is around here somewhere. She's on the city council."

One of the men with Elizabeth called out, "Good afternoon!" to a nearby guard. It took me a second to remember that voice: I'd heard it a few weeks earlier, right before I found Andy Jennings silently sobbing in the stairwell.

I studied the man, imagining him without the receding hairline and patchy beard. Then I jutted my chin in his direction. "That's gotta be Frank, Andy Jennings's dad—he's also on the city council. He and Rae's mom are feuding over this Save Our School project. He wants it, she doesn't. Andy's being an asswipe about it, giving Rae a hard time."

Lucas squinted at Councilman Jennings. "We gonna beat the shit out of Andy?"

"Not ruling it out." Elizabeth and the other council members stepped into the elevator. When the doors closed, I asked Lucas, "Ever hear of an EIR?"

He shook his head.

"Stands for Environmental Impact Report. It can make or break Eclyra Energy Solutions's plans for the drilling rig. Wonder how you get one?"

"EIR?" Lucas asked, doing a search on his phone. "How do you spell 'Eclyra'?"

"E-C-L . . . ."

Lucas had stopped listening. For a big guy, he moved fast. He was already standing at the empty Planning Department counter. In one move, he had swiveled one of the open computer terminals in his direction. He pecked at the keyboard, just like he'd done in Coach Gillman's office.

I whispered, "Don't!" It dawned on me that there were cameras *everywhere*.

He ignored me.

"Lucas! Stop!" I hissed.

Lucas snapped photos of the monitor with his phone and swiveled the computer back in place. The next thing I knew, he had plopped down beside me again.

"Are you out of your mind?" I murmured.

"You're welcome," he said, unfazed as always. He was busy blowing up my phone with texts—texts of photos he'd stolen off a government employee's computer.

"Lucas Cruz!" announced a shrill voice.

I almost lost my lunch.

"Parking?" the cashier asked.

"That's me!" Lucas chirped, all smiles.

26

RAE

Unfiltered Views from Your Average Awesome Autistic

THE CURSE OF THE MASK

The symbol for comedy and drama is two masks: one smiling, the other grimacing. In ancient times, Greek actors used these masks to express emotions to the audience. Brilliant, right? If everyone wore one now, life would be a lot less confusing. It would be soooo much easier for spectrumites to understand what people are really thinking.

You see, we're missing the gene or whatever it is that grants neurotypicals the ability to conveniently "read" another person's hidden emotions.

Me: *How was your weekend?*

Friend: *Great. Just great.*

Me: *Cool! That's wonderful.*

Friend: *My parents got a divorce, and the dog died!*

Me: *Ohhh. I'm sorry!*

We don't expect sarcasm or see the punch line coming, either . . .

Friend: *Why can't Ray Charles see his friends?*

Me: *Because he's blind?*

Friend: *No, because he's married!*

Ironically, if you're on the spectrum, you may be the one who slaps on a mask—to *hide* your emotions. Take my "normal" mask, for instance. It's a beauty! Developed over four summers of acting camp and three years in high school Drama Lab, it works wonders for blending in. When wearing it, I manage to have the "right" expression and the "correct" response in most social settings.

My mask is all about forced eye contact, grinning and nodding so I can give the impression of interest even when my mind is a million miles away. If people only knew the truth of how incredibly *boring* they can be at times!

By hiding my true nature, I don't seem (as) odd. I can (sometimes) avoid being bullied at school. The "normal" mask is like having a shield to protect me from being harshly judged by others, because no matter how many times people have called me names, it still hurts! I don't know how to let things "roll" off me, and I will never learn to develop a "tough" skin.

Quite the opposite.

I'm super sensitive about being judged. Years of being misunderstood and teased have resulted in me having a REALLY hard time trusting anyone. But the mask is both a blessing and a curse. Even though it kinda-sorta protects me, it's soul-crushing. It makes me feel like something is MAJORLY wrong with the REAL me.

What happens when I wear the mask is, I get anxious. I get REALLY depressed. Basically, I start to hate myself. I guess I have to ask: Is it better to be myself and suffer the pain of being misunderstood? Or is it worth keeping the mask on while my sense of self quietly dies?

Noodle licked my hand as I knelt on the floor of my bedroom and fastened a sparkly mask on his head. He knows the voice and hand signals for *Give me a paw, Give me a kiss,* and my favorite, *Pose.*

I raised my left arm above my head like a ballerina and said, "Pose!"

Noodle tilted his head, and I snapped the perfect shot of him. Then I removed the mask, gave him a biscuit, and uploaded the image. Then I pressed *Publish,* just as Mom tapped on the door.

"Come in!" I smiled sweetly, closing my laptop. I'd been working for days, writing my blog post and deep-diving into research on the oil rig. Mom had threatened to take away my power cord if I didn't get some exercise.

She watched me unfasten the mask from Noodle's furry face. "Did you finish the English paper?"

"Rewriting," I answered, being as vague as possible.

"It's due tomorrow, right?" She regularly checked my class updates. Like she had nothing better to do.

"It makes me anxious when you question me. Jill said I need to tell you when you do that. I know you're trying to help, but you're making me second-guess myself!"

"Alright," Mom said. "I'll be more aware of that."

"And I'll get off my butt." I slipped on sunglasses. "Walking time!"

"Want company?"

"I'm going to Braden's."

"Oh. Okay." She glanced around my room, lingering. "Are his parents around?"

"I don't know."

"If his parents were home, I'd be more comfortable."

"I'm sure you would." I swept a pile of notes on the oil project into my messenger bag and slung it over my shoulder.

"It's natural to want to be close to someone, to kiss and touch—"

"Mom!"

"What?" she asked, following me downstairs to the kitchen.

I secured Noodle's harness, hoping to get out of the house without suffering through the same conversation about good decisions and safe sex.

Mom lifted an apple from the fruit bowl and bit into it with a distinct crunch, followed by the click of her jaw. TMJ again. I instantly and desperately wanted to throw the toaster through the window. Mom's right hand rose again, and I watched with horror as the scene unfolded in slow motion: the apple closing in on her face, her mouth opening, her gleaming teeth approaching, just millimeters from the fruit . . . .

"Stop it," I begged. "Stop eating!"

She hesitated for a second, as if just now noticing the apple in her own hand, and withdrew it from her face. Putting it down on the countertop, she picked up a tangerine this time.

The anger began to uncoil. "Thank you." I took a breath to collect myself.

"So. About Braden," Mom started in again.

"Do you trust him?" I snapped.

"I barely know him."

"Do you trust *me*?"

She stopped peeling the tangerine. "With my life."

Emotion welled up in me.

"Do you trust *me*?" she asked.

"With my life," I said without hesitation.

We split the tangerine, and I felt energized. Hopeful, even. And I wanted Mom to be proud of me.

"This is what I've been working on." I pointed to my bag, stuffed with color-coded files, each containing articles I'd printed out about oil and gas wells. "Petroleum, also called crude oil or oil, is basically made of two elements: carbon and hydrogen, also known as hydrocarbons. Natural gas is made up of a different mixture of hydrocarbons, like ethane, propane, and butane. It's lighter than oil and found above petroleum because it's less dense. Pressure and heat determine whether hydrocarbons turn into oil or gas. Both are non-renewable, fossil fuels formed from the remains of dead animals and plants over thousands of years. People use oil for fuel, electricity power generation, heating, even plastic."

Mom thumbed through a file. "I see you researched both sides—environmental groups *and* energy companies." She nodded to herself. "Your notes are so detailed."

"Uh, yeah. I'm autistic. I can't do it any other way," I reminded her.

Mom grinned and started reading another file. "Why the sudden interest? I thought you were leaving this part to me."

"It's my school. The air I breathe. I care about my fellow students and teachers."

Mom raised her eyebrows.

I elaborated. "I do care, Mom, in an I-don't-want-you-to-get-sick-and-keel-over kind of way."

Mom handed the files back to me. "Outstanding work, honey."

With her approval, I felt my energy levels soar. I puffed up, proud of myself. "There's more." I pulled out the entire contents of my bag and spread them across the counter.

Mom checked her watch. "I want to hear everything, but I have to read a report before the agenda meeting . . . ."

But now that I'd started, I couldn't stop. "Neighborhood activists inspired the LA City Council to vote in favor of a new system of annual inspections on oil and gas facilities, but so far—nothing! The office that oversees the sites has only two employees. It's ridiculous! Hundreds of active wells aren't being checked. Seems like unless people's noses are bleeding, unless they're suffering headaches or complaining about foul odors, nothing changes. Worst of all, the oil companies are turning in their own annual reports! That's like having students grade their own SATs. It's so wrong. We can't let that happen to Pacific Crest."

Mom held up a hand and nodded. "Our job is to make people recognize that this has the potential for toxic land use, fundamentally at odds with residential neighborhoods and school grounds. But Rae, let's pick this up after dinner."

"One question: Do you think the petroleum platform causes cancer?"

Mom paused. "My gut says yes. But four million dollars spent by the city on testing says no. You can see why people are so divided over this."

"But it's better to be on the safe side. Shouldn't the city council require more research until the issue is less confusing?"

She wagged a finger at me. "You weren't working on your English paper."

"Busted," I laughed, holding up my hands.

"It's wonderful that you're paying attention and asking questions, Rae. The world needs more people like you."

I knew Mom literally meant she wished people had my traits—autistic traits like deep-diving into detail and doggedly digging up facts. My heart swelled.

"Go! Walk! Sweat!" she insisted. "And please be back in time to finish your homework before dinner. We can talk more then."

She gave me the sweetest look with her eyes full of love. It helped me so much—more than I'd realized that I needed.

"And say hi to Braden for me."

I promised I would, though I had one detour to make first.

I walked through the neighborhood with Noodle, calmed by the pleasing scent of the eucalyptus trees. I thought about Braden and wondered if he thought about me half as much as I thought about him. Unlikely.

Braden had parents and a supercute little sister at home to keep him busy. He always had his cousin Connor around to play video games and Lucas to talk sports. And then there were the cool, smart girls from journalism. Did he kiss them, too?

I hated my monster voice. I really freaking did.

My pace picked up, as if I could outrun my unconscious. Soon enough, I found what I'd set out looking for.

The drilling tower lived behind a short driveway and a tall, solid locked gate that hid most of the rig from view. The tower's tattered canvas covering flapped in the breeze. I couldn't see if anyone was working on the platform at the moment, and the steady flow of cars behind me made it impossible to hear any clues. Posted on the gate were many signs, however:

NO TRESPASSING!

THIS AREA CONTAINS CHEMICALS KNOWN TO THE STATE OF CALIFORNIA TO CAUSE CANCER AND BIRTH DEFECTS OR OTHER REPRODUCTIVE HARM.

I could look at that information in two ways: One, that warning had been plastered onto apartment buildings, shopping malls, and offices everywhere, so it didn't really mean there was anything particularly evil about the rig. Or two, the rig was a killer hiding in plain sight, and people were too lazy to care.

27

BRADEN

onnor and I played video games in my den, polishing off the pizza we'd picked up from Mulberry Street for an early dinner. My appetite was fine, but my mood was sour. Rae's nonstop grind mode put me to shame.

I thought *I* was a hard worker—until I met her. She was like Spark with her favorite toy: relentless. Try as I might, my invites for cold brew or Froyo couldn't tug her away from her grip on researching petroleum platforms and her dedication to blogging. Not so long ago, it wouldn't have bugged me one bit if a girl didn't answer my texts right away. Apparently, now I was *that kind of guy*.

When I kept losing every game we played, Connor finally asked, "Wazzup, cuz?"

"Nothing," I fibbed.

Not only was I missing Rae, but the stolen photos Lucas had texted me from City Hall seemed to pulsate from my pocket like a beacon. *Guilty! Guilty! Guilty!* All he'd managed to capture was an image of a contact page and the table of contents, so I reasoned with myself that this was a worry thought as opposed to a Real-Life

Problem. Mimi Kim sure would be proud at our appointment tomorrow. Maybe I'd even tell Mimi about Rae, since I didn't know my next move with her.

As if by coincidence or conjuring, my phone vibrated in my pocket with a text from Rae.

Here.

When the doorbell rang, Jenji yelled, "Braaaaden! For youuu!"

Rae stepped inside with Noodle at her heels. She wore black leggings, sandals, and an Eagles concert T-shirt with the neck so stretched out, you could see a lacey black bra strap. I had to tear my eyes away from her lingerie.

"Howdy!" I said, managing to sound both nerdy and chipper.

Her eyes swept from the television to me to the empty pizza box and back to the television. "Can you turn that off, please?"

I quickly palmed the remote and shut down the system. The driving, electronic game music cut out, and the room suddenly grew quiet.

"That's better."

I made room on the sofa, but Rae chose to sit on the floor.

Connor petted Noodle. "He's so cute!"

"I know, right?" Rae pulled her bag onto her lap and removed a colored folder. "Here's what I've got so far on petroleum platforms. Let's get the kids at school to change their minds. With enough community input, we might be able to stop the project."

Trying to demonstrate my enthusiasm, I presented my phone. "I have some research too. *I* think they're hiding something in the EIR."

Rae and Connor squinted at the blurry screenshots. "You do realize you're missing four-hundred-fifty-four pages of evidence, right?" Rae said.

"Wait. What?" I was beyond confused.

Rae handed me a different folder. "These are chapters from the EIR—one on air quality, and another on hazardous materials."

"Can I see?" Jenji peeked around the doorframe.

Our pit bull darted out from behind her to sniff Noodle's butt. Rae cooed softly and petted Spark's ears.

"Jenji, stop spying," I snapped. "It's . . . confidential."

"No, it's not." Rae looked up from petting our dog. "Environmental Impact Reports are publicly available online."

"Ohhh." I fanned through the pages Rae had handed me, feeling like a dork. "What do you call someone who's quick to panic *and* misinformed?"

"Rude?" Jenji offered.

"Awfulist?" Connor suggested.

"Neurotypical?" Rae weighed in.

"Sorry, Jenji." I patted the cushion, inviting her to sit down. Instead, she did a forward roll onto the couch, ending up in a headstand.

Still upside-down, Jenji focused on the report in my hands. "Is that homework?"

"City council members do study projects before they vote. It could be about a hotel or a subway line or a drilling rig, like this one." Rae talked a mile a minute.

Other than my concern that she might have a third lung, I absolutely loved seeing her get so passionate about things. She took a breath and then kept going.

"Eclyra Energy Solutions has something called 'mitigation' to deal with potentially adverse effects of their operation, like pollutants. They also promise not to dump particulates near fresh air intakes, and to randomly test their trucks, which spew crud into the air too." She rolled her eyes. "A hollow promise—big whup."

My hand touched my chest where I felt a sudden twinge. Was it possible that my lungs were disintegrating already?

Rae plucked a piece of fluff from between her toes, and I momentarily lost sight of my imminent demise. The sky blue nail color of her pedicure, the shape of her foot, the delicate ankle . . . . It was getting harder and harder to focus on Rae's words.

"The rig near school is one of *hundreds* in LA," she was saying. "The city controller says there are 'thirty-plus years of inattention.' People with nosebleeds and nausea. Neighborhoods in low-income areas suffer the most. I mean, don't they always?"

Nosebleeds. Nausea. Neighborhoods. Reality came into sharp focus, and I forced myself to keep my gaze directed at Rae's face. I was supposed to chime in now.

"We're not exactly low-income, but public schools like Pac Crest are hardly drowning in cash," I said, once again fixating on my long-gone lungs and wondering about the success rate of a transplant. "How are we going to convince anyone to forget the money Eclyra Energy Solutions is promising to give the school district?"

"Save Our School, right?" Connor nodded sarcastically. "Where the school gets rich, and everyone lives happily ever after."

"Or they're wrong and everyone dies," I added.

"No!" Jenji rolled back off the couch, landing on her feet and locking her arms around my waist. "Don't say that!"

"You're a really good sister," Rae said, watching Jenji.

Jenji sniffled and started to untangle herself from me.

Connor flipped through the Environmental Impact Report. "Acidizing. Alkanes. Particulate matter. We learned about them in Chem class."

Jenji hung on Connor's every word. "Is the high school toxic?"

"Well, I don't think you need to worry too much, Jenji," Connor stalled. "That platform's been there for decades, right? I figure—"

Rae jumped in. "For sure the rig contains cancer-causing chemicals. They release methane, too, which is a planet-warming gas worse than carbon dioxide. A better question might be: Will it leak gas? Or *has* it leaked gas? Because when that happens, we're talking evacuations, explosions . . . even death."

I clapped my hands over Jenji's ears. "Uh, Rae?" I tried to make eye contact with her as my kid sis stubbornly peeled my fingers off her head, one by one.

Oblivious, Rae forged ahead. "The only oil facility permanently shut down is in Cutter Ranch, where a natural gas and oil well leaked methane gas that caused a fatal accident three years ago." She dug through her bag and removed another file. "According to the *LA Times*, Ramon Ortiz and his brother Alejandro were just cooking in their kitchen before their house in Cutter Ranch suddenly exploded."

Rae handed me a red folder—presumably her research on fatal accidents, given that she'd drawn a skull and bones on the cover. I, in turn, passed the folder on to Connor like a game of Hot Potato.

"Cutter Ranch. Is that even in California?" I said, trying to play it down for Jenji's sake. Okay, for my sake, too.

Connor flipped through the red folder.

Rae leaned forward, elbows on her thighs, and rested her chin on top of her hands. For a split second, I caught a flash of the pale skin on her bare hip. Everything in me turned hot and electric. She shifted, and there it was: her tattoo.

Seeing it, Jenji's eyes rolled around like a soccer ball spinning against the goal net. "Are you Braden's *girlfriend*?"

Connor raised one eyebrow at me.

"Nope," Rae said. The corner of her mouth twitched, holding back a smile.

Ouch. Third-degree burn. She'd sent me back to the minor

leagues. Maybe she'd decided that dating a rude, neurotypical awfulist was a bad idea.

Rae stood up. "I need to go. I told Mom I'd be back in time to finish some homework before dinner."

"Want a ride?" I asked, giving it one more try.

"No, thanks. I prefer to walk."

Obviously, I was on a roll.

But then, out of nowhere, Rae reached up and kissed me lightly on the mouth. All my nerve endings flared, blazing now, even as I begged them to quiet down.

We moved apart, and she met my gaze for half a second. Surprise flickered across her face, and her eyes glittered. Seeing the fiery energy that burned there, I decided to take that as a sign to get her alone—to do that again.

Then she looked away.

Jenji crossed her arms. "You told me you weren't boyfriend-girlfriend!"

Exactly. Even my kid sister could see the mixed messages. *Way to go, sis!*

"We're not," Rae said, adjusting her bag over her shoulder. "Braden, we have to warn the kids at school what's really going on. The city council is going to make a decision soon."

I was speechless, still reeling from being kissed and being banished to the friend zone in the same moment.

Rae looked at me again. "One way to convince kids it's a bad idea is if you go to Cutter Ranch."

"Why me?" I asked, my voice sounding a little rough.

She shrugged. "You're a journalist."

"Sports editor," I corrected her, trying to clear my throat.

Connor snapped shut the folder. "Rae's right."

"Come on, cuz!" I shook Connor's shoulders softly. "I'm not

saying she's wrong, but seriously, who's going to listen to us? And besides, a house blew up there. Is that really where we should be going? What if—"

"You're doing it again, cuz." Connor stared at me. "Awfulist."

An hour later, we entered a neat, clean planned community of houses that all pretty much looked the same except for paint colors. Connor checked the address on his phone, and I parked in front of 10622 Solito Drive. The Ortiz house.

Or what was left of it.

The house had been demolished. All that remained was a square of rubble with a *For Sale* sign stuck into the ground out front.

Connor slammed the passenger door shut. I reluctantly turned off the engine and joined him on the sidewalk. A few little kids on bikes rode around the street, jumping curbs and popping wheelies. After a minute or two had passed, and nothing bad happened, I gradually let myself relax.

I FaceTimed Rae. Seeing her close-up, right there in the palm of my hand, almost took my breath away.

"You made it." Her voice was flat; I thought she'd be more impressed.

Something in my chest started to cave in. Was it hurt I was feeling, or embarrassment? Maybe Rae was playing games?

But I didn't really believe that. All things considered, I had probably read too much into the kiss. Maybe she didn't feel . . . anything. After all, she'd clearly said she was *not* my girlfriend.

Connor made a heart shape with his fingers.

Thanks, cuz. Thanks a lot.

Ignoring him, I aimed the screen at the empty lot. Someone had installed a chain-link fence, but the lock had been broken off and anyone could invite themselves in—us included.

Connor and I stepped over weeds as we moved deeper onto the lot. The kids on their bikes glanced our way. A gust of wind rippled through, and I shivered, suddenly cold.

"Are we freaking ourselves out for nothing?" I asked. "I mean, Cutter Ranch isn't Pacific Crest. Would they really let something like this happen?"

"Yes!" Rae snapped, sounding impatient. "No one thinks anything horrible is going to happen until it does."

I tried to keep the anger out of my voice. "One of my best friends got killed in a hit and run, so please—I don't need the lecture about horrible things happening."

"I . . . I didn't realize . . . about your friend."

I could barely speak. "His name was Hojun."

Connor cringed. We rarely spoke his name.

My eyes burned with pent-up emotion. I *so* did not want to be there—thinking about Hojun, lamenting the fact that I seemed to be frozen in the friend zone.

I marched ahead, silent, until a piece of charred something snapped under my foot, like I'd trampled a crispy femur. "Ugh!" I darted back onto the dried lawn, almost doing a faceplant in the process. On closer inspection, I realized I'd stepped on a brittle tree branch.

Onscreen, Rae complained, "I'm getting motion sickness. Please! Stop waving the phone."

"Um, look, there's not much else to see here. Can we talk later?"

Click. Conversation concluded. Fade to black. The end. Because people loved to be hung up on. It is known. A universal concept, really.

Honestly, it stung being hung up on. I had to wonder: Had I made up whatever that moment had been, that kiss between Rae and me?

Connor and I started back to the car. He swung an arm around my shoulders. "You okay?"

"Not sure, I guess." I could never bullshit Connor for long.

"She's not easy. Rae," he continued. "But I think she's one of the coolest girls I've ever met."

I nodded in agreement.

Connor went on. "I also think she's really into you." The kids on bikes were still hanging around, and Connor waved. "Cool bikes," he said when they rolled up.

The oldest one, about twelve, spoke for the other two. "You guys friends with the Ortizes?"

Connor cleared his throat. "We didn't know them. What were they like?"

The kid looked down at his handlebars. "Alejandro used to babysit us. He let us stay up late playing video games."

"Sounds like a cool guy," I said.

The kid shrugged and looked out at the horizon. The two younger kids rolled their tires back and forth, anxious to cycle on. All the anger drained out of me.

"Nobody's buying the house. I wouldn't either," the kid said, futzing with the brakes.

"Because it's dangerous?" Connor asked.

The kid shook his head. "On account of the ghosts. When you die and it's, like, totally unexpected and wrong, the person doesn't know they're dead. They keep haunting the last place they were alive."

The other two kids nodded in total agreement.

"Sorry about your friends," I said softly. I would've liked to tell them that in time it got better, but really it only got different. You kept on missing your friend.

Maybe that was what they meant about ghosts.

28

By the time Saturday rolled around—the night of the spring musical performance—I needed a change, anything to brighten my mood. To distract myself, I spent the morning on Pinterest, checking out new hair color ideas. But I couldn't get that image out of my head: the lifeless lot that used to be the Ortiz home.

To make matters worse, I'd said something wrong to Braden on our FaceTime at Cutter Ranch. And right after that delicious, not-as-innocent-as-it-seemed kiss! It had woken something up in me, and I was craving more. But as we FaceTimed, his voice had changed, sounding brittle. And his shoulders were rounded suddenly, like talking to me was just too much burden to tolerate—like it was too much work to even be together on a call.

Braden would never be unkind to me, no matter how awkward the situation was. But I knew my social skills weren't reliable. I didn't know how to handle things like this. Part of me feared I'd blown up yet another relationship.

Another part of me ached that Braden hadn't shared Hojun's death with me. I finally texted him about it.

> Me: Why didn't you tell me about Hojun?

> Braden: I don't like to talk about it.

> Me: I felt like an idiot. I didn't mean to upset you.

> Braden: If I were bold (like someone I know), I could speak my mind. But I tend to keep stuff to myself. I'm weird. You've said so yourself!

Maybe it sounds obvious, but I learned from Zach that even though two people could be mutually attracted, they had to "get" each other. Zach didn't get me, and after the breakup, I decided no neurotypical ever would.

Until Braden.

He indulged in my special interests, and I never realized how hugely important that was to me. Rescue dogs. Understanding autism. And now the focus on the oil company's plans. Sharing these things with Braden gave my life purpose, and I'm not exaggerating about that. He helped push away the depression that liked to sneak up on me when I least expected it.

Of course, me being me, I also considered how things would be when it was over between us. The sadness. The aloneness. Was Braden even still going with me to the after-party tonight?

Unfortunately, I couldn't ask Arman what he thought about all this, though I'd be seeing him soon enough.

Once I made up my mind about the hair color, I set down three black plastic bowls on the bathroom counter. The sharp smell gave me a little thrill. I slid on plastic gloves and dyed the top third of my hair, from my scalp to my ears, a deep plum color. The middle third, I did in fuchsia. And starting just past my shoulders, I painted the tips a pale lavender. Good hair days made me a happier, more confident person.

"Five minutes!" Mom's voice from downstairs brought me to the present. It was time to drive to school for the performance.

I followed the sound of Billy Joel's "Scenes from an Italian Restaurant" and found Mom humming at her desk, paying bills. She looked up. "Hair is stunning!" Then she went back to her spreadsheets.

"Thanks! Um, can't you send some of those to Dad? Though I doubt he cares about them. Or us."

"He cares." Mom paused to look at me. "And he's your dad."

"Define 'dad.'"

I hadn't even seen him for weeks. I can't describe how much I hated packing up and spending the weekend in Manhattan Beach. His wife, Jodi, never let me out of her sight, especially around my little half brother, Chance—or "Fat Chance," as I secretly called him. I was a stranger in their house. They didn't want me there any more than I wanted to be there.

Mom set down her pen. "He called me a few minutes ago. I know you're not going to like hearing this: He's on his way to the show."

"But he's not invited." Obviously.

Mom got up and came around the front of her desk. "I sent him a ticket a long time ago, Rae. When I didn't hear back, I assumed . . . . Well, it doesn't matter. What matters is, you deserve to be seen, and to have a better relationship with your father."

My lower lip trembled. "This is completely unfair. You're ruining this! You're stripping away any sense of good feeling I have about myself."

Mom rubbed her temples. "I'm so sorry. Springing this on you at the last minute makes me want to dig a hole and bury myself in it. There's literally nothing I can do about it."

"Of course not. Because Dad is an asshole."

"Don't call him names."

As we drove to the school, I closed my eyes, trying to meditate him away. It defied logic that Mom was standing up for the man who had walked out on us.

She slowed for a red light. "You won't even see him in the audience."

"You better hope I don't," I growled.

"What does that mean?"

"It means that I'm angry! That I want to tell him how much he's let us down. That he's the single biggest disappointment in my life."

Dad could never get past the surface. Nor would he ever understand that I was born different and that it was not a choice. That beneath it all, I was fine—happy, even—to be the way I was.

Mom pulled up to the auditorium and parked. We sat there, quiet, as I watched the Drama Lab kids scurry inside the stage entrance. I knew I had to go in too, but I couldn't seem to make my legs move.

"I love you." Mom gently patted my hand. "Everything's going to be okay."

I desperately wanted to believe her.

As I rushed backstage, the lights, the voices, and the energy were all *too much*. Out of habit, I searched for Arman. Instead, I ended up almost colliding with Andrew.

"Watch where you're going, for chrissakes!" he fumed, shielding himself with a large roll of electric tape. "You're gonna hurt somebody."

I backed away and rushed off to hide in the girls' bathroom. My breathing was too fast, and I felt the panic threatening to take hold. As I leaned against the cool sink and shut my eyes, my phone *binged*.

Braden: Big performance tonight!

Seeing his name pop up brought me such relief! I replied right away.

Me: Are you still coming? Please say yes.

Braden: Uh, yeah! I bought tix for tomorrow night too! You nervous?

A jolt of energy raced over me like I was being electrocuted. The realization that Braden was still in my life made me ridiculously giddy.

Me: Not at all. I don't suffer from stage fright.

The bathroom door opened, and a noisy group of girls tumbled in. I slipped into a stall and quietly climbed on top of the toilet seat, hoping to avoid them.

Me: But everyone's talking at the same time, running around. Sensory overload.

Braden: What helps with that?

Me: I'm used to hanging out with Arman. Now he's with Andrew's crowd.

Braden: Talk to Arman. It's not always black and white. Not everyone will be on your side. But everyone won't be against you either.

Then he sent the dove with olive branch emoji, followed by:

Break a leg!

What would that feel like? Reaching out to my former best friend? Would Arman turn his back on me again? Time to find out.

I ventured backstage, pushed through the chaos, and found Arman sitting at a dressing table, brushing on powder in front of a mirror. He stared at me in the reflection, but I just stood there, at a complete loss for words, thinking, *This was a terrible idea.*

I opened my mouth to speak, but the words still didn't come.

Arman set down the brush and swiveled in my direction. We were face-to-face. "Are you alright?"

"I'm sorry!" I squeaked. "I know I must've really done something hideous."

He patted the empty stool beside him. "No, love, not at all."

I lowered myself onto it and stared at the powders and wigs organized on the table.

"I'm sorry too. If I'm being honest, I have to admit, I completely overreacted." He picked up an eyeliner. "Close your eyes."

Unexpected, I thought, closing my eyes and trying to process the fact that I got an apology in return for an apology. I didn't even mind the tugging sensation on my eyelids. Instead I just concentrated on the soothing sound of Arman's voice.

"I was feeling sorry for myself about Spencer dumping me. Aaaannnd . . . well, you can say stuff, am I right? Insensitive or off-putting, maybe. But you don't mean it that way. I should be over that! I've missed you more than you know."

The tugging stopped, and I opened my eyes. "What about Andrew? How can you guys be friends?"

"We can't." Arman tossed the eyeliner back on the table. "He promised to start a new LGBTQ group using the funds from Save Our School. Then I find out, he promised *everyone* there'd be money for *everything*. Armani-designed cheerleading uniforms. A planetarium. Saltwater pool." He looked at himself in the mirror. "Why did I believe his empty promises? I'm such a fool."

"No," I said, feeling my lips curl up at the ends, into a smile. "You're an optimist."

We got into costume just in time, and Mr. Barsanti directed everyone to take their places. "Have *fun!*" he insisted. "When you do, the audience can feel it too. It's like there's a string reaching from you to each person sitting out there. You can bring joy. Actors have that power. You all have it! So use it. Let it out tonight!"

The energy coursed around the auditorium, just like Mr. Barsanti said it would. There was nothing in the world like bringing joy to other people and then having it bounce right back. The entire show seemed to go by in minutes. Laughter and applause exploded in all the right places.

Being in the ensemble and dancing in our monkey costumes was the best part. It wasn't serious. It was silly—actually, it was beyond silly. And the audience loved us!

"And can I just say? It is such a privilege to work with every one of you," Mr. Barsanti said afterward. "I have the best job in the world."

But my anxiety level began creeping back up as Arman and I threaded through the crowd in the lobby. Everyone kept bumping and brushing by me, and the other actors were holding smelly bouquets that made my head hurt. Then I saw Braden pushing through the bodies to get to me—so tall, he was hard to miss.

"I love the hair," he whispered in my ear. "You are the cutest thing I've ever seen."

Before I could respond, I saw my parents waving. "I'm Hank Gordon," Dad said, thrusting his hand out at Braden and then Arman. "You were terrific, Rae. What's with this wild hair? Wooh! You've really outdone yourself." He pulled me to him abruptly and kissed my cheek.

I wanted to wipe him off. His aftershave mixed with the heavy smell of the roses he waved around almost made me black out.

Mom swooped in, along with her friends Olivia and Nicki. "I'll take those home for you," Mom said, whisking the roses away.

I grinned, secretly pleased. We both knew she would be discarding Dad's gift. Meanwhile, Olivia held a bunch of bright yellow, fragrance-free sunflowers in her hand.

"You're a star!" she gushed. "The show was so funny!"

Nicki held her arms out and waited for me to walk into them. "You were darling." She gave me a light squeeze. "Everything was so professional! The singing, the costumes, even the lighting."

Lighting. That was the stage crew. I instinctively looked over my shoulder, expecting to find Andrew Jennings lurking there.

Dad smiled so big, I could practically see his molars. "I was telling your mom that I've been reading books about autism. Now I understand your aversion to bright lights, why you lock yourself up in your room. But goddamn, if you're not better! I mean, look at you. Acting onstage, just like all the other kids. Fitting in." He cleared his throat. "You've even got two guys buzzing around."

All this time, I wanted to say, *and you still don't get me.*

Dad kept talking and smiling, all teeth. I tried to filter out the noise of a hundred different conversations all around me. I heard Dad say something about dinner and steak.

My voice returned, barely a whisper. "Mom and I don't eat red meat."

Dad waved me off. "They have other things on the menu. Bring your friends."

"We can't," I said firmly. "We're going to an after-party."

"That's it?" he huffed. "I fight the 405 for ninety minutes, don't see you for weeks, and now you're running off to god-knows-where?"

"The after-party is at Rich Wood's house," I clarified. "Chances are, there will be alcohol. Maybe weed."

Dad looked horrified.

Mom spoke to Dad. "We weren't sure you were coming, and Rae's friends are expecting her. This is a big night."

Dad scratched his beard, obviously uneasy.

"Why don't you come with us girls to Casa Encantada? Pretty sure they've got steak tacos. And really good margaritas," Mom enthused.

Superhero Mom. She always knew what to say to him—don't ask me how. But Dad accepted her invitation, and I was free.

It was easy to forget my parents once we got to the party. I let the music thrum through my body and laughed so hard when Braden danced with Arman and me. He'd warned me that he couldn't dance. Now I believed him.

When Braden left to use the bathroom, Arman and I slid down the wall and sat on the floor, watching everyone from a distance. "I like this one."

I peered into the crowd. "Which one?"

"Which one!" he said, gently teasing me. "Braden!"

I play-hit my forehead with the heel of my hand. I can be so dense.

A burst of laughter came from the kitchen, where Andrew and the stage crew guys were doing shots. They saw us looking over, and the next thing I knew, they were hovering over us.

Andrew sort of tumbled over next to Arman and looped an arm around his shoulder. "Have a drink with us!"

Arman shifted, uncomfortable. "That's okay."

"Arman, I confess that I find the stage crew work often outshines the actors, but you know what, buddy? You are seriously talented." Andrew was slurring his words. Then he poked Arman in the chest and said, "You are one good-looking guy."

"Why, thank you," Arman said, lifting Andrew's arm off his shoulder.

"And I just want ya to know, that LGBTQ advocacy group we talked about? It's handled."

"Right."

"Just listen, will ya?" Andrew insisted. "Word on the street, even the mayor's in favor of activating the well. Soon's that dough's in our hands, you'll see nothing but pride flags waving on every corner of school." Andrew struggled to his feet and waved his drink around. Some of it sloshed on his shoe. "To saving our school!"

His friends echoed him. "Save our school!"

Arman and I stood up too, and a million things whipped through my mind. Explosions. Toxic chemicals. Invisible particulates. Alejandro Ortiz. I wanted to tell Andrew off, but I didn't even know where to begin.

Arman wrinkled his nose. "Politics should never be discussed at a party. Etiquette 101. Mind your manners."

Andrew's face went blotchy. "After all I've done for you? Don't tell me to—"

Braden came up behind him suddenly and just stood there. He was taller than Andrew by a good six inches.

Andrew stood still. "'Sup?"

"Ta-ta, Andrew," Arman said with a wave. "Thanks for dropping by!"

"What was that about?" Braden asked, turning to watch Andrew and his buddies retreat to the kitchen.

I was suddenly exhausted. "Can we go?"

"Yay! I don't have to dance anymore," Braden joked, sliding car keys from his pocket. "Seriously, what did Andrew want?"

I sighed. "To steal my friend."

Arman brushed a nonexistent piece of fluff from each arm. "Many try. None succeed." Then Ross came up and asked him to dance, and you could see his face light up.

As Braden and I headed for the door, a slow song came on. Arman and Ross held each other. My best friend—the least self-conscious person I knew.

I walked down the street with Braden, away from the loud music and the odor of too many people crammed indoors. When we got to his car, Braden opened the door for me, which seemed so old school, but I kind of loved it. Maybe next time, to shake things up a bit, I'd open the car door for him.

As we drove, I watched the glow of the streetlamps and the way the trees looked like black cardboard cutouts against the sky. Once we arrived at my house, Braden parked on the street and turned off the ignition. But he didn't make a move, and I felt my heart die a little.

Then he put his hand on mine and slowly rubbed his thumb back and forth against my wrist. It may have been the sexiest thing a guy had ever done with me. I hoped a kiss would be next . . . .

The porch light flickered on. Mom must've been lurking on the other side of the door.

Braden noticed the glowing fixture and released my hand. "I should probably go."

I studied the floor mat. "Well, goodnight," I said.

But what I wanted to say was: *This has been the best night of my life, and I seriously wonder if things could get any better.*

29

BRADEN

Record temperatures for April reminded me that summer weather had kicked in early. With the semester halfway over, I looked around at Simon and Jerome and the other Life Skills boys and realized how much I would miss them when the school year was over.

According to Ms. Hinojosa, the hardest part of being a special education teacher wasn't the kids; it was their caregivers. Some parents loved her. Others blamed her or called her incompetent. Some even falsely accused her of child abuse. Between the advocates and attorneys, between the lawsuits and the school admins who barely gave a second thought to special education, choosing to be a special ed teacher took grit.

The second hardest part was paperwork. It was endless: tedious forms that had to be filled out, lesson plans, evaluations, 504s, IEPs. What made it worthwhile, Ms. Hinojosa said, was the kids. She'd told me about students who had come back twenty years later to tell her she's awesome. She'd also told me about students who seriously hurt her. Through it all, she loved it and could not imagine being anything other than a special ed teacher.

I think she was trying to drop hints about a future career being in a school somewhere.

But my immediate goals focused on what was going on in *this* school. Right now, I was thinking about keeping Pac Crest students safe from the fate of the Ortiz family—and about how to make the haters stop bullying Rae. Beyond that, I didn't expect much more of myself. Then again, Rae had already inspired me in surprising ways.

Without warning, I found myself trying to remember the exact taste of her lips.

My phone vibrated with a text alert, piercing my daydream. Rae had sent me a Bloomberg link, where I learned that more than half of the oil and gas rigs in the United States leak methane. She wanted to know when I was going to write about the potential effects on Pac Crest.

I chuckled to myself. Being with her was a bit like being assigned to a group project.

I slid my phone into my back pocket and turned to Jerome. I had gotten used to his hands, all herky-jerky, fluttering around like they had a mind of their own. He tapped his iPad, where he'd found video of orcas in captivity, their huge bodies hovering over the surface of aquarium tanks, their dorsal fins flopped over, as they did the tricks they'd been trained to do. It was beyond depressing.

Jerome's gaze shifted to the window. Then he tapped his iPad again and wrote: *These whales live here until they die.*

Two things I'd picked up about Jerome since I'd started in the Life Skills classroom: 1) His grammar had gotten better, and 2) He understood everything. Before I could think of some intelligent response to his whale comment, he'd started crying.

"I get it," I said at last. "They shouldn't have to perform at all."
Jerome cried harder.

I stammered an apology as Noah offered him a book. Feeling useless, I reluctantly moved toward Simon and some other kids playing Social Skills Bingo. On days when it seemed like I helped them, my own worries faded. On other days, like now, my body buzzed with an unnamable fear.

During lunch period, I shuffled to the journalism room, still feeling like crap and relieved Rae wouldn't see me like this. I didn't want to bum her out or look like an overly sensitive dope.

There sat my carefree classmates. Lucas had sunk into the ragged sofa, surrounded by the power trio: Naomi stood behind the sofa, tapping a pen against her thigh. Alicia sat to one side of Lucas, snapping the lens cap on and off her camera. Shanice sat to the other side, sipping a green smoothie that probably set her back fifteen bucks.

My go-to turkey-avocado wrap suddenly looked particularly unappetizing. "Bon appétit," I said, handing the wrap to Lucas.

"Fake IDs are ubiquitous, and most parents don't lock the liquor cabinet," Naomi said. Then she waited, staring at me as if expecting me to weigh in.

"As long as they use a ride service," I responded sluggishly. "If they want cirrhosis, that's their problem."

Alicia looked up from her camera. "What about kids blacking out?"

"From now on, are we all drinking Diet Cokes and cucumber water at parties?" Lucas asked. "And how do I sign up for that?"

Shanice took a micro-sip of her smoothie. "The drinking age in Italy is fourteen. We aren't hearing about teenagers dropping their pants in Florence and waving their willies around."

Underage drinking didn't really concern me right now, but I

went through the motions. "Kids have been getting trashed since the invention of beer. That doesn't mean every tipsy guy is going to wave his—excuse me, did you say *willies*?"

Naomi, ever the news boss, kept her eye trained on me. "How about a piece on athletes who drink?"

I sucked in my lower lip, like I was seriously considering her question. "I'm actually on another lead. Maybe Lucas could take a crack at it?" I backed off toward the teacher's cubicle.

Lucas frowned like I'd tossed him a bag of dog poop.

Mr. Hackbarth was hunched over his desk as usual. "In or out," he grumbled.

"Would it be okay if I wrote a story about the oil platform?"

"So, you're telling me you're no longer a sports editor." This was a news story. I was supposed to bring up the idea to a news writer in a meeting—for instance, the meeting I'd just ducked.

"No, no. I'm still on sports."

He stared at me—not friendly, not mean.

"I'd interview student athletes, who spend the most time near the rig."

Mr. Hackbarth continued staring. "What's the purpose of journalism?"

It sounded like a trick question. Or one he wanted to answer himself. I waited.

"You need to give citizens information that will assist them in making the best possible decisions about the world." He scribbled on scratch paper and handed it to me.

I stared at the paper with a local phone number and name: *Shadi Shokrian.*

"One of the best student editors in the history of Pac Crest. Also captain of the girls' tennis team. She's got stage II breast cancer."

By now, I understood the worry train was a waste of time, but I couldn't help but probe my neck for a bump. For all I knew, malignant tumors were multiplying in my own lymph nodes. I *had* been feeling more tired than usual lately. And hadn't my mother just asked me if I'd lost weight? It took everything I had to stop myself from getting on board that train. It just felt so real.

Assignment in hand, I catapulted away from the journalism room to buy a bag of chips and give myself a second to figure out my next move. At the vending machine, I saw my locker neighbor, Mallory—a three-sport, all-star goddess.

"Braden Bernstein," I introduced myself, unsure if she had ever registered my existence. "I'm doing a survey about the impact of the oil well for *Neon Vikings*. Can I ask you a few questions?"

"Aren't you the sports editor?" Mallory asked.

So, she *did* know who I was. "Yeah."

"What's the oil well have to do with sports?"

"School athletes are the ones who spend the most time on the track and field near the well."

Mallory squinted at me. "You're not one of those Save Our School people, are you?"

"Nope."

"We're supposed to be phasing out fossil fuels and using renewable energy. Why can't they install solar cells over the cafeteria instead?"

"Good point," I said, taking notes on my phone. In the back of my head, I was thinking that after three and a half years as locker neighbors, this was the longest conversation Mallory and I ever had.

"We should be more forward-thinking," she said, moving down the hallway. "Did I answer your question?"

I was dismissed.

I jammed to the track and field. There it was: the drilling derrick—so obvious, so strange, and yet we had all just accepted it being there because, well, it had been there for decades. I found Brittany Chu doing stretches near the lacrosse goal and asked, "What do you think of the rig?"

She looked over her shoulder at it, for just a second. "Uh, I don't."

"There's research that points to it being dangerous."

"Braden, I need to focus on my hammies right now . . . ."

Another dismissal.

Inside the gym, I found some varsity volleyball players doing drills. I asked this guy Mike, a middle hitter, what he thought of the oil well.

"It looks like it belongs in a third-world country. They should get rid of it! Pac Crest is known for its elite athletic program."

Right. Okay, then. "Do you know anyone who's gotten sick from the oil well?"

Mike looked at me thoughtfully. "You mean cancer?"

I stood up taller, alert. "Yeah."

"I heard about this coach. Retired guy."

"You happen to know his name?"

A few minutes later, I raced back upstairs, bursting to tell Lucas what I'd learned. He was right where I'd left him, at one with the sofa, only now he was hunched over his laptop. Without looking up, he said, "You owe me."

"Uh, hello? Turkey sandwich?"

"That doesn't make up for Naomi dumping the alcoholic athlete story on *me*."

"Do I smell cigarettes?" I definitely smelled cigarettes. "Anyway, listen. Coach Zanetta—remember him? He's got cancer. What do you think about contacting him about the rig?"

Lucas squinted at me. "Stick to half-court buzzer beaters and miraculous finishes, Braden." Then he looked off into nowhere. "When people get sick, they want to blame it on something. The environment. Genetically engineered cherries. UFOs."

Before I could argue, the alarm rang. Over the loudspeaker came the instructions to exit the building, which we all knew by heart at this point. "Seriously? Another bomb threat?"

We grabbed our backpacks and headed out. "If you care so much," Lucas asked, sarcastic as always, "why don't you write about it?"

"Ha, ha. And what? Interview you, my anonymous source?"

He gave me a knowing smile that stopped me in my tracks.

People streamed around me to get to the stairwell. "Dude? You know something about this?"

Lucas yawned, still walking toward the exit. "You're holding up the exodus."

I jogged to catch up and gave him a backhanded slap on the shoulder. "Do you?"

Lucas let out a *pffft* sound and pushed through the metal double doors. "Yeah, right."

30

Peering out my bedroom window, I gazed at the glowing, enormous supermoon. Only when the full moon coincided with its closest orbit to Earth did it look this massive. The technical name for it was *perigee syzygy* or *full moon around perigee*—both names that sound like poetry. Staying up late to witness one of nature's coolest sky shows was so peaceful.

My phone made a soft *bing*.

Braden.

I had begun to count on his mood-lifting goodnight texts. Tonight, I sent back the full moon and howling wolf emojis.

Now that I was madly-in-like with this tall, sweet boy who drove the ugliest SUV in the world, I worried that I'd inadvertently do something insensitive and ruin everything. At the same time, I knew if I did not just act like myself, I'd become so strangled with anxiety that I'd wither and die—and, you guessed it, ruin everything.

As soon as I heard Mom softly snoring down the hall, I was ready to express my true self.

Alone with my thoughts, I found the right words.

AUTIEFREAK.COM:
Unfiltered Views from Your Average Awesome Autistic

SPACE

Why do I crave solitude? My therapist Jill calls it *self-care*. Other people call it *selfish*. I call it essential. Here's what can happen when I (and other spectrumites) don't get adequate alone time:

- We suffer from migraines from sensory overload.

- Cortisol (stress hormones released by the adrenal glands) courses through our veins, convincing us that forces are gathering to cause deep trouble.

- We slowly drown in self-doubt (aka meltdown).

- Things go blurry.

- At our worst, we can't see or talk or get off the floor (aka shutdown).

Alone time is predictable and restorative. Attending school is not. And since the littlest things can throw me off, I have to make constant adjustments.

Like the other day at school, when I ran out of my favorite lip balm: Chapped lips may not be a big deal in a neurotypical person's world. In mine, they kind of are. I was aware I was getting to the bottom of the tube, but thanks to a sketchy sense of executive functioning (the ability to organize), I didn't plan ahead. By third period, my lips felt so dry that I couldn't stop licking them, which only made them worse. I could barely focus on the teacher's lecture. On top of the daily sensory assault of cologne-wearing guys, and girls who stand too close, and lights blinking in the gym, dealing with chapped lips is utterly exhausting. It depletes me.

The remedy: alone time. By myself, there are no obstacles. I can connect to other people online who care about dog rescue. I can walk. I can read. I can stargaze.

It's not optional. Alone time is an emotional and intellectual necessity. It's how many of us who are neurodiverse regulate. To survive and thrive, we need this space.

From the looks I get at school, I doubt anyone would believe me. They think I'm being standoffish because I don't talk to a lot of other kids.

"You're not autistic, because you can talk."

"You're not autistic—you're just giving off attitude."

"You're not autistic, because you get good grades."

In my last session, my therapist suggested I could do a better job of explaining myself. Easy for her to say. She hasn't met my classmates. But I have become an excellent observer of them. Most fall into the following categories:

- Sheep. Blindly follow whoever is in front. Memorize trends. Sit in the cafeteria as close as possible to Populars.

- Populars. Social. Decorate their lockers for every holiday. Volunteer at every event. Talk too loudly. Laugh constantly. You never know if they're laughing about something funny or if *you* are the joke.

- Jocks. Sense of self-worth is based on their stats and the size of their biceps. Use body spray. Believe their athletic skills will make them succeed in life.

- Stoners. Philosophers, actually. May surf. May skate. Intelligent but have given up on school. Understand society is bullshit.

- Nerds. Always forget Picture Day. Have same hairstyle since first grade. May emit body odor. Wear off-brands. Are lovable.

- Freaks. Anyone different. Feel a heightened sense of emotion or can be seemingly devoid of emotion. Crave understanding yet want to be left alone.

Yup, that last one is me. Statistically speaking, I know there must be other autistic girls on campus, but I have yet to meet them. I'm friends with boys on the spectrum, and they are crazy-fun-loud-emotional goofs, but they aren't exactly like me.

Thankfully, I have found incredible auties online! Maybe the journey could be a little less terrifying if I could hang out with an autie girl IRL. Maybe it could be the BEST feeling in the world. There are things I have NEVER shared with my mom, and I know I could share these things with a room full of girls who have the same diagnosis. Together we could escape from everyday struggles.

We would amplify each other's superpowers.

31

BRADEN

Lucas was waiting for me in the student parking lot to ask for a ride. "Car's in the shop again. Someone stole the catalytic converter."

I nodded like I knew what that was and unlocked my car. As I turned off campus, Lucas scrolled through the radio stations. We settled on the Dodgers game. Their pitcher had just been hit by a ball.

"Ouchie!" Lucas exclaimed. "Last month, groin sprain. Now this. He needs to see a witch and burn some candles."

"Is that a thing?" I asked.

"Many people swear by it. And if you want the witch to give you a reading, it's like a thousand bucks."

"I think I'd prefer getting smacked by the ball."

As we drove through traffic, Lucas stared moodily out the window. Then he turned to me. "So, how's the story going?"

"Crumbling faster than a cupcake dipped in milk. I don't know where to start."

"You know, Braden, I take back what I said." Lucas sounded

serious. "You want to take on the man? Get up in the oil corporation's grill? Do it."

I had to smile. "I thought you wanted me to stick to slam dunks and buzzer beaters?"

He sighed heavily. "I've been thinking about my dad. How he's banging someone, putting our family at risk. He's totally selfish. Then I'm thinking: *Here's Braden. Perfectly willing to screw himself by writing a story to help other people, when half those people couldn't give two shits.*"

"Don't make it sound so heroic," I cautioned. "I'm paranoid about methane giving me pleuritis."

He gave me a look.

"It means difficulty breathing from inflammation of the pleura."

Lucas shook his head. "Point is, you're not doing this for personal gain. A bunch of people are going to call you out for questioning the wisdom of ramping up a petroleum platform for financial gain."

Just what I needed: more stress, more confrontation. Hadn't I left the basketball team because it was making me miserable? "Did I tell you that Mr. Hackbarth's source never returned my call?" I complained. "And what if Coach Zanetta won't talk to me? For fuck's sake. I don't know what I'm doing."

"Trust me, no one does." Lucas grinned. "But I have faith in you. When the world is on the brink of destruction—toxins spreading, pleurae swelling—that's when *you* come out swinging!"

I frowned. "Are you high?"

He thumped both thighs. "When do we start? I want to help."

Suddenly, the weight I'd been lugging around on my shoulders lifted. "You're serious?"

"Yes," Lucas replied. "Also, hungry."

"We can start right now . . . ."

"Can we stop at Shake Shack first?"

I glanced at him. "What about your catalytic conversion?"

"Converter. It'll wait. Story ain't gonna write itself."

In a way, having Lucas by my side was like having a fierce, chubby lion guarding me. I turned in the direction of Shake Shack. "I owe you."

"Cool. Can you loan me ten bucks?" he asked.

As we stuffed our faces with junk food, I did a quick Google search and found Coach Zanetta's phone number. Crumpled to-go paper bags and soiled napkins scattered on the floor of my car barely registered once Coach Zanetta answered his phone and agreed to be interviewed right away.

Lucas and I drove to his condo in Culver City, where a visiting nurse showed us to Coach Zanetta's bedroom. We found him reclined in a bed that looked straight out of a hospital room. His *YALE* sweatshirt sagged off his shoulders like he was a coat hanger. The tanned, sinewy drill sergeant I'd remembered from freshman-year PE had aged into droopy cheeks and grayish skin.

We sat on low, rickety folding chairs beside the bed, giving us a view straight up Zanetta's nose. A canula had been inserted into each nostril, effectively connecting him by plastic tubing to a gurgling oxygen machine. Feeling faint, I forgot my questions. I forgot the name of the pink flowers on the side table, even though they were my mom's favorite. I think I forgot to breathe.

Maybe I'm experiencing early-onset dementia, I thought stupidly.

Lucas adjusted his position on the plastic seat, causing it to creak loudly. "I hope I don't break your chair, Coach!"

Zanetta slowly leaned over the side of the bed to survey Lucas. "You said it, not me."

He didn't have the strength to straighten himself up again. The nurse appeared and readjusted the pillows until he was more or less upright.

Then he got right to the point. "They don't know where the cancer started."

My anxiety multiplied faster than a melanoma.

"I didn't notice it until I felt a bump on my right side." He rubbed his gnarled hands over a spot below his ribs. "It had already spread to my lungs and lymph nodes. My advice, gentlemen? Make hay while the sun still shines."

And what was to stop cancer cells from invading me? Didn't I run on that track ten months a year, inhaling the same invisible particles that had caused poor Coach Zanetta to look like a corpse?

Suddenly, my underarms were soaked. My skin felt like it was on fire. Fueling my panic was a sense of guilt. I was a shitty person who cared only about myself. That knowledge kept me weighed down, tethered to my chair.

After Hojun died and the shock wore off, I never thought I could ever feel that scared and sad ever again—until that moment, looking at Coach Zanetta.

My phone buzzed in my pocket. I snuck a look. It was a text from Rae.

> I'm working on expressing daily gratitude. Thank you for always sticking up for me and for sticking up for all the students, even the ones who mock us. You're one of the strongest people I know. I'm so lucky you're in my life.

Reading her text, I felt way better. Her unexpected stream of words was organized with Rae's typical honesty and certainty, and they gave me confidence. They reminded me that I could endure my discomfort with this fucked-up situation, sitting with Coach as terribly sick as he was. Gradually, my mind began to clear. I grasped the bottle of water that the nurse had offered me and gulped it down.

This was different from Hojun's disaster. There was a slim chance I could stop someone else from getting hurt. It was too late for Coach Zanetta, but the least I could do was get the story right.

I turned on my phone record function. In a voice that sounded stronger than I felt, I asked: "What makes you think the drilling platform is to blame?"

"For over forty years, I taught at Pac Crest," Coach Zanetta began. "I spent more time on that field than anywhere else. Maybe toxic fumes only leaked for a few weeks or months. Or maybe it was years."

"There was a class action lawsuit ten years ago," I reminded him. "Cancer victims already tried to sue the school district and the previous company that owned the platform." I had done my research. The lawsuit I'd remembered was real, but it just didn't go anywhere.

"Someone smart—like you and two-ton Teddy here—needs to make 'em think again," Coach Zanetta wheezed. He couldn't seem to catch his breath, and I cringed as his coughing fit worsened.

I threw a glance at Lucas. He gave a slight nod, but when he didn't get up, I followed his lead. We had to keep going. "So you were generally healthy before . . . this?"

"All I can tell you gentlemen is, I've avoided sugar since I was a teenager. I've eaten a plant-based diet for years. I lifted weights and ran five or six miles a day until nine months ago." Coach Zanetta stopped to cough again.

"Awful." I shook my head. "I'm so sorry."

Coach looked over my shoulder, his eyes bleary. "I didn't say yes to you comin' here for your pity," he said in a hoarse voice. "Write your story. That platform needs to be decommissioned. It's a dinosaur, kind of like me. It should be extinct."

"We're gonna make those jerks pay, Coach," Lucas declared. "And you're right. I do need to cut back on the sugar." He gave Coach a gentle fist bump.

The next day at school, a few kids gave me fist bumps, and one freshman girl asked if she should be wearing a gas mask to school. With Lucas's help, I had finished a rough draft from the front seat of the Ford the previous afternoon, after leaving Coach Zanetta's place. I was doubtful I'd get the oily odor of french fries out of my car, but it was worth it. We published "Retired Coach Says Oil Well Made Him Sick" by the deadline.

Mr. Hackbarth liked the piece. Well, he actually didn't say he "liked" it; he just didn't say he didn't. He did have one question: "Where's a quote from Shadi?"

His former student, the one with breast cancer, hadn't called me back. "I left her a message." I shrugged.

A lot of Pacific Crest students must have seen the article, but most said nothing, and I figured they probably didn't care. Then I stepped out of Spanish, my last class of the day, and two stage crew kids across the hall gave me the stink eye.

Outside on the front lawn, Taylor and Kennedy—in their form-fitting *Save Our School* T-shirts—beckoned me to the bench they were sitting on.

"Braden, why are you against us? Why are you against the well?" Taylor tilted her head to one side, awaiting my answer.

Kennedy *tsked*. "Did psycho girl put you up to this?"

"I'm going to pretend I didn't hear that," I said, more calmly than I felt. "And if you think you can sum up someone's entire life from seeing them at school for a few minutes, you're completely nuts."

"Spare me the lecture." Taylor squared her shoulders. "Can you imagine if Pac Crest had the money to offer Latin? To repave the tennis courts?"

I softened my approach. "C'mon. Tell the truth. Did you actually *read* my article?"

Kennedy and Taylor glanced at each other.

"I'd be shocked if you had. Who has the time at an incredibly high-performing school like ours?" I tried to defuse the situation. "With all the extracurriculars, the mind-numbing hours of homework . . . ."

Kennedy straightened her top as Andy walked up to the bench. "I trust Andrew." She pouted.

I kept talking like he wasn't there. "Did he happen to mention that even with budget cuts, Pac Crest students still manage to score high on exams and get into top-tier colleges? Or that a drilling rig might actually make you really sick?"

Taylor looked at Andy and then back at me, as though suddenly unsure of which team she should be rooting for. Kennedy crossed her arms and looked impatiently at Andy.

"Braden," Andy said in a soothing voice that also strove to be menacing. "I am not the enemy."

Thump. Thump. Thump. The blood pumped in my chest like I'd just done the hundred-yard dash. Two of the stage crew minions had edged closer to us. I realized that I was on my own—not a friend in sight.

"We're dudes," Andy continued. "We hold a girl's handbag while she's in the bathroom. We think of nice compliments to make a good impression. So here you are, a damn good sportswriter, writing about stuff you know nothing about."

It was getting harder and harder to keep my hands from balling into fists.

Andy lobbed another insult. "I get it! You want to keep Rae happy. She's loco, but you know what she's like. Hell, she even tried coming at me once . . . . And now you're whipped. Hah! She's driving you to do stuff for her—"

"Careful." I cut him off. "Who's driving *you*, Andy?"

"I prefer Andrew now." He smirked, raising his voice for the gathering crowd.

"You expect me to believe you've suddenly got a hard-on for petroleum companies?"

"As sappy as it may sound, Braden, I'm just looking out for the greater good." He stood stock-still before me, as though expecting a punch in the face—one that I sorely wanted to give him.

A semblance of logic surfaced. Breaking Andy Jennings's nose really wasn't the story I wanted to tell. I turned and swiftly crossed the crowd, kids stepping out of my way.

I trotted down the stairwell to the parking lot, texting Rae to offer a lift home if she wanted to meet me at my car. She must have been close already, because she beat me there. I sighed with relief, seeing her safe and adorable, and—for the moment—untroubled by Andy and his crew.

"You up for a kiss?" I ventured.

She looked at me for a full minute, and her eyes sparkled. "Mmm-hmmm," she finally murmured.

I placed a finger carefully below her chin, tilted her face up, and gave her a soft smooch. "You up for being my girlfriend?"

Her sapphire blue eyes widened for a moment. She looked at her shoes. Years passed. Finally, she answered me in a flat voice. "Yes."

I took a step backward and gave a wary smile. "Your enthusiasm is heartwarming!"

She looked confused.

"What took you so long? You paused!"

"You asked me a serious question. I had to think about it. Which, of course, means I had to overthink about it." She reached up to me, linking her hands behind my neck, and pulled me to her for a kiss. Then she stopped again. "Before we suck each other's faces, there's something you should see."

Rae led me around to the driver's side of my car. The door had been keyed with fourteen-inch letters. Scratched deep into the paint, someone had written: *LIAR! LIAR!*

Thump. Thump. Thump. Adrenaline raced in my veins. I traced the damage with my fingertips. "I can't believe this."

"Oh, I can." Rae nodded. "You're not a sheep."

I didn't get the reference. "Why'd you wait so long to tell me about my car?" I said, unable to keep my voice from rising.

Rae shrugged. "You asked if I wanted to kiss. Then you asked if I wanted to be your girlfriend. With all that going on, how am I supposed to process your car being keyed?"

Not so long ago, this would've confused me. I would've felt frustrated because Rae didn't understand how upset I was about having my car vandalized. Now I knew it just meant she was risking emotional overload already: dealing with bullies saving the school from environmental danger, having a new boyfriend in her life after she'd been burned in the past. Rae should not have to carry all that alone. No one should.

I dialed it back. "I'm sorry. I'm upset."

"It gets worse," Rae said.

She showed me her phone, where *Neon Vikings* was open on the screen. Andy had already written a letter to the editor:

> *I strongly disagree with Braden Bernstein's scaremongering*
> *tactics to mischaracterize the oil/gas proposal. For every*
> *person he's persuaded to speak out, there are hundreds more*
> *who would completely disagree.*

> *People get cancer. It's tragic, and my heart goes out to them. But don't blame the oil rig and the good people who want to elevate our high school and make it one of the nation's best, like it used to be. Sorry, dude. That takes money. Lots of it.*
>
> *We have to wonder about this fake news. Is Braden hungry for attention because he didn't get any when he was on the basketball team?*

My blood boiled. "They're not going to stop with my car. They're going to punish my friends. Especially my girlfriend."

Rae twisted a thread on the hem of her T-shirt until it finally snapped off.

"Could you deactivate from social media for a little while?"

"No," she said quietly. "I won't let the haters win. I have to keep in touch with the dog rescue groups. And I want to keep blogging."

"How about just for a week?" I pressed.

She frowned.

"Never mind. It's just . . . seeing the car like this . . . ."

Rae took my hand, and I felt a little better. But this was a threat, not a random worry thought. More worries were sure to follow, about Real-Life Problems this time.

And my biggest worry was that someone might hurt Rae.

32

RAE

After class the next day, I waited for Mom at my usual spot in front of the gym. When I turned my phone on, it *binged* with new notification alerts from AutieFreak.com, signaling I had new comment activity.

A tremor of excitement went through me as I anticipated the possibilities. I logged on to my website and saw my latest post on the PAWS Act, along with the banner I'd uploaded: a photo of a proud veteran and his new service dog, both part of the Puppies Assisting Wounded Servicemembers program. The PAWS Act, as my post explained, provided service dogs to veterans diagnosed with PTSD, including complimentary training of service dogs as part of the vets' treatment. But when I navigated to the Comments page, that thrill turned into physical pain as my stomach seized up.

Disturbed.

Freak.

Fugly.

The only friends you'll ever have are imaginary. Or future prison cellmates.

You obviously inherited the MENTAL gene from your mother.

Tears pricked my eyes, and my nose started to run. I rubbed my face hard with the sleeve of my T-shirt. This time they were rejecting me as a human being.

How could people be so mean? And why didn't I see this coming? Braden had predicted the sheeple at school would lash out, especially now that Andrew Jennings had it out for me. He'd tried to warn me, asking me to take a social media vacation.

"That's letting the haters win!" I'd argued. But if I didn't protect myself—if I didn't anticipate and plan for how people might react to my posts—my emotional survival was in jeopardy.

Autistic women are thirteen times more likely than non-autistic women to die by suicide. Until recently, I didn't think I'd make it. When Zach broke up with me, I convinced myself that the world wasn't made for me. I fell down so deep, I didn't think I could ever get up again. The only thing that made me okay was Mom saying: *You're enough. You're brave. You're strong. You're going to be okay. Every other time you had to go through something hard, you got through it.*

Then suddenly things got better than I could've imagined. I decided I wanted to work with service dogs, and I met Braden. His support gave me something totally new—more confidence and belief in myself than I'd experienced for years. No way would I shy away from posting about the PAWS Act or any other issues that were important to me.

But I couldn't stop the haters from hating.

How could I have been so naïve as to have expected to find my tribe by blogging? Over and over, I had to face this thing about me being different, this thing that made other people despise me. Why had I expected anything else?

I logged out of my website as Mom pulled up to the curb. "How was your day at school?" she asked cheerfully.

"Okay," I replied. Technically, school had been fine. It was my online world that sucked.

I don't remember driving home or walking through the front door, until Mom gently set down her bag and said, "You're quiet."

Demonstrating I wasn't, I let my bookbag slide off my shoulder to the floor with a thud.

Noodle scampered into the entryway to greet me, and I plopped to the ground to play with him. My dog never failed to bolster my spirits.

Braden cheered me up too. What was it about being with him that was so different from being with other neurotypicals? I could be myself. Unmask. He believed in me. Compared to the bullies and cyberbullies who tried to tear me down with their callous comments and thoughtless remarks, at the end of the day it was Braden's opinion that mattered most. He never told me that I was too fixated on my special projects; he supported me like a boyfriend ought to do.

I really hoped he wasn't too anxious about the sheep who trashed his car so we could get back to preparing for the council vote on the oil rig. Whether they realized it or not, my schoolmates needed our help.

"Did you know the city council of Culver City banned oil drilling and by 2030, they'll have thirty-eight wells shut down for good?" I asked Mom a couple hours later. We were eating an early dinner:

quesadillas oozing with three kinds of cheese, topped with slivers of ripe avocado and fresh *pico de gallo*—one of my favorite meals.

"Yes." She studied my face.

I had just finished watching the recordings of three previous council study sessions on the drilling platform. "Mommy? I couldn't do what you do."

"If a dog's life was on the line, you would. Wouldn't you?"

"Definitely." I looked down into Noodle's warm brown eyes and kicked off my shoes. "I also read the city's website . . . all those letters you wrote the governor, supporting prison reform and affordable housing, opposing the streamlining approval for the petroleum company. No one appreciates you!"

Mom smiled. "Ah, I think there are a few who do."

"Not Councilman Jennings. He just loves to hear himself talk. Gawd, he's boring!"

Mom looked off in the distance. "He's going to term out in three months. I hear he's been looking for a job at Eclyra Energy Solutions . . . lobbying the city council."

I sat up straight, shocked. "He can't!"

"It's unethical, but not illegal. He can come up with some angle, like he's not really lobbying the city because the corporation has changed hands, or the project has been modified in some substantial way, making it different from what they're presenting right now."

"That sucks! Resign from the council in protest. Slam him on social media!"

"I see it differently," Mom said, shaking her head. "I'm trying to find solutions. Even small progress is still progress."

It made perfect sense. It also made the tightness in the center of my chest ease up. Screw the haters. I was going to double down on blogging.

I looked down at my phone, still on the floor next to my backpack. Texts from Arman. Missed calls from Braden. They'd obviously seen the cyberbullying.

I'm trying to find solutions.

Even small progress is still progress.

"Okay if I schedule a call with Jill?" I asked Mom.

She looked at me intently. "I hope talking about my work hasn't upset you!"

"Of course it has." I slipped my bra off beneath my shirt. "People can be awful."

"They can also be incredible. Like you with your mad research skills! Your potential is limitless."

Hm. I didn't know about that.

I started taking care of the dishes and was just about done when Jill got back to me. I excused myself from the kitchen and ran upstairs for privacy.

Over the phone, I told Jill about the blog and the trolls. "I'm so angry and hurt right now for people talking shit about my mom!" I tried to keep my voice down in case Mom was in the hallway.

"You have every right to feel emotional," Jill replied. "But studies indicate that repeatedly expressing anger actually increases the possibility that you'll get angry again. The only way to prevent that is to stop obsessing over what the trolls did. Don't hang on to it."

"Easy for you to say! No one hates you."

"Anger makes us push people away, Rae, makes us want to isolate ourselves."

Welcome to my world.

"Sadness can do that too," Jill observed. "But when we're sad, it's something we can pass through. It's softer. We're more open to help. We can work through the emotion."

I scoffed, unimpressed.

"I'm not saying you should *dismiss* your anger. I'm asking you: Is it possible for you to consider not getting stuck in it?"

I looked at my desk—at the files I had created with leads on forever dog homes and data on drilling rigs. I didn't have time to get stuck. Like Mom, I needed to find solutions.

Even small progress is still progress.

AUTIEFREAK.COM:

Unfiltered Views from Your Average Awesome Autistic

PLAYING CHESS

When I was a little kid, a friend was just someone I played with—not because I needed "socialization," but because they liked the same things as me: dinosaurs or dogs or *The Simpsons* or whatever. A friend was someone who could offer me a new way to play and learn about my special interests.

Now that I'm in high school, a friend is more like a chess piece: They're either on my team or they're not. If you factor in online friends, though, I've got a kick-ass team. Shout out to Brenda! She's like me, and she's an incredible artist and animal activist. (Quick plea: Don't buy from breeders! Secondhand dogs make first-rate pets. :-)

My mom thinks IRL friends are more valuable than online friends, but she totally doesn't get it. The internet is such an incredible resource for me to find people who think like me and care about the same things! It drives me crazy: Mom thinks an hour or two max is sufficient for my daily online time. Personally, I don't believe in any online time limits.

We don't agree on exercise either. Mom's a gym rat, while I think a leisurely walk around the block with my rescue pup more than satisfies my physical fitness requirements. And on the topic of manners, Mom is a real hard-ass. She nagged at me for ages about apologizing to a dreadful bully in my grade. Grant you, I pushed him down, even though I'm five foot six and he's probably six feet tall. The creep so had it coming, and Mom backed down once she heard he'd called me freak and tried to get me to perform some sort of super-autistic magic trick.

People assume if you're "high-functioning" like Bill Gates or Einstein or Mozart, then you possess unique talents and are übersmart. Excuse me. I'm no genius. I have no special talents. Here's a pocket guide to help you if you're a "normal" and trying to figure out what your autistic friend is like:

- We do better when we have a set schedule. So, if we go out for Froyo on Fridays and you suddenly change our plans to tacos on Tuesdays, don't be alarmed if we get upset. We may even cry over it!

- We crave understanding and love. Even if we don't want to hug or look you in the eye, it doesn't mean we don't desperately need your friendship.

- Our special interests are not obsessions! Think of them as our passions and be patient if we talk a lot about them. Special interests give meaning to our lives.

- Expect us to withdraw every now and then. It's not personal. Navigating the neurotypical world takes a lot of energy and we must have time to recharge.

- Self-care is essential to our health. Allow us the space to meditate, to do nothing, to read, or to stare at the clouds. Without judgment.

Being friends with an autistic person isn't really so different from any other sort of friendship: It's complicated. Just like chess.

33

BRADEN

My phone vibrated with a text. I figured it had to be Rae. *My girlfriend.* I loved the way that sounded.

Not that I could actually daydream about my new romantic status or check my phone. Not while worrying about Rae getting bullied. Not while sitting at my kitchen table with Mom and Dad, who were more freaked out about my car being vandalized than I'd expected. And definitely not while being quizzed by the two Pacific Crest police officers who had finally arrived to take our report.

Detective Figueroa sat back in the kitchen chair, big as an NFL fullback, taking notes on a legal pad. His hair was graying at the temples, and he wore black technical pants and a black, short-sleeved golf shirt—*FIGUEROA* in embroidered block letters across the right side of his chest. He seemed like a chill guy, ready to play a round of eighteen. Well, except for the gun on his right hip.

Figueroa's partner, Officer Stanten, looked half his age and seemed twice as serious. Maybe it was her traditional black, starched uniform. Maybe it was her solemn expression. Maybe it was because she asked questions I didn't feel like answering.

"*Any* idea who did this?" Stanten had asked me the same question twice already, phrasing it differently each time. Kind of like me asking my parents for tickets to Coachella.

"I'm not sure." As much as I disliked Andy and his sidekicks, I was not a snitch. I turned to my parents. "Doesn't insurance pay for this kind of stuff?"

Dad furrowed his brow. "Even if it did, you can't let bullies get away with it."

"Vandalism is a crime," Mom said, backing him up.

"And vandalism is *expensive*," Dad reminded me. "This is my car we're talking about. In case you forgot."

I fidgeted, anxious to read my texts and get going. Rae was expecting me to pick her up.

Stanten spoke again. "Maybe there was a misunderstanding with a girl?"

"I don't think so."

"Or a boy?" She studied my reaction.

My private life wasn't her business. "I wrote a story for my school's online newspaper. Some people had a problem with it."

Dad seemed genuinely confused. "What could you possibly write in the sports pages to elicit this kind of a response?"

Unless I wanted to be trapped at this table for the next decade, I had to reveal something. "There's this club at school, advocating for the Eclyra Energy Solutions oil pumping deal so the school can score big money. They call it the Save Our School club, which sounds like a no-brainer. Until you factor in student health and the environment."

I paused for a breath.

"My friends and I think it's a terrible idea. I interviewed student athletes and a retired coach who's dying from cancer—people who've spent a lot of time on the field closest to the well—and then I wrote a story about the potential for environmental danger. It pissed off a few Save Our Schoolers."

"You're not on sports anymore?" Dad asked. "Why am I always the last to know?"

"I'm still sports editor, Dad."

"The old oil tower is controversial. Everyone's been talking about the city council vote, taking sides," Mom wondered out loud. "Could an angry mob be dangerous to our son?"

Wait, an angry mob? I hadn't actually said the word *mob*, had I?

"We'll interview all the suspects, Mrs. Bernstein," Figueroa informed her. "Don't worry."

Wrong answer.

"Don't worry? In the current climate, with school shootings and kids carrying assault rifles, I shouldn't worry?" Mom's eyes flashed, like the time Jenji wasn't at her designated carpool pick-up spot and it took us an hour to find her. Turns out, she'd been delayed rescuing a stray cat.

Figueroa leaned forward toward Mom and gave her his card. "We'll conduct a thorough investigation. Anytime you want to discuss it, we can. Here's all my contact information."

Dad touched Mom's forearm. "Don't blow it out of proportion, Shannon."

Mom snatched her arm away, fuming. "Please. This is serious."

Mom's hyper-protectiveness had kicked in after Hojun died. When it came to Jenji and me, any threat—from pesticides to pedophiles to salmonella to GMOs—was a Big Deal. Come to think of it, maybe that was a good topic to bring up at my next therapy session.

Officer Stanten pivoted to me. "Earlier, you said you and *your friends* think the oil project is a mistake. Who else is being targeted?"

Rae was the bullseye. But she had made it clear to me after the cyberbullying that she was determined not to report anyone. She thought it would make things worse for her.

"What was the question again?" I stalled.

Stanten straightened an invisible hair out of place. "Other students being targeted?"

My phone vibrated again. Now I peeked at it. Rae had sent the woman shrugging emoji. I was late.

Detective Figueroa closed his notepad. "This time it was a car. But recently there's a pattern of students hiring other students to do their dirty work. One of my current cases involves a young man who Venmo'd money to another student in exchange for stomping on someone's face. Or more accurately, he bought silence in the event this face-stomper got caught."

Andy was too spineless to do any real damage on his own. With the upcoming city council vote, though, he might turn up the heat on his little Save Our School campaign. I had no idea how far he'd take it—or who he might enlist to join him.

I rubbed my eyes, dreading doing what I was about to do. If anyone found out, people would call me a rat. But worse, so much worse, was the real possibility Rae might dump me for betraying her privacy.

"I didn't actually see him key my car," I said at last. "But Andy Jennings takes the Save Our School club personally."

Figueroa's eyes narrowed. "Andrew? Councilman Jennings's son?"

How did he know Andy? "Yes, sir." I had never called anyone *sir* before.

Mom's voice returned to normal. "Has this child been in trouble before?"

The detective grinned. "Let's just say if I know a kid's name, then they've done something to get my attention, right?"

Mom cracked a smile. "I was wondering why they sent a detective for a vandalism case."

I didn't buy it. If Andy turned out to be responsible for keying my—I mean, Dad's—car, would anyone of authority ever say squat to him? Because, *hello*, he was a councilman's son!

"How do you know Andrew?" Figueroa asked me in a casual way.

"We've known each other since kindergarten, but we never really hung out." A bead of sweat formed over my lip.

I could only pray Rae would understand. I realized I'd do pretty much anything for her, and that scared me more than carbuncles or kidney stones or even hired thugs.

"Andy and his friends have been truly horrible to a girl named Rae," I continued. "We've been working together on this story. And, yeah, her mom is also on the city council."

Figueroa closed his notepad. "Mm-hmm."

I was wading into deep water. "She's super smart. Reads a lot. She's on the spectrum." Rae never shied away from her autism diagnosis, so why should I?

Figueroa leaned forward. "Last question: How do you know her?"

"She's my girlfriend."

My parents' inquisitive looks did not bode well for me. Parents typically loved to meet their son's girlfriend and ask a million questions, closely followed by the requisite weigh-in with unsolicited advice and opinions. This could get out of control fast. If I wasn't careful, Mom and Dad could be inviting Rae over for tea and scones and arranging family movie nights once a week.

The officers seemed satisfied and pushed out their chairs. We thanked them, and then I headed straight to my room, hoping Mom and Dad wouldn't follow.

Shit. Shit. Shit. What did I do? I thought. Rae had specifically told me she did not want to rat on Andy. What if she broke up with me?

I ducked into the bathroom to brush my teeth, just in case this was my last chance to kiss her. I leaned down to spit in the sink, and the next time I lifted my head to look into the mirror, Jenji was standing there, staring back at me.

I almost hit the ceiling. "How many times have I told you to stop spying?" Toothpaste sprayed out of my mouth.

"You can brush your teeth for a year," she said evenly, "and you'd still have baboon breath."

"Stank you. Stank you very much," I responded.

"Why didn't anyone tell me the police were here? Maybe I would've liked to talk with them. Maybe I could've helped."

"Uh, because it wasn't any of your business."

Always the tae kwon do show-off, Jenji dropped into a fighting stance and took a swing so fast, she could've clocked me if she hadn't stopped the heel of her hand a half inch from my jaw.

"Love you too, sis."

"Zoe's brother says he heard about your car."

"Yeah?"

"He knows who did it, but he wouldn't say who."

"Can you keep a secret?" I asked.

She solemnly nodded her head up and down.

"I think I know who's behind it, too. Maybe. But it won't make a difference, Jenji. Not unless Zoe's brother was there when it happened."

Jenji nodded sagely. Who could say what went on in my kid sister's mind?

When I finally pulled into Rae's driveway, she was already waiting outside for me, in a puffy jacket two sizes too big and black Ray-Bans masking her eyes.

Dad had taught me to always pick a girl up at her door, but Rae had already pushed off the planter she'd been leaning against and was heading for my car. So I got out of the old Ford with the lovely *LIAR! LIAR!* label freshly removed, courtesy of the neighborhood auto shop, and popped a mint in my mouth just in case dreams came true.

When I opened the passenger door for Rae, she tilted her head up to look at me, and I saw her perfect, pillowy lips. Aching to touch her, I started to move in for a kiss.

"You're twenty-three minutes late."

I paused. Had I been a football kicker, the ref would've called it *No good!* Thanks to my poorly planned trajectory, I'd missed the goalposts entirely.

"Blame it on the police officers handling my case," I said, trying to sound exasperated instead of rejected. "They asked so many questions."

"Figueroa and Stanten?"

I nodded, gobsmacked. "Wait. What? You know them?"

"I don't want to talk about them." Her face darkened, and she changed the subject. "So you got your car back. Still ugly."

I cleared my throat. "Technically, it's my dad's car." I wanted to ask again about the police officers, but I didn't know how.

Rae tugged a tube of lip color from her pocket and swabbed it across her lips. "I have to text Mom when I'll be back."

"I get it." I tried to sound cheerful. "My folks have me on the Find My Friends app. Feels more like wearing an ankle monitor."

"Are your parents worried about social isolation and depression too?" She seemed to soften.

Something about the color of her eyes and the open expression of her face made me want to fold Rae up in my arms and never let her go. "That, sure. And car wrecks. Abductions. Ax murderers." I opened the passenger door.

She hesitated.

"Tell your mom we'll be back before dark."

That seemed to satisfy her, because she got in and buckled up.

As I turned the ignition, the radio blared, and Rae flinched. I immediately cranked down the volume, but I wanted to smack myself for looking like an insensitive idiot.

Being someone's boyfriend really was a lot of work sometimes.

34

RAE

I struggled to parse Braden's words from the background clatter of the car radio. Gathering reconnaissance on the oil rig operation was crucial, but I was starting to regret my decision to venture out at all. Mentioning the detectives' names had been a careless slip, and the music was making my head throb. It sounded like someone was yelling at me.

"Please just turn it off!" I said as I clamped my headphones over my ears.

Braden switched to sports radio: crowd droning, then someone screaming about a goal. "Better?" he asked.

"No!" I winced. My frontal lobe threatened to tear itself from my skull.

He switched off the radio and shifted into drive. Reaching for my phone, I pressed the play icon. Within minutes, I felt calmer.

A tap on my upper arm interrupted me. I pressed pause on my phone. "What?"

"Um, what're you listening to?" Braden asked.

"It's a podcast about the PAWS Act. Veterans with PTSD can

now be paired with service dogs. PTSD is an invisible disability, like autism. Autistics should have the same rights. All of it is so overdue."

"Sounds incredible. Listen, Rae—"

I hadn't finished my point. "Have you heard of K9s for Warriors? They train rescue pups in their service dog lineup. Isn't that just the best ever? It all came about because lawyers wrote this transformative legislation. I mean, I never thought about law school before, but now I can see how that education could really benefit me in the future!"

"Totally worthwhile . . . umm . . . ."

There was so much to share. "There's even been legislation passed to make it illegal to fake having a service dog, and—"

Braden tapped my arm a second time.

I clenched my jaw, annoyed to have been derailed from my thought process again. "If you keep interrupting me, I'll have to start over from the beginning!"

"Would you mind removing the headphones?"

I did as he asked. I *was* going to have to start over. How else to explain such an important new law and not leave out crucial details?

Braden drummed on the steering wheel. "So, I know how passionate you are about your special interests. It's charming as hell to watch you in action and see how your mind works. Um, how do I say this? It's like you're missing page six from *The Girlfriend Handbook*. You're not supposed to listen to a podcast, err, in the middle of a date."

"Why not?"

He slowed for a red light. He was pressing his lips together and making a *pop* sound as though trying to figure out what to say. "I guess because it makes the other person feel left out. As if they don't matter and you don't need them."

I needed Braden more than he knew. I slid off my sunglasses, realizing how odd I must have been acting. The headphones went back in their case and the phone into my pocket. "Is it available online? *The Girlfriend Handbook?*"

"It's not a thing." He shook his head. "Sorry, I was trying to make a point."

I had missed the joke. Again. "Maybe I should blog about a girlfriend handbook for neurodiverse girls."

"I love the way you think, you know that?"

My insides went to mush. It was the highest compliment anyone could ever give me.

The light changed to green. We drove on in silence for a few minutes, my thoughts pinwheeling with new themes related to dating, love, and sex for my blog.

I threw a sideways glance at Braden. Every detail was intriguing: the way he slouched in the driver's seat, the muscles flexing in his forearm, the freckle on his right wrist. The impulse to make him pull over and climb into his lap almost overtook me. I sat on my hands to stop myself from touching him.

Unexpectedly, Braden reached across the center console and softly tugged my left hand from beneath my thigh. He held my hand in his, moving his thumb back and forth across each finger. His touch set off a tingling sensation that traveled from my fingers and branched out to my arm, and soon my entire body seemed to buzz. The gentle hum of the air-conditioning cushioned me from the outside world. We drove like that, and I felt so safe in the car with Braden.

When he broke the silence, I almost shushed him.

"On behalf of OCD sufferers everywhere, I *have* to ask," he began. "Why can't you talk to me about the cops?"

Without thinking, I pulled my hand back and stuck it beneath my leg.

I desperately wanted to trust Braden. Except if I couldn't forgive myself for hitting Mom, how could I expect him to?

Chemicals churned in my brain. Fatigue weighed heavily on my eyelids. The sense of shame reached an unbearable level. "I need to go home," I said finally.

"Wait, what?"

"Let me out!"

Braden pulled over and tapped the brakes too hard. I felt the shoulder belt snap me back in my seat.

He put the Ford in park. "What just happened?"

"I'm sorry. I'm on the verge of having a panic attack." I clutched the door handle, accidentally smashing my pinky. I immediately stuck the injured digit in my mouth—it tasted like whatever Braden had used to clean the car.

I gagged and pushed against the door. In my rush to get out, my foot caught the curb, and I pitched forward. The next thing I knew, I found myself sprawled on the pavement.

Braden flew out of the car and helped me to my feet. "Are you okay?"

Things weren't tracking. They never did when I panicked.

"I'm sorry, Rae. I—" Braden brushed some dried grass off my pants. "The cops said some things. And I said some things too. Maybe more than I should've. I told them Andy's been bullying you. I'm so sorry . . . ."

Braden's voice, full of remorse and something that sounded almost like love, stopped my spiral. He reached for my hand and gave it a squeeze. Slowly, I understood this had absolutely nothing to do with Mom and me.

When Braden let go, I could still sense where his fingers had pressed against mine, and I craved that sensation again. "I don't want anyone to hurt you," he murmured. I realized he was blushing. "And most of all, *I* don't want to hurt you."

I looked down, suddenly shy.

Braden dug the toe of his sneaker into the grass. "You know I like spending time with you, right? You're different."

Different. There it was.

"I've seriously never met anyone like you. And I wouldn't change a thing."

Ohhhhh. He meant *that* kind of different. I didn't realize how badly I needed to hear that from Braden, I was alright just as I was.

I focused on the threads of my jeans where a new hole had formed over the right knee. Even though the shame soaked my skin and drenched my spirit, Braden deserved to know the truth.

"A few weeks ago, I slugged my mom in the face," I confessed. "It was one of the worst days of my life. Mom didn't know what else to do, so she called the police. That's how I met Officer Stanten and Detective Figueroa."

"O-kayyy." Braden's eyes went big and round, reminding me of a Boston terrier's.

My stomach flopped, and I felt weak. As usual, I'd said way too much.

"It sucks that happened," he went on. "The thing about moms? They still love us when we do stupid shit. At least, the good ones do."

Tears blurred my vision. I dropped my chin and pressed my head into his chest. Overwhelmed, I stood there.

Braden gave me a squeeze—firm yet gentle—and let go before it got uncomfortable. Then I wrapped my arms around him, urgently needing to feel his body against mine. He immediately hugged me back. Crying released the tension I'd been holding in, and I felt calmer.

I wiped my eyes. "Medical plaza closes in an hour," I reminded him.

He smiled and brushed his fingers lightly across my cheek. "Really? You sure?"

I nodded. "The council's voting in a week. We need to go spy on that oil rig now."

Minutes later, we were staring down from the eighteenth floor of the medical plaza adjacent to the rig. From here, you could see how extremely close it was to both the medical facility and our school. It was one thing to know a controversial drilling operation loomed next door. It was quite another to see kids sprinting around the track just across the fence from a potential health hazard.

Huge oil splotches marred the surrounding concrete around the base of the giant pump. Bulky white cylinders, big as elephants, took up a third of the area. Three mysterious rectangular storage units rose along the north side of the site. Flanking the center unit were two steel-shelled tanks on wheels—they looked sort of like trains.

Two workers in white hard hats stared at indecipherable machinery housed in a dingy steel case. Other workers drove around in what looked like industrial golf carts—checking on what exactly, I didn't know.

"They look like Lego figures," Braden observed.

"At least people are there, I guess. Most petroleum companies that go bankrupt simply abandon their sites. They're called orphan wells, and they can leak methane. And no one's there to do anything about it."

"Um, that's terrifying." Braden's phone rang. "Hello?"

The voice on the other end of the phone was familiar, and loud enough for me to hear most of it. "Good . . . Braden. This is Frank Jennings . . . catching you . . . good time?"

Braden made a face and pressed the speaker icon. "Um, yeah?"

"I have a few things to discuss with you about your article in the school paper," Jennings continued. "If you could possibly manage the time, are you available to come to my office on Friday? Say, three o'clock?"

Braden confirmed the meeting, and I thought of what a condescending jerk Frank Jennings had been to my mom. She never used to drink wine on weekdays until all this trouble with the site started.

"I don't get it," I asked. "What's he want from you?"

"Take your pick." Braden ticked off on his fingers. "I ratted out his son. Wrote an article exposing the dangers of his pet project. Put his new job in jeopardy . . . ."

I stared at the strange activity below, hidden from most of the world by tall gates. "For decades, they pumped 550 barrels of oil a day here, and 350,000 cubic feet of natural gas. And that's just here at this one site."

As we walked back to the car, the sun dipped in the sky, casting an orange glow over the trees and the sidewalk.

"Even in the article, you didn't link the environment to the cancer cases," I continued. "You couldn't prove it."

"How could I?" Braden asked. "I'm a high school junior barely passing Chem!"

"Cancer clusters happen all the time, with no clear link to environmental pollution."

"Cancer cluster?" he said, picking at his hangnail.

"It's when a statistically significant number of people in a certain area get cancer during a specific time period."

Braden opened the passenger car door for me. Then he got in the driver's seat.

I felt it my duty to warn him. "We don't have enough data on people with asthma, lung cancer, thyroid cancers . . . ."

He pressed the heels of his palms against his eyes. "But there's an 8,000-foot-deep well next to campus, possibly burping benzene, barium, and a bunch of other lethal crap into our lungs."

I blurted out, "I think Councilman Jennings is counting on that being hard to prove."

Braden sighed. "Are you playing devil's advocate, or have you changed your mind about everything? If I didn't know better, I'd say you were batting for the other team."

He was talking in puzzles. Little pulses of dull pain began to throb behind my left eye, and I rubbed my temples. We sat there, not saying anything.

"Naomi and Alicia thought it was solid. Even Shanice was on board, and she's always so skeptical . . . ." His voice faded, and for a moment all I heard was *Naomi . . . Alicia . . . Shanice.*

When Naomi and Alicia interviewed Arman at the blood donation, I was impressed. They asked smart questions. They had style. They fit in.

But they didn't know as much as I did about oil and gas platforms. No way I was going to settle for adequate. I was all in.

The throbbing radiated from my left eye all the way to my jaw.

"Maybe you just woke up on the wrong side of the bed." Braden took my hand in both of his.

Devil's advocate. Other team. Wrong side of the bed. I yanked my hands away. "Speak plainly!"

"I thought I was." Braden paused. "It feels like you're criticizing me, and it's making me really insecure. I hoped you'd be a little more supportive."

My processing wasn't working properly, obviously, because I thought the exact opposite. Wasn't I being supportive by pointing out the weaknesses in our research so he could be prepared?

I tried to talk in a way that Braden would understand. "If Frank Jennings is calling you, then you've got him on the defensive. I *am* on your team. I'll always be on your team. I want us to *win*."

35
BRADEN

n bed, I scrolled through Rae's text chain and imagined her electric blue eyes, her slender ankles, and other stuff that's kept guys awake since cave man times. I wanted to think about Rae. Only Rae.

But the specter of Councilman Jennings kept intruding. I would have to face him the next day. Dread ruined my dreamy haze, and I thought of excuses not to see him: Swine flu. Acid reflux. Traumatic amnesia. As sensational as they were, these excuses had nothing to do with my real anxiety trigger.

Uncertainty.

Not knowing what to expect from Jennings made me toss and turn. Around midnight, I rolled on my side. There on my nightstand, nestled between an empty protein bar wrapper and my prized LeBron James bobblehead, sat my trusty copy of *The Worry Cure*. The most recent chapter that Mimi and I had gone over was the most uncomfortable one for me so far. It was about living with uncertainty.

As usual, I was living up to Connor's nickname for me: I was an awfulist. When I pictured my meeting the next morning, I saw a catastrophe. What if Jennings demanded I take back what I'd said to the police about his son bullying Rae? What if he called me out for questioning the platform deal and his judgment as an elected official? What if he wanted me to be bros with Andy?

I flashed on one of my dad's philosophies. Dad always said that in this life, the most important thing (other than Never Give Up) is your name. When people think of you, you want them to see you as good, trustworthy, and honest. I worried that Jennings could ruin that for me and totally trash my reputation. He was influential and powerful. He could hurt me if he wanted to.

Why had I written that damn article in the first place? Sure, part of me had wanted to impress Rae. Another part of me was fed up with how people keep destroying the planet. I couldn't fend off illegal poachers killing elephants. I couldn't prevent dragnetting from wiping out sea life. What I might do, and this was a big maybe, was encourage someone to think twice about the consequences of a drilling operation near a school. My school.

Unable to sleep, I threw off the covers. My eyes adjusted to the darkness. I could make out everything around me—night vision.

Seeing in the dark reminded me of Jake Olson, the blind college football player in my X feed, who could hike a ball with absolute precision even though he lost his sight at age twelve. He can still see when he dreams—forgets he's blind until he wakes in the morning. I couldn't imagine living with his day-to-day level of uncertainty.

Yet he seemed happy: perfect snaps on the football field, three-hundred-yard drives on the golf course, a cuddly guide dog named Quebec who rode with him in the cart. Once he posted a video of himself jumping off a high dive. His caption: *The trick is not to look down.*

Waiting outside of Frank Jennings's office at City Hall the next day, I tried to channel some of Jake Olson's fearlessness. But the chips I'd eaten at lunch kept repeating on me, and I thought I was going to be sick. The feeling worked its way back down and sank into my feet.

The secretary had taken my name and directed me to wait outside of the imposing, polished wood door leading to the councilman's office. I sat on a padded office chair and watched people walk along the shiny tile floors, their footsteps echoing as they moved from elevators to offices and back again. Their tense hush reminded me of the viewing stands during match point at Wimbledon.

Councilman Jennings finally opened the polished door and welcomed me inside his office. I'd planned my approach as a confident stride, but it soon became more of a terror-induced shuffle. He shook my clammy hand and gestured to a lopsided seat in front of his desk. I immediately sank down into it.

He, on the other hand, sat on a leather throne—a swivel chair that placed him several inches higher than me. "Thank you for coming in," he boomed, all smiles. Pristine-looking plants lined his desk, probably fake. Alongside them was a display of framed photos of himself on the tennis court, a large sailboat, the red carpet at movie premiers.

"Of course," I croaked. My mouth was dry.

"I know you had a long day: AP Lit, AP US History, Life Skills, Advanced Journalism."

The guy knew my schedule. Creepy.

"I read your article on the Eclyra Energy Solutions project," he gushed. "You're one of those cerebral types! They're obviously teaching you guys *something*."

Wait, compliment or diss?

"So, I hate to be the one to say this: Your teacher should *not* have let you write about Eclyra. I blame him—or her." He chuckled. "Or *they*." He shook his head. "Pronouns are supposed to make things more specific, but nowadays, all they do is confuse people. Like your story. It's confusing readers!"

I realized three things more or less simultaneously. First, Jennings was kind of an idiot. Second, he clearly hadn't realized that most kids never bothered to read the school paper. Third, I wasn't used to being bullied—by a rude adult, no less.

I didn't like it.

Councilman Jennings was still babbling. "May I suggest you consider writing a follow-up? You know, balanced journalism, some input from another point of view. You can interview me! And I can walk you down the hall to meet other council members, too."

I punted. "I'm not prepared to do that today."

Jennings got out of his chair and sat with one hip on the desk, his leg swinging casually. "So. I understand you've been really sticking up for poor Rae Wolf at school. My son has told me about her . . . challenges."

At the mention of her name, I crouched down slightly, the way an offensive tackle does when he's protecting the QB.

He rambled on. "Now, let's presume you got the story *right*. Well, things might go much easier for Rae—and you." He chuckled. "In politics and in high school, rumors are hard to control. Your article made a few people wonder, and when folks don't fully understand an issue, tempers flare."

I gritted my teeth. "What rumors? The people I interviewed didn't make up their concerns—or their cancer. And at least one of them is definitely dying." Poor Coach Zanetta. I owed it to him not to back down.

Jennings nodded thoughtfully. "Tragic. Awful."

You'd think he'd lost a bet on the Dodgers instead of acknowledging the fact that someone was *dying*. He didn't seem all that concerned over cancer clusters or chemo or playing Russian roulette with the health of Pac Crest students—my classmates and me.

I pulled a pen and a notepad from my backpack and went on the offensive. "Why does the council have to vote next week? What's the rush?"

He ignored my questions and straightened his tie, as though to remind me of my place. "I'm no lawyer, but if the class action suit failed, why dredge this up again?"

"Mr. Jennings, seriously, who even reads the school paper?"

His voice got louder. "Overprotective parents! I've heard from several of them. We need to nip this in the bud, before I hear from more of them. I'm sure you wouldn't want your article to have any . . . unintended consequences."

There it was—the adult bully who'd raised the school bully. Like father, like son.

My face must have given away my disgust, because Jennings glared right back at me. I cleared my throat. "On second thought, let's talk about that follow-up article. Starting with the EIR."

Jennings went still.

I checked my notes. "Yeah, we read the Environmental Impact Report." *We* sounded better than *I*. "According to the California statute, you must give 'major consideration to environmental protection in regulating public and private activities.' Basically, you shouldn't approve a project where a better option exists."

Lifting his rear end off the desk, Jennings sat down in the seat next to mine and morphed back into Mr. Cordial Councilman. "They have better technology now. More protections for people." Jennings sat back as though trying to psych me out, make me think it was a done deal. He was using psychological warfare, just like in sports.

"Um, didn't the last company make the same promises? Before they went bankrupt and left us all hanging?"

"That's why the city is collecting money *up front* for the eventual capping of the well. But until then, we have a terrific opportunity to help kids like you have more choices of AP classes!"

Well, he sure had the wrong guy, because that sounded like an absolute nightmare.

When I didn't respond, he prattled on. "Wouldn't you like the journalism department to offer more travel opportunities so you can go to more competitions? Imagine spearheading a new quarterly magazine—in print! You could be editor! *That* would dazzle the college admissions people."

I took a good hard look at the councilman. His suit coat had been dry-cleaned too many times, and the collar had gone shiny. He had a nervous tic: blinking too much. It was the middle of the workday, and he wasn't busy—he was meeting with me, a high school nobody.

He was desperate.

Suddenly, whatever fear I'd had of him disappeared. This guy couldn't do anything to me! I hadn't done anything wrong. "This isn't about me."

"No?" He chuckled softly. "That's not what I heard. Your car . . . ?"

"That's costing my parents five hundred dollars," I fumed. "Andy should pay."

"Andrew? He had nothing to do with it. That's—well, rumor." Jennings stood up again and returned to his office chair throne. "What's *fact* is, they're close to cracking the case on the Pac Crest bomb threats, which have been an exorbitant waste of tax dollars and a drain on the time of our fire and police services."

The hairs on the back of my neck rose.

"Detectives will find the people who are responsible. Very, very soon." Jennings shuffled some files. "We're talking jail time."

Why had he changed the subject to the bomb threats?

"The most likely culprit is a student. A clever hacker. A kid who took in thousands in bitcoin to disrupt the school day and postpone exams. Do *you* know who's responsible?"

I suddenly realized that we *hadn't* changed subjects. He was threatening me.

Jennings toyed with his tie. "People have devoted a great deal of time and money to the platform project plans. You probably have big plans of your own: where you want to attend college, what you want to do with your life."

I shrugged.

That's when he dropped the hammer. "Thing is, detectives already have a confession from someone calling from out of state—someone who worked in cahoots with a local student. They have an IP address. Next, they'll have a name."

My armpits prickled. "I hadn't heard that."

He swiveled in his chair and stared me down. "Under the law, if you know someone who commits a crime and you don't come forward, you are complicit. This is all hypothetical. I'm not saying *you* did anything wrong. It'd be dicey, though, if a friend, a *close* friend of yours, did something illegal. There'd always be that question in people's minds . . . *Did Braden know?*"

The backpack almost slipped from my lap.

Recollections stacked up: Lucas hacking into school servers, changing his grades. Lucas hacking into Coach Gillman's computer, uncovering private photos of the coach's girlfriend. Lucas illegally accessing a city computer, even though what he "stole" was public information.

Lucas always seeming so pleased about getting out of class during the bomb threats . . . .

I was wrong. Jennings *could* hurt me. And the people I cared about.

36
RAE

The familiar smell of melted butter and maple syrup made my stomach growl. Mom placed plates of steaming scrambled eggs and fluffy gluten-free pancakes on the table for our Friday tradition: breakfast for dinner. The menu consisted of "safe" foods that I could reliably count on being appetizing. Plus, the whole thing took barely ten minutes from prep to table.

I busied myself gathering frozen berries, tangerines, and yogurt for our fruit smoothies. Over the noisy blender, I heard my phone and looked longingly to the charging shelf.

Bing.

I got away with lots of things: Staying up late. Spending too much time on the computer. Wearing the same comfy jeans six days in a row. But phones at the table? Uh-uh. I had dutifully plugged my phone into the charger and left it on the shelf. Mom was a stickler, so I saw no point in telling her that because of her rule, I was missing updates from Braden on his meeting with Jennings.

Bing.

Torture.

Unconcerned, Mom drizzled hot sauce on her eggs. "Noodle was nosing around your backpack. Your lunch was untouched. You must be starving."

"*Noodle* was nosing around? Not *you* invading my privacy?" I speared an entire pancake on my fork and stuffed it in my mouth, hoping my poor manners might provoke Mom.

Bing.

My jaw hurt. I plucked out half of the saliva-saturated pancake wad and swallowed the remaining half.

Mom stared.

I inspected the half-chewed piece still in my hand and decided it looked okay. So I ate that, too.

Bing.

I kept going, systematically. First pancakes. Then eggs. Then smoothie. Slowly, I felt my body regulate. The food revived me in a way I hadn't realized I needed.

I got up to clear my plate. "*Now* can I see what happened during Braden and Councilman Jennings's meeting?"

Mom set down her fork. "Meeting?"

When I told Mom about Jennings calling Braden into his office, she told me to ditch the dirty dishes and call Braden right away.

"*Call* him? No, no, no."

"Why not?" she asked.

I gave her a look. "Do I really need to explain texting to you again?"

Mom hovered over my shoulder while I texted Braden. He responded immediately.

Braden: Councilman Jennings is a cabron!

Me: A what?

> Braden: It's a Spanish cuss word. Not from
> Spanish class, of course. Naomi taught me. She
> speaks 5 languages.

I felt a prick of jealousy.

> Me: Of course she does.

Braden's next text was a photo: Lucas sitting at an empty table, giving two thumbs-up while looking over his shoulder at another table, filled with dishes of exotic-looking food.

Bleep.

A different alert notification had sounded, this time from AutieFreak.com.

My hands started to tremble. I tried to brace myself. Chances were, it was just more trolls who had found my blog.

I logged in to my admin account and navigated to the Comments page. As I scrolled, a shadowy hopelessness drooped over me.

Bitch.

Got it from her mama.

Freak of nature.

You don't belong.

"Whatever it is, we can talk about it."

I heard Mom's voice like it was far away, like she was on the other side of the room instead of next to me at the kitchen counter. I felt the wetness on my cheeks. Numb, I didn't even care when Mom started reading over my shoulder.

"This is outrageous," she said bitterly. "I'm contacting the principal. And Detective Figueroa. Enough is enough."

"Don't," I pleaded. "Besides, I don't even know who they are."

We continued reading the thread. The comments were shitty and mean and *redundant*.

Mom pointed to the screen, having read ahead of me. "That's more like it."

Interspersed with the trolls' remarks, I saw new comments and started to feel oh-so-much better.

> *School is not a safe or happy place for me either.*

> *Life started to suck when I turned thirteen.*

> *For once, I'd like my personal qualities to not be measured by a test!*

The thread continued, all sounding as though these readers were girls like me. A few at first, then more new followers weighing in, going one-to-one against the trolls.

> *I hate the way people see us as the label, someone less than whole.*

> *It's very hard for a non-autistic to imagine what's going on inside an autistic person.*

> *Meltdowns are not tantrums! They're triggered by things like sensory overload and specific people. Like YOU.*

> *Stop trash-talking Rae, my new favorite blogger!*

I looked up at Mom, utterly amazed.

"That's my girl." She beamed. "People forget all the strengths of being a spectrumite. And one of yours is your stick-to-itiveness."

She was right. It was a huge, key trait. Bullies weren't going to derail my blog. I wasn't backing down.

I responded to each positive comment, sharing how grateful I was that these readers had found a place for neurodiverse girls who have their own way of being. Then I excused myself and went upstairs. I needed alone time. After being told again and again that I did not belong, I wasn't enough, and that this world was not made for me, I had finally found my tribe. All the negativity I had faced, with the constant pain and humiliation and doubt, all the hurt and the constant stress, it could not shatter me. It made me stronger and more determined. And now the joy I experienced was so intense, tears kept falling out of my eyes. To be myself and to find others like me . . . felt better than I could've ever imagined.

The inspiration welled up inside me.

AUTIEFREAK.COM:
Unfiltered Views from Your Average Awesome Autistic

YOU BELONG

"You don't belong."

One anonymous commenter wrote this. What makes anyone think this is acceptable to say to another human being?

"You don't belong."

It's like saying this world was not made for you. And I'm guessing what you really mean is, "Be silent. Go away. You're a freak, and I want nothing to do with you."

It may surprise you to learn that I *do* belong. I belong to a group of neurodiverse people online and in real life. I belong to a dedicated community of people who are into rescuing dogs and helping people. I also belong to a family that loves me.

This may even shock you, but I have a boyfriend who is kind, funny, and quite good-looking. I belong to him, and he belongs to me.

You do not know me, and societal prejudice is not a good look for you.

My mind is strong, and I am less restricted by societal norms than you are, which gives me freedom to be an extremely creative thinker. My long-term memory is amazing, and I can "see" memories. My special interests help others. And while I have many strengths, I recognize I have plenty of work to do on myself.

What about you? Have you thought of the work you could be doing on yourself?

Maybe you have the perfect cheerleader's body and everyone's vote for student council. It doesn't matter. You still have work to do. That would be a good use of your time instead of putting me down. You don't know me. In fact, maybe you're trying to hide your less-than-perfect attributes by criticizing me.

For the rest of you readers, whether you're verbal or nonverbal, conventionally pretty or quirky, introverted or extroverted, remember this: YOU BELONG.

Don't let anyone put a doubt in your brain about that. Especially you.

37

BRADEN

Even as I sat with Lucas at a clean, square table at his favorite Filipino restaurant, as though everything in my world was perfectly calm and normal, Councilman Jennings's threats seemed all too real. If I didn't do what he asked—revise my article—Rae could face a shitstorm at school, and Lucas could end up in jail.

I had to warn them. I had to protect them.

"Gotta be honest, this was a surprise," Lucas said, perusing the menu. "I didn't think you liked Filipino food."

I shrugged. "Never tried it."

Lucas took it upon himself to order everything. The waitress repeated the order: *Adobo. Pancit bihon. Corned beef and lumpia. Bilo-bilo.* Then she headed to the kitchen.

A red patch of eczema had cropped up on my elbow. Or maybe it was psoriasis. Both are triggered by stress. I scratched it.

"Let me ask you a question." Lucas leaned his elbows on the table. "With the feminist movement, don't you think women should occasionally pick up the check?"

"Yeah. Definitely." As if *I* knew who should be paying.

"Tatiana always had me pay. I didn't have the balls to question it," he groused.

My phone vibrated and I checked it, distracted.

"Does Rae ever pick up the check?"

"Um, she's not a fan of restaurants. You know, noise and crowds—they bug her. And she has this 'safe' foods list."

Lucas nodded. "It's sweet that you're taking her out. Girls like Rae, you can't fool around with them. You don't want to break their hearts."

"Well, I would never want to hurt her," I said firmly. "I think she's cool and pretty, and I feel very lucky she lets me be a part of her life."

Lucas sat back and crossed his arms. "You know, I get what Rae's going through. I mean, anything that makes us unique also makes us a target. Is there anything I can do for her? Break Andy's nose? Hack his social media?"

"I'm sure your quiet support would go a long way. And really, there's no reason to . . . break the law." I searched his face.

He just laughed.

Two waiters began noisily setting platters on the table. Lucas pushed what looked like a taquito onto my plate. "Not letting you get away with being a picky white eater," he informed me.

I took a tiny bite. "Wait, is this pork? You know I don't eat pork!"

"Lumpia? It's beef." He quickly slid the dish to his side of the table and swapped it out for a bowl of noodles. "Here. Try the pancit."

Seeing Lucas happily dig in only made my stomach knot up, but I dutifully slurped up a spoonful of broth followed by a forkful of noodles.

Satisfied, he continued chowing down. "This is worth getting fat over."

"You're not fat," I said, in a weak attempt at a joke. "You're four months pregnant."

He cackled, enjoying himself. "I'm really glad you called me, man."

I pushed the noodles around my plate, at a total loss for how to bring up his possible role in the bomb threats.

The waitress set down the check. "I got this. You can get it next time." I counted out the bills. "I mean, you've got thousands stashed in your mattress, don't you? Or is it all in crypto currency?"

He belly-laughed. "And that's why I just took a job working the graveyard shift at a Starbucks warehouse. 'Cuz I've got bank!"

Time to get to the point. Was poor Lucas getting framed by Councilman Jennings, or was he actually phreaking our school? Either way, Jennings's threats weren't going to deliver themselves.

I lowered my voice. "I've got a source who told me the cops are onto the swatter who's been calling in the bomb threats. They think he's getting bitcoin to delay exams."

"Why are we whispering?" he mocked me.

"Dude," I snapped, my voice returning to normal. "They think it's you!"

Lucas's eyes went wide. "Who is 'they'?"

"Councilman Jennings."

"The fuck's he got against me?" Beads of sweat dampened the hair around his face. He wiped at it with his hand, then a napkin. "I've pulled a lot of crap in my day, but I had nothing to do with that."

I wanted to believe him. "Well, Jennings didn't say your name, but—"

"Jesus, Braden! I'd never jeopardize my citizenship status doing anything so dumb! I don't miss the Philippines. I'm not going to tell you it's been easy for us here, but this is home."

I nodded. Lucas was a lot of things. Lazy. Irreverent. Obnoxious. One thing he wasn't: a liar. "He's trying to intimidate me by threatening my friends. Says he's losing votes on the oil rig deal. Because of the article."

"The article," Lucas repeated. "In the *high school* paper? Seriously?"

"I get you did nothing wrong . . . but Jennings said the police have some sort of confession from an out of state source."

"He's full of shit," Lucas scoffed. "Jennings is a douche."

I tapped my fingers on the table, thinking out loud. "Think the councilman plays sports?" Lucas wedged a toothpick between his front teeth, waiting for me to formulate my idea. "I mean, he's basically doing a ball fake. Got us defending in one direction, but I think he's coming the other way."

"Then we'd better figure out a counterattack," Lucas said.

Having an ally on my team now, someone to brainstorm with, gave me some confidence. I wiped my hands off on my jeans. Only one problem: With just days left before the city council vote, I had no idea what the strategy should be.

38

Arman and I reclined on our lounge chairs by the pool at my house, under the stars. I had wrapped myself in a fuzzy blanket, even though Arman didn't think seventy degrees qualified as cold. I didn't feel like educating him on autistics and temperature control issues. Instead, I curled up, knees to my chest, and hugged myself to warm up.

Arman had a new astronomy app, and he pointed his phone at dim dots in the sky. "That's Saturn. And there's Jupiter."

But all I could think about was Braden's text:

> There's something I need to talk to you about. I'll swing by after dinner.

Absent-mindedly, I scrolled through social media. Braden's article, "Retired Coach Says Oil Well Made Him Sick," had been reposted. Yay! That was a good thing. Word was getting out. Then I glanced at a comment from Naomi the News Boss: *Love you and everything you write!*

Another comment from Alicia: *Score! You can write something that doesn't have a score.*

Even serious Shanice commented: *Who knew? The man can write. You pulled it off.*

Smart Naomi. Cool Alicia. Witty Shanice. A cold empty sensation roiled through me. I shivered, suddenly freezing.

Did Braden secretly like these girls? Everyone said he was the nicest guy they knew. Could he have asked me to be his girlfriend out of pity? The hard truth was, a neurotypical made a better match for him than someone like me. Someone who was missing page six from *The Girlfriend Handbook.*

"That faint light over there is Mars!" Arman prattled, slowly panning his phone up at the sky. "Don't you feel so small and unimportant?"

His voice faded into the background as my mind pulled me down. A sense of dread settled on my chest, so heavy I had to place my own hand there for a minute.

I had published a blog post saying Braden and I belonged to each other. And at the time—just last night!—I would've bet my life on it. So why was my body telling me, *Run? Danger! Escape!* I had nowhere to go, and I couldn't shed my own skin. Enormous amounts of energy seemed to leach from my pores.

I'm missing page six from The Girlfriend Handbook.

I'm not good enough.

I'm not good enough.

"So much for the solar system." Arman's voice penetrated the darkness.

Wanting to disappear, I pulled the blanket tighter around my body. Finally, I explained about the journalism girls. "I hate feeling like this!"

Arman *tsked*. "People love to flirt. Just because someone made a suggestive comment doesn't mean—"

"Naomi speaks five languages," I sniffled from under the blanket. "And she wears these cool vintage clothes that make her look fashionable without trying. She's . . . she's not like me."

"Maybe that's why he likes you." Arman gently tugged at the blanket, trying to pull it away from my face. "Remember all the drama when I couldn't decide whether or not to come out to my parents?"

I hunkered down deeper in my dark cocoon. It had taken less than a day for doubt to dim the joy I'd been experiencing. Doubt had always been my worst enemy. Now it was making me question my relationship with Braden.

"I ended up making a list, remember?" Arman continued. "Just writing down the pros and cons sort of unlocked me."

The blanket fell away from my shoulders. This was a superb idea. Pros: why Braden and I belonged together. Cons: why that was impossible.

I started taking notes on my phone and reading them out loud. "Cons. One, Braden met me at his lowest point, when he'd quit basketball. Two, he could do better. Like date the journalism girls." In a meeker voice, I mumbled, "Three, Braden feels sorry for me."

Arman nodded. "Ahem. And the pros?"

I wracked my brain to produce pros, but more cons kept popping into my mind. *I'm not good enough. I'm not good enough.*

"You're frowning," Arman observed. "Did you know that if you frown as little as a thousand times, it makes a wrinkle?"

"Shut. Up."

Arman pretended to lock his lips and throw away the key.

A pro came to me. "One, Braden is honest." Then another: "Two, we're both passionate about dog rescue and the environment." And another: "Three, Braden smells better than any human I've ever met. Four, I can't stop thinking about him." I looked up from my notes. "Maybe four belongs on the cons list?"

Arman laughed. "Go on."

Then I started crying, like the breakup had already happened. I remembered how awful I'd felt when Zach dumped me and realized, looking back, that I hadn't even loved him. My brain flung me to the future and the certainty that not only was Braden about to dump me, but I would never find anyone as good as him again.

"Oh, honey." Arman tried to console me, but I just pulled the blanket up over my face again and let the tears come. "Don't cry."

My muffled voice—nasal from crying—sounded pathetic as I defended myself. "Tears release hormones and cortisol. They make you feel better."

But having bloodshot eyes and a big red, runny nose doesn't make you *look* better. And of course, *that's* when Braden texted to say he was five minutes away and could he stop by now?

Unable to speak, I held up my phone screen so Arman could read it.

"Shake your sprinkles, woman." He stood quickly and offered a hand to help me up.

"You know," I muttered, "I don't have to let him in." Every muscle in my body felt weak. My energy had been depleted by all the schoolwork, plus all the research, plus a habit of forgetting to eat lunch this past week.

Arman motioned with his hand, impatient. "And I don't have to lust after Regé-Jean Page. But where's the fun in that?"

Together we walked back through the house. In the kitchen, Mom looked up from her tablet. "Did you see Saturn?"

"Wasn't it wonderful?" Arman gushed before I could tell Mom that I, in fact, had not.

Upstairs, Arman quickly brushed my hair.

"Got any mascara?"

I gave him a blank stare.

"Okay. Lip gloss?"

I swiped some across my lips and sniffed the pomegranate-scented tube, wondering why it mattered.

At the front door, Braden seemed surprised to see Arman. "Hey." He nodded, his chin jutting ever so slightly up.

Arman mirrored the move. "Hey yourself."

Braden watched him go and turned back to me. "Was I interrupting?"

"Yes," I said matter-of-factly.

"Can I come in?"

I blocked the doorway and crossed my arms over my chest.

Nearby, I could hear Mom in the kitchen, pouring water into the kettle for tea.

Braden looked past my shoulder as if something lurking in my home had caused all the trouble. "If I did something to upset you . . . ." He didn't finish his sentence. He focused on me again, and I knew it was my turn to speak.

"Get on with it! Are you going to ask Naomi out?"

His eyes widened. "No!"

"Shanice, then? Or Alicia?"

"Where's all this coming from?"

"Did you read their comments on your article?"

"We're friends. Just friends."

"Why?" I demanded. "When you could have someone who wears the right clothes. Someone who fits in. Says the right thing at the right time."

"*You're* my girlfriend, okay?"

I tried to let that soak in. My negative self-talk was programmed to fuel doubt, and it was hard to undo.

"You're bold, Rae, not afraid to speak your mind." His voice dropped and sounded gravelly. "Do you have any idea what that does for me?"

He stared at me in silence. My logic and intuition said to believe him. Not that the same logic and intuition had been helpful when I'd seen the girls' comments in the first place.

"Not exactly," I admitted.

"I can't stop thinking about you," he said slowly. "Every time I know I'm going to see you, I'm higher than when the Kings score a goal, or when the Yanks win the World Series—or when the Lakers don't suck. And every time I have to say goodbye, my chest hurts a little. None of that has ever happened to me over a girl."

He cradled my jaw in his palm and kissed me lightly and quickly. Butterflies stirred in my lower abdomen. Eyes glued to the floor, I thought I might cry all over again—happy tears this time.

His voice firm, Braden said, "It's you I want."

I leaned forward and rested my head against his chest. I could hear his heartbeat. I synced my breathing with his. He ran his fingers through my hair. My brain slowed down.

Braden kissed my hand and then my wrist. The butterflies in my belly fluttered their wings. "Whenever something bothers you, promise me you'll tell me right away."

I nodded and snuck a quick peek at him. His eyes were sort of glossy.

"Is it sexist," he said, his voice huskier than I was used to hearing, "if I think you look hot when you're jealous?"

"Depends. Am I hot when I'm *not* jealous?"

"Don't get me started."

Whether it was chemistry or pheromones or just plain lust, it was pulling at us both. I had the distinct desire to start unbuttoning Braden's jeans and lead him to my bed. My fingers itched to touch his bare skin. Then my brain reminded me that the clattering sound I was vaguely aware of—silverware being placed in a dishwasher—meant my mom was nearby.

I flashed an embarrassed smile. "I won't. Tell me, what happened at your meeting?"

"That's what I needed to talk to you about. Councilman Jennings is being very shitty. I think he's making stuff up to scare us."

"Scarier than an operating oil rig in our backyard?"

"He made it out like Lucas could be in some sort of serious trouble." Braden took a step forward into the house. "And I'm worried he's going to come after you. Or get Andy to do it for him."

Mom swept by. "Oh! Hello, Braden! Good to see you."

"Hi, Ms.—I mean, Elizabeth," Braden said, dorky and adorable.

Then Mom gave me a pointed look. "It's getting late."

"Yes, Mom," I said sweetly, "we were just saying goodnight."

Mom nodded and went upstairs, glancing back and clearly expecting me to follow.

Braden leaned against the doorjamb and hooked his thumbs into his belt loops. I wanted to grab his shirt and pull him inside. Instead, I put both hands on his chest and walked him backward, out of the doorway.

"What's this?" he asked, clearly disappointed.

"For once in my life, I'm not going to let my impulse control issues get the upper hand. You heard what Mom said. And nothing can get in the way of going to Tuesday's meeting," I reminded him. "And we have to get ready. Everything we say goes on record. We only have three minutes to talk. Do you know how hard that's going to be?"

"Not as hard as walking away from you right now."

He gave me another kiss, longer this time, and I realized what people meant when they used the word *swoon*.

Then he pulled away. "Wait, what do you mean, they give us three minutes? Are you saying we're supposed to speak? When was this decided?"

"That's three questions."

39

BRADEN

Monday started out horribly. I overslept. Then my car battery died. And that meant Dad had to drive me to school, like in the old days before I got my license. As he moved with the long line of cars leading to campus, he thumped on the steering wheel, impatient.

Trying to sink into the passenger seat, I forced down a KIND bar and endured the inevitable punctuality lecture.

"Five minutes of extra sleep is not worth the pressure!" Dad glanced over at me. "Geez Louise! You're getting crumbs in the leather."

I tried to pluck an oat flake from the seat cushion, but it disintegrated, the powder wedging deeper into the leather creases. Dad sighed. He was going to need a vacuum. Or a bourbon. But I had bigger worries: Was poor Lucas getting framed by Councilman Jennings?

Dad squinted through the windshield. "Is that . . . Connor?"

My cousin was standing on the school's front lawn and shouting something, along with Joe, Alex, and several other Scouts, clearly identifiable in their Class A uniforms. Scouts *never* wore their uniforms to school. Everyone already assumed they were kind of geeky and clannish, all about helping old ladies cross the street and making baskets. No one equated neckerchiefs and badge sashes with badassery.

As Dad's car rolled closer to campus, I heard honking and saw what the Scouts were shouting at: Andy Jennings, bullhorn in hand, and a small crowd of stage crew guys mingled with a few ASB officers, including Kennedy and Taylor. I cracked the window, and we heard their angry voices. "Save our school!"

The Scouts chanted too: "Green not greed!" and "Save our lungs!"

"Oh, my god," I said, flabbergasted. "What are they doing?"

"Student activism is alive and well." Dad scanned the crowd. "Which one is Andrew Jennings?"

If you ever saw my dad pissed off, you'd understand my reluctance to answer his question. Picture the manager of the New York Yankees getting tossed from a game against the Boston Red Sox. That was Dad. He'd never put his hands on anyone, but he could sure make a helluva scene.

I unbuckled my seatbelt. "I'm good. I'll walk the rest of the way." I slipped out before he could ask me any more questions.

As I jogged onto the front lawn, I saw that the *Save Our School* posters were gone; they'd been replaced with anti-drilling posters. On second glance, I saw that these were the old *Save Our School* posters—only flipped and repurposed.

Andy was furious, ripping down poster after poster and inspecting the flip side of each one. The tell-tale sign of the Scouts' handiwork was the duct tape. Scouts used the sticky silver stuff for everything from shoe repairs to finger splints.

I was on the verge of asking Andy to do something colorful to himself when Connor blocked my path. He was holding a gigantic new coffee thermos. "Kona?"

Joe and Alex linked their arms around me and swept me into a wave of other students heading for the school lobby, away from Andy.

Connor held out his thermos, offering me a swig of coffee.

I hesitated. "Have you had a fever in the past week, or been around anyone else who's been sick?"

"Awfulist," he muttered.

I took a sip. Then I slurped some more.

The morning bell rang. As we hurried to homeroom, Connor shrugged out of his uniform. Layered beneath was a happy face T-shirt that said *Happy*.

"Why didn't you ask me to help with those signs and stuff?" I asked, feeling a bit left out.

"We came up with the plan last night, and we knew you'd try to talk us out of it. And once you get started," Connor said with a grin, "you always win." That was a nice way of telling me I was a serial rule follower and total nerd.

Joe rolled his uniform into a ball and held it beneath his arm. "When Connor told us about the Ortizes' house blowing up, I was like, whoa."

Behind me, Alex put a hand on my shoulder. "What he's trying to say is, we give a shit. And since the vote is tomorrow night, there's no time to lose. We couldn't put off our civic duty."

"By 'civic duty,' you mean stealing someone else's posters?" I asked.

Alex gave my shoulder a bro squeeze. "I prefer the word *recycled*."

I stopped by my locker to grab a textbook for first period. Mallory nodded at me, shutting her own locker. "People say stuff on social media," she said sympathetically. "Don't take it too hard."

"Huh?" I was lost.

"You tackled a prickly subject. Kudos. Screw the trolls."

I whipped out my phone and checked Instagram.

"Retired Coach Says Oil Well Made Him Sick" had been reposted again over the weekend. A lot. At least forty people had commented on being worried about getting cancer—and being scared to death to go to school.

Another dozen or so had commented on the loser theme. Me, that is—the quitter who'd abandoned his team, according to Andy's letter to the editor. The punk who made shit up in a pathetic quest for popularity. The guy dating a weirdo.

I felt a rock in my stomach.

Rae and I had started something, and a big part of me wanted to take it back. I worried about Rae getting bullied even worse than before. I worried about my car getting vandalized again. I worried that Lucas might be arrested.

As the day went by, I could barely concentrate on lectures or what anyone was saying to me. My eyes couldn't focus, and I kept blinking and squinting. My hearing was fine, but nothing penetrated the thick haze of nervousness clouding my brain.

Kids involved in athletics high-fived me in the hallways.

ASB kids looked away, like I didn't exist.

Drama peeps stopped to hug me, even the ones I barely knew.

Nate, my conversation buddy in Spanish, stopped me between classes to tell me, *en español,* that the boys' basketball team planned to protest at the Pacific Crest City Council meeting.

My stomach clenched. If I'd wanted to be the center of attention, I would've done something more on point, like string a papier-mâché penis up the flagpole.

During lunch period, I suggested to Lucas that we get some fresh air.

"I'd rather smoke, but if you insist," he drawled.

We wandered to the front lawn, where Rae, Arman, and some other drama groupies were selling *Green Not Greed* T-shirts. Rae looked happy and busy, offering change to someone. Arman was by her side, posing in a fitted *Green Not Greed* T-shirt. Rae must've been wearing an XL, because it fit like a sleep shirt. With her pajama pants, it looked like she'd come to school straight out of bed. Her multicolored hair was a little wilder than usual, too.

Arman waved a T-shirt at me. "Braden! They're going fast! I think the blue would complement your coloring."

I didn't know what to say to that.

Arman did a one-eighty so we could see the design on his back: a ripped dude wearing a mask over his nose and mouth, standing defiantly beside an oil well. "I designed them myself. I modeled the guy after you."

Lucas belly-laughed.

"Right." I smirked. "How'd you get these done so fast?"

"My talents are many. Especially with help from my Uncle Mike at Wizard T-Shirts," Rae said as she pretended to pat herself on the back. "We're almost sold out!"

I bought one, and Arman insisted I put it on immediately. I pulled my hoodie and T-shirt off and slid the shirt on. It was way too tight. "What size is this?"

Arman nodded. "Size Perfect."

Helpless, I turned to Rae, who was folding shirts.

"I trust Arman," she said.

"It's a look. Not sure if you're pulling it off, though," Lucas teased.

Andy, Kennedy, and Taylor walked by, wrinkling their noses like they smelled an open sewer pit. "You've gone to the dark side, bro," Andy said, directing his comment to Arman.

Arman folded a shirt, ignoring him.

Taylor said, "Rae."

Rae stopped folding and peeked up at her.

"Did you forget to brush your hair? It looks terrible."

Rae looked stricken, and I found myself speechless.

"Personal hygiene? Hello?" Kennedy adjusted her sweater that didn't need adjusting.

Arman glared. "You're going to wish you hadn't said that. Once you say something, you can't unsay it."

"Arman! Don't be mad." Taylor pouted. "We miss hanging out with you."

"They're doing you a favor." Andy grinned at Rae. "You should thank them."

"You cruel piece of shit," I said, advancing on Andy. My fist itched to slam into his nose.

Lucas grabbed my forearm hard, stopping me. "Not here."

"Have a nice day," Andy said, walking away with the girls.

Rae wiped her eyes. "It's okay."

"No, it's not," I told her.

"I know." Rae's blue eyes were bloodshot and brimming with tears. "I just said that because I thought that's what you're supposed to say when someone is really mean, and you don't want to show that you're on the verge of crying."

I fought off the urge to cuss out loud. It felt so helpless to think about all the jerks who had made Rae feel like she was some sort of loser for having messy hair or struggling to get the joke or feeling anxious in noisy crowds. I saw how people treated Lucas sometimes because he was overweight. He shrugged it off like it was no big deal, but it always bugged the living shit out of me. Like being chubby or having your brain process things differently was a crime or uncool or made you unworthy.

What Rae really needed was a friend. Someone who didn't think twice about being kind. Someone who could make her smile. Someone who made her feel like she could be herself—like being herself was enough. Because that's what she did for me.

I whispered in Rae's ear, "Even on a bad hair day, you're adorable."

Her face lit up, and I felt my nerves shrink back from the edge. A warm, comfortable feeling took their place.

"May I?" Arman asked, pointing to Rae's hair. When she nodded, he began carefully combing her hair with his fingers and pulling it back into a loose ponytail. "There. Okay, woman. Shake your sprinkles. We've got T-shirts to sell!"

Across the lawn, I saw Andy and Taylor getting farther and farther away. Lucas was watching them too. "Time to go, Lucas."

"We gonna beat the shit out of Andy?" he asked, even more eagerly than the last time.

We caught up to them, and I put my hand on Andy's arm to slow him down. "Get the fuck off me," he hissed.

"I know you keyed my car, *Andrew*," I replied evenly. "And you want to get into it with me, great. Game on. But you leave Rae out of it."

"You know I *keyed* your car like you *know* that the oil deal is evil." He looked me up and down. "Your girlfriend's got a problem. Everyone can see that. Except you."

"She never did a damn thing to you."

"She belongs at a special school," Andy sneered. "But no one says shit because of who her mom is. And as long as that crazy bitch continues to roam this campus, me and my friends will be on psycho patrol."

"Psycho patrol," Lucas repeated. "Good one. You come up with that yourself?"

Andy turned his sneer toward Lucas. "You smoke, right? I thought nicotine was supposed to curb food cravings."

Taylor tried to hide her smile. "You're terrible, Andrew."

Kennedy giggled.

"Ooh, fat jokes," Lucas fake-laughed. "Never heard me one of those before."

I stepped between them. "Look. I'm not asking. I'm telling you. Leave Rae alone."

"Or what?" he asked, throwing an amused smile to Taylor. "Are you going to throw a basketball in my face?"

"Me?" I pointed to my chest. "That's funny. No, not me."

"Then who?" He nodded at Lucas. "Lard-ass?"

"Andrew . . . Andy . . . ." I shook my head. "Don't you remember what happened the last time you faced off with my girlfriend?"

A momentary look of confusion played across his face.

"Will Rogers Park," I reminded him helpfully. "Ring a bell?"

Andy's cheeks and neck flushed red-hot.

"That's right, Andy. You landed on your ass. And you looked like one too."

40

RAE

I hung out with Mom in her bathroom as she got ready to leave for City Hall. Her cosmetics were scattered across the marble counter. "We're expecting a lot of folks tonight," she said, checking her makeup in the magnifying mirror.

As always, she looked polished. Tonight, she wore her green blazer and a silk blouse. Even I had tried to dress for the occasion. I'd chosen new black velvet leggings with a hot pink tank and an unstructured gray blazer—my mature look—ha!

Mom hummed, pretending to be Just Fine.

"I like it better when you're genuinely worried about an upcoming vote," I told her. "At least I know you're being yourself."

"Humming relaxes me." She stuffed her reading glasses and lipstick into her purse. "You sure you don't want to drive with me?"

"No, thanks. Braden'll be here soon."

"What you two have done to raise awareness is extraordinary. You stood up to people who were not very nice to you. You fought for a cause that you believe in."

"Hopefully not a lost cause."

Mom tucked a strand of hair behind my ear. "Embrace your special you. You might be exactly what is needed."

I felt the back of my throat swell up. Mom had inspired me to try, like she did, against all odds. I gave her a big squeezy hug.

Braden pulled up a few minutes later. Usually, he asked me a question or two when he picked me up. Not tonight. We drove in comfortable silence.

I closed my eyes and meditated. I wanted my mind to be clear.

When I opened my eyes, I set my intention for the night: *Trust the universe. Accept that there will be loud mouths, overly perfumed bodies, and unfriendly faces.* I had to prepare myself for those who would attack me because of my beliefs—or because they didn't think I belonged at their school or at City Hall. But I also predicted there would be IRL friends I could count on, like Arman and Connor and Lucas.

Braden and I walked toward the large, ornate building amid a stream of people. Having so many arms swinging near mine, with everyone bunched up on the sidewalk, made me twitchy. Then Braden reached for my hand. This small, public gesture meant more to me than he could've imagined.

Zach had kept me a secret. I didn't think about it at the time. Or maybe I did, but I didn't understand what it meant: He was ashamed of me. The simple pressure of Braden's fingers around my own flooded me with joy.

When I stole a glance at his face, though, I saw that his jaw was clenched. He blinked too much. I tried hard to think of something to say that would make him stress less.

"Were you aware that K-9 Ministries sent seven therapy dogs to Thousand Oaks after the Borderline Bar shooting?" I asked. "Sometimes these dogs sit for hours, being pet by trauma victims."

Braden lifted the corner of his mouth in a half smile. "Are you suggesting I am about to become a trauma victim?"

"No. Not at all. Just thinking about how dogs naturally comfort humans. They lower people's blood pressure. I thought the image might be useful."

"We don't know what's going to happen tonight."

"Try thinking about Tri-State Canine in New Jersey," I pressed. "They send comfort dogs to help school shooting survivors. Such amazing animals!"

"I bet." Braden gave my hand a gentle squeeze. "Do you mind if we talk about dogs after the meeting? No offense to Tri-State Canine. You're the one saving my life tonight."

I'm no dating expert, but I really liked whatever was happening between us. Braden was clear about his needs and his appreciation. I vowed to do the same.

Braden pushed open the heavy glass doors to City Hall. Inside, I recognized the journalism trio: Shanice, Naomi, and Alicia. They took turns giving Braden a peck on the cheek.

When he put a hand lightly around my waist, I relaxed into him, my side fitting neatly against his. I reasoned the girls' greeting held no hidden meanings. They weren't trying to steal my boyfriend. I made a mental note to reach out to them after the meeting. Maybe I would let them interview me about my blog after all.

Mr. Hackbarth, Braden's journalism teacher, rounded a corner. He shook Braden's hand, grumbling, "Why the aversion to tucking in shirts? This isn't a picnic. It's a serious event."

"Of course," Braden said, fussing with his clothes.

Mr. Barsanti had overheard. "Cut him some slack, Gil. The clothes don't always make the man."

The adults teased each other, which I found entertaining until we had to squish inside the elevator. The doors thumped shut, and I felt trapped. Once they reopened, I escaped first. I found refuge in council chambers, my back firmly against the wall closest to the exit.

Braden waved to Jenji, who was seated between two adults who I assumed were Braden's parents. His mom responded with a victory fist pump, and his dad gave a quick salute. Suddenly, I wished I knew every last basic thing about Braden. What were his parents' names? Who was his first kiss? Did he think about me as much as I thought about him? I wanted him to share everything about himself, and I wanted to share everything about myself with him, too.

For several minutes, we watched kids squeeze onto the polished walnut benches and adults hunt for open seats. Nobody wanted to be in the adjacent "spillover" room, observing the meeting on a monitor. I didn't want to be in either place. Everywhere I looked, mouths, mouths, mouths, sucking in all the oxygen.

Leave some for me! I pleaded.

Snippets of conversation filled my ears.

Yeah, it's crazy in here.

Eclyra sent some Ivy League heavy hitter.

The council already met in secret. This is all for show.

My history teacher's giving extra credit for being here.

Arman waved me over. He was wearing his *Green Not Greed* T-shirt. I couldn't endure venturing through so many shoulders, elbows, and torsos. I hung back and hoped he'd understand.

The athletes arrived and sat down on the floor, right in front of the podium. Scout families, teachers, and strangers filled the space. "We've reached Fire Code capacity," announced a microphoned voice. "Open chairs are next door."

Discouraged, those still milling about began filing out to find seats elsewhere.

As planned, Braden went up to the front of the room and dropped our prepared comment card in the request box. Now it was set: We'd be on the night's agenda, speaking together like we'd practiced. As he rejoined me at the back of the room, I noticed that he looked a little pale.

"This proves how much I like you. Volunteering to speak at the center ring of this circus . . . . Oh, god!" He smiled at me weakly. "Do you get it?"

For different reasons, both of us were tolerating being uncomfortable for a cause we cared about. Braden battled anxiety. I struggled with sensory issues. Uncomfortable together.

"I get it," I whispered.

The volume in the room suddenly rose, and I shrank against the wall. Hugging myself, I shut my eyes and tried to remember positive things to shield me from the onslaught. Over and over in my head, I said:

Not everyone is against you.

Fly your Freak Flag.

You are good enough. You are good enough.

"Awfulist!" A voice pierced my mantra. Braden's goofy cousin, Connor, waved excitedly at us from the aisle. "Oh, hellooo, Rae!" He had saved seats for us.

Braden stepped toward his cousin just as a woman with a large handbag bumped me.

Instinctively, I pushed her off. She stumbled into another woman, who carried a shih tzu in her own giant handbag. They gaped at me like I'd done something wrong.

"*You* bumped into *me*," I said through gritted teeth. No apology? No responsibility? Fury roiled through me.

The situation began to spiral. Pungent cologne. Pulsing lights. Air so thick, I could barely breathe. I ripped off my blazer. The women skirted away.

Braden turned back to me. "What's wrong?"

"I feel like I'm on the verge of a panic attack."

"Let's get some air." He lightly touched my wrist.

I snaked past him. "I'll be okay. I just need a breather."

In the bathroom, I locked the stall door and reminded myself to inhale. *Seven seconds in. Eight seconds out. Repeat.*

When I returned to Braden a few minutes later, he had saved a spot for me, right at the end of the bench. I hadn't asked him to do that. He didn't give me a pitying look or act worried. He just knew that simply sitting in this room drained me.

At the far-left side of the podium sat Frank Jennings, next to Mom. To her right were Mayor Bloom and the two other council members, both gray-haired men in dark suits. From the front row of the viewing section, Andrew turned around and gave me the Death Stare. I glowered back. Game on, as Braden would say.

"Good evening." Mayor Bloom spoke first. The conversations faded as he introduced the issue of the night. "As a reminder, we must limit speakers' comments to three minutes each."

Then Mayor Bloom called the first speaker: Mr. Jerold Hartley, an Eclyra Energy Solutions executive. He stood at the lectern, facing the council and thanking them. On two ceiling-mounted monitors, we saw in close-up as he straightened his tortoiseshell glasses. He looked like a law professor, not an agent of evil, but that just goes to show you.

"The environmental analysis for the site suggests student health will not be endangered," Hartley began. "Furthermore, the claim that pressurized methane gas beneath the campus poses a threat is unsubstantiated. On a macro level, we don't deny fossil fuels contribute to climate change. There are practical steps available now that could quickly curb emissions and provide a tremendous opportunity to plug orphaned wells. California has an estimated 5,500 of them! Your city can avoid that future headache because we stand by our promise to plug the existing wells when they are no longer productive. Until that time, the schools will share in the profits."

Hartley spewed data. I loooove data! But I was bursting to find out what Eclyra Energy Solutions would do to help us avoid that "headache."

Instead, Hartley jumped to another topic. "Our reports conclude that the supposed risk of cancer does not exceed the air quality management district threshold."

Councilman Jennings piped up. "Can we have that study up on the screen?"

A city employee seated at a side table typed at her laptop, and Hartley proceeded to info-dump us with colorful graphs and slick statistics.

Mayor Bloom called the next speaker, high school PTA president Kathleen Carmona—another one in favor of the project.

"Safety is number one, two, three, and four," Mrs. Carmona announced. "This well was operational *for years*. There's no proof it harmed anyone! We can't let this deal slip by. Not when we finally have an opportunity to build up the school's programs after years of scaling back."

I squirmed in my seat, restless for Braden's and my turn to talk.

Andrew was next. Unbelievable! In a suit and tie, he was his dad's mini-me. "The key to school pride," his voice boomed from the speakers, "is having Eclyra Energy Solutions as our educational partner."

His sheeple clapped.

"Whether it's new uniforms or more theater productions or an expanded robotics program," Andrew bleated on, "I know I speak for all students when I say, we want to feel school pride."

How dare he claim to speak for me? I bit the inside of my cheek to keep from speaking out of turn. Councilman Jennings beamed at his son. *Nauseating.*

Next up was the boys' track team captain. "My teammates and I run by that rig every day, and you know what? We don't need to breathe any crap—er, I mean toxins—into our lungs. I have a scholarship to Colgate, and I don't need cancer, okay? Don't poison us!"

"Yes!" I blurted out. Huge mistake.

Councilman Jennings shot me a warning glance. Mom's eyes searched for mine. This time when I bit my cheek, I tasted blood.

Braden gave my hand a quick squeeze and whispered, "Rebel!" Like what I'd done was a good thing.

A girl wearing a *Save Our School* T-shirt was called next. "Drill, baby, drill!" she screeched. "Next year, I'm a senior. And you bet my tennis teammates and I want new uniforms and repaved courts!"

Cheering rose from various spots in the audience. It started to feel like the whole world was against Braden and me. But then the drama peeps took turns at the mic. I was so proud of them. Had there been an award for best speaker of the night, I would've given them all First Place.

"Be right back," Braden whispered as the next speaker was called to the lectern. "Gonna get us a couple bottles of water."

A minute later, somebody started to sit beside me. "It's taken," I said firmly. The person sat anyway.

It was Zach. My ex.

"Big night," Zach whispered.

I recoiled, and my first instinct was to flee. I tried to get to my feet, but Zach quickly reached out and easily pressed me back down.

"Chill, boo. Just want to say, I hope you win."

I couldn't figure out whether Zach was being sarcastic or serious.

"I saw you with Braden and everything. So, yeah. You guys are totally right. We don't need this shit."

A girl seated in front of us snapped around with a loud "Shush!" It was Taylor.

Zach flipped her the bird. "Mind your fucking business, Taylor."

Her mouth twisted like she'd sucked a lemon.

In my peripheral vision, I saw someone waving a hand. Arman caught my eye and pointed to his mouth, and then to me. *My . . . mouth.* It was hanging open, I realized. I quickly closed my lips.

"Good luck, boo." Zach rose, heading across the aisle to join some of his teammates, just as Braden returned.

"What'd he want?" he asked, handing me a bottle of cold water.

Before I could answer, the woman in charge of sifting through comment cards called out: "Braden Bernstein. Rae Wolf."

"Oh, god," Braden said.

"Don't worry," I told him. "You're already a star. At least in your dog's eyes." I'd written and practiced this joke earlier that day. It worked. He smiled.

We strode toward the front of the room.

"You got this!" Connor cheered, high-fiving Braden.

Arman called out, "Break a leg!"

Life Skills Simon stood up and yelled, "Captain America!"

From the back, Lucas shouted, "Badass! Get 'em, Rae!"

Mom cracked a smile.

"Everyone, everyone," Mayor Bloom called out, "please be respectful."

Then Braden and I were side by side at the lectern. Councilman Jennings peered down at us, menacing, from the raised podium.

Braden fetched a stack of index cards from his back pocket. His voice wavered as he started to speak. "Most people here know me from sports or journalism. I'm not exactly your go-to guy on hydraulic fracturing or acid well stimulation treatments."

People laughed. In a friendly way. Peeking over my shoulder at the audience, I saw mostly smiles. Most of these people liked Braden and seemed genuinely interested in what he had to say. His moist fingertips smudged his note cards, but he still ticked off the points we'd covered: safety, climate change, long-term health effects.

I counted the number of times he said *uh*. Nine.

"Honestly, just reading the studies on this stuff gave me insomnia for weeks." As he went on, he said *uh* less often. "Okay, so according to our research, strong evidence indicates that frac fluids *can* lead to local environmental contamination."

Councilman Jennings interrupted. "In all due respect, Mr. Bernstein, how did you conduct research? Reddit? Anecdotal quips found through a Google search?"

Braden froze, unprepared for bullies.

I took over. "Try the German Society of Toxicology. The largest toxicological organization in Europe."

The line between Jennings's eyes deepened.

"Here's a handy compilation of resources." I stepped forward and placed a copy before each council member, pausing to smile at Mom.

Returning to the lectern for the audience copies, I almost collided with the ASB girls—the student body duo who'd always scared me. But something seemed to have changed.

"We've got this," said Kennedy.

"Let us help," Taylor added.

Unsure, I turned helplessly to Braden. This had to be a trap.

But Kennedy lifted the copies from my hands and whispered, "We're so sorry about before. We were wrong. Obviously."

Taylor chimed in. "About everything." And they began to hand out our resource booklets, row by row.

Incredible.

Meanwhile, Braden's face flushed. Flipping to his next card, he had inadvertently dropped them all.

I knelt beside him to help reorganize his notes and then remembered how reassuring it was when he held my hand. So I braided my fingers through his and squeezed. Miraculously, his color returned.

"Back to our regularly scheduled program," he joked as we stood up.

People chuckled.

"Unfortunately, this next part isn't funny," Braden quipped. "The reports reference so-called acceptable levels of contamination. Sorry, but no soil, water, or air contamination is acceptable."

"I know we're students," Braden said, starting to wrap it up. "We're young. We have a lot to learn. Even so, until we know more—and for the sake of our health and the environment—let's tap the brakes on the Eclyra deal."

The timer sounded. Braden gave me a shaky smile, and I gave him two thumbs-up.

Applause echoed around the chamber as Councilman Jennings thanked Braden in an unconvincing tone. "It's very reassuring to see student activism. Obviously, this crowded room, filled with so many young people who are in earnest, trying to educate themselves, is a testament to the strength of our Pacific Crest Community."

I hated the way he was trying to come off so wise, so knowledgeable, so compassionate. What a slimeball!

"Today's students face huge challenges. It's so tempting to accept easy answers," Councilman Jennings continued as the clapping began to fade. "To seek out a heartfelt TikTok conversation, or to do a search on Instagram and think to yourself, *Yes, this must be the truth!* But you know—"

A wolf whistle pierced the air.

I whirled around. Lucas had his bottom lip over his teeth and was making an extraordinarily loud sound. The applause rose again, sounding more robust than before and drowning out Jennings's voice.

Mom held up her hands, quieting the room.

Next, it was my turn. Braden lowered the mic for me, and his eyes were so warm and reassuring that I couldn't help but smile. He tried to offer me our note cards, but I waved them off. I didn't need them.

"My name is Rae Wolf." I made eye contact with each council member and took a deep breath. "Oil and gas platforms sure are in weird places. Do you know where they are?"

None of the council members answered. I wrestled the wireless mic from its holder and turned my back on the stage. I approached Arman instead. "Do you?"

He tilted his head toward the mic. "No idea."

I walked across the aisle and held the mic before Connor. "Do you?"

"Can't say that I do," he said.

This wasn't all that different from performing in a theater production. Playing up the drama, I waded further into the aisles and stopped near Alicia. "Do you know why someone thought it would be wise to put an oil rig near homes? The coastline? Our school?"

"No!" she answered.

"Do you?" I asked, moving the mic to Ms. Hinojosa.

"No!" she sang out.

"Well, I'll tell you. Oil and gas platforms are hidden all over the place. Behind gates. Under tarps. Lurking beneath innocent-looking wooden structures. They're hidden in plain sight. And you know what happens?"

People were shaking their heads.

"Residents complain," I continued. "Bloody noses. Headaches. Bad odors. Oil spills. Explosions. Cancer. Then the city says they'll create setbacks or even decommission the platforms. Only what keeps happening?"

I faced the council again.

Silence.

I swung back to the audience. "What. Keeps. Happening?" I thrust the mic out to the audience.

"Nothing!" someone said from the fifth row.

"What happens when people complain about oil rigs? *Louder* this time!"

"NOTHING!" screamed a whole lot more people.

"Nothing," I repeated quietly. Then I turned back to the council. "It's been three years since the disastrous Cutter Ranch gas leak. Who knows what untold damage is being caused to their community? Residents are traumatized. People died! And that oil rig? It's still open for business!"

I paused to let it sink in.

"After a 1.8-billion-dollar settlement—after a community subjected to an environmental nightmare—Cutter Ranch *is still open*."

I faced the audience again.

"Are *we* going to be the next Cutter Ranch?"

"No!" Lucas called out.

"No!" Simon shouted, standing up again.

Then a chorus of voices yelled, "No! No! No!"

Councilman Jennings's voice crackled harshly over the speakers, jarring me. "We are Pacific Crest, not Cutter Ranch. Big difference, Ms. Wolf."

Mom broke her silence. "Councilman Jennings, this time is reserved for public comment."

Jennings looked ready to burst into flames.

Mom nodded to me, and I continued. "We *have* to move away from fossil fuels. It's the right thing to do for the planet and for our community. Please tell us that we can learn from mistakes. That you care more about our health than making money!"

The three-minute buzzer sounded.

I slid the mic back into its holder and looked over at Braden. He was staring at me with an expression of wonder. Or disbelief. I still struggle to tell the difference.

I heard clapping, so I started clapping too. At first, I thought it was one of those oddball things I should've known not to do, and I wanted to slap myself. But by the time Braden gave me a one-armed hug, I knew it was okay.

As we threaded our way through the crowd, the room erupted in crazy applause. It was validating and exciting and awful at the same time. I leaned into Braden's ear. "It's too much. I've gotta go."

We pushed open the chamber door and almost slammed directly into Andrew and his stage crew BFFs.

"Excuse me," I said.

Nothing. They stood there in the lobby, blocking our way.

"Excuse me," I said, louder now.

Andrew's minions whispered, apparently enjoying the show.

"Don't make her say it again," Braden said in a low voice.

Some of the crowd poured out of the chamber door behind us, congratulating us.

"Erin Brockovich!" Mr. Hackbarth called out. "Or do I call you Greta Thunberg?"

I couldn't contain a smile. "Rae Wolf works."

Then he noticed the roadblock. "What's going on here?"

Andrew turned sharply to the others. "Get out of the way."

The herd parted. Good thing, too. If they hadn't, I wasn't going to wait. Not now—not after this amazing moment.

Braden and I pushed the heavy glass doors open and escaped together into the cool night air.

41

BRADEN

Rae and I settled onto a park bench outside of City Hall. I was sweating, my heart still thump-thump-thumping like I'd gone into fourth-quarter overtime.

"You okay?" Rae asked.

"I will never forget the way you spoke tonight," I said once I'd caught my breath. "Not for the rest of my life. I still can't believe how much grit you have. Enough, I guess, to lend me some because, wow—so embarrassing. Can't believe I dropped my note cards."

Rae kicked off her sneakers and tucked her cute feet beneath her. Then she leaned against my shoulder. I loved the way she fit against me, the contact points where her arm pressed against my side and her cheek rested against my chest. It made me want to stay very still so she wouldn't change her position.

"When will they vote?" I wondered out loud.

"A crowd that large? Could be hours. It's impossible to say."

We looked at the sky. You could see a few stars, and we were alone. I stopped sweating and my breathing slowed down. I became acutely aware that we were, indeed, alone.

Rae seemed to feel it too. She looked around and, when she was satisfied no one was watching us, climbed into my lap and nuzzled into my neck. "I don't even have the words to describe how proud I am," she whispered. "How good you make me feel. How happy I am since I met you."

I tried to kiss her.

She pulled back. "Let me finish, please. This is hard for me to say, and I may never get the nerve to say it again!"

"That some kind of joke? You're the gutsiest girl I've ever met! And you are definitely going to say these things to me again. Multiple times a day, if I have my way. Because, yeah, the feeling is mutual."

She studied my face like she was trying to memorize it. "For as long as I can remember, I have felt misunderstood and unliked by most of my peers. Over time, I found tools to help me cope. Like therapy and meditation. Like special interests and time alone. But none of that compares to what it's like to be seen for who I am. *You* see me. I feel it. I have felt it since that first day in Life Skills, even before you knew my name."

"Oh, my god. You blew my mind!" I said, hoping I wasn't interrupting. "Without you, I'd still be overstudying, obsessing, expecting the absolute worst. I'd still be pretending to be the confident athlete and scholar who had it all handled, all the while lying to my friends and family about how miserable I felt."

Rae's mouth twitched before she wrapped her arms around me, nuzzling her face in my neck.

"Worst of all," I continued, "I'd still be lying to myself, telling myself that I was just fine. I wouldn't have the courage to face the fact that I needed help, needed therapy. Needed you. Without you, my anxiety would have erased any good thing I've ever had in my life. And Rae, I'd never be as happy as I am now."

Then she slowly slid her hand across my stomach. The sensation practically sent my eyes rolling back in their sockets. I kissed her cheek where it met her mouth and then concentrated on her indescribably soft lips. I cupped her delicate jawline then traced my finger down her neck and beneath the collar of her T-shirt. Then I put my mouth where my finger had been.

She didn't slap my face or tell me to take a hike, which I thought was a good sign.

There wasn't a lot of talk after that.

I totally lost track of time until I heard a sliding door slam nearby. I opened my eyes and saw a wheelchair being unloaded from some kind of van.

"Oh, my god. I can't believe it," I said quietly. "That's Coach Zanetta."

Rae moved off my lap and jabbed her feet into her sneakers. Together we ran to the curb, where I said hi to Coach and offered to help his nurse while Rae guided them to council chambers.

Back inside, we made kind of a commotion at the chamber door, so I wasn't surprised when Mayor Bloom called Coach Zanetta to speak next. I brought the mic to his wheelchair.

"Two years ago, I retired," Coach began, wheezing heavily. "I was looking forward to spending the rest of my life chasing my wife Lianne around the house and tinkering on muscle cars. Dying early is going to put a crimp in the plan. I'm not sure Lianne will ever forgive me."

Then Coach started coughing. It was a hard cough, and he couldn't seem to catch his breath. His face and neck turned bright red, but finally he caught his breath. He raised a hand in thanks, and the nurse quickly wheeled him out of the exit to respectful applause from the entire chamber.

The whole thing was so alarming. More than that, it was just so sad.

You could see that the council members felt it too. Rae's mom wiped a tear from her face. The mayor kept sipping from his water bottle, like if he didn't keep drinking, he'd start bawling. Jennings and the other two council members just nodded. I couldn't tell what that meant.

When Mayor Bloom introduced the next speaker, my heart clamped up. "Shadi Shokrian?"

Hackbarth's former journalism student walked to the lectern, her gait slow. Her face was washed out. She wore a colorful LA Dodgers cap, but you could tell she was bald.

"I have to thank Braden Bernstein for reaching out to me," she said, right off the bat.

It was all too much. The stakes were too high. Coach Zanetta, and now this poor woman! I started sweating and I felt dizzy. My mouth was dry. Weak, I wondered if I was dehydrated or my medications were having a bad side effect. If I couldn't convince people tonight, did that mean I was guilty of somehow being responsible for every other person who stood to be poisoned?

I turned to Rae.

She was the picture of calm. Her big, blue eyes seemed to understand everything I thought and felt. There was no judgment, only love. How could I tell? I guess it's like they say: When you feel it, you just know. Love is undeniable.

Shadi continued with a soft accent. "I apologize for not returning your call, Braden. I was on week three of chemo and feeling so sick."

She paused to take a deep breath.

"Like many of you here, I played sports in high school. I was a tennis player and loved every minute spent running on the court. I've always been active—hiking, biking . . . . Believe it or not, I'm a gym rat!"

She made a muscle with her bicep. It looked more like a glorified string.

"I practice meditation and yoga daily." She playfully wagged her finger at the council. "And you should too!"

Then Shadi seemed to lose her train of thought for a moment. No one made a sound. She gathered herself again.

"I've had genetic testing done, and I've been found negative for everything I've been evaluated for, including the BRCA genes. Yet here I am. Stage III breast cancer. And the only thing I can point to is this oil well."

Shadi started crying then.

You could see the expressions on the council members' faces. Elizabeth looked stricken. She found tissues in her pocket and walked them over to Shadi, who took one and dabbed at her nose.

Councilman Jennings gestured to the city attorney. "Please make a notation in the record that the city has done their due diligence, and though Ms. Shokrian is completely deserving of our sympathy and should be given every courtesy that we can afford her, the reports are clear. Her claim is entirely unsubstantiated."

"Ah, go to hell, you slimy sleazebag," I said out loud.

"She shouldn't have to listen to this! It's cruel!" Rae called out, backing me up.

The three-minute buzzer sounded.

No one dared tell Shadi that she was out of time. "As we learned tonight," she continued, "it's difficult to find concrete environmental links to illness. But I stand with Braden and Rae, and I beg you to face this situation with humility. To admit that there is so much we don't know, and that whatever gain the school reaps can never be worth the risk to human life."

She thanked the council for the opportunity to speak and shuffled two steps in the direction of her seat. Before she'd even sat down, just about everyone else in the room rose to their feet. We gave Shadi a standing ovation.

My eyes welled up, and I pressed them with the heels of my hands.

"You found Shadi, and she came through," Rae said.

The rest of the meeting was a blur. A few people droned on, especially from Councilman Jennings's side. It all got to be very repetitive and insulting. Either you were an alarmist who didn't understand the financial upside, or you were too selfish to care about health and the environment.

Around midnight, the council finally voted. The vote was three to two.

We won.

42

RAE

 text alert woke me up. Bleary-eyed and half asleep, I reached for the phone on my nightstand. The text was from Braden:

Good morning, WINNER!

He included the kissing face, the first-place trophy, and the sunflower emojis.

When the vote was announced last night, I'd jumped up and down, barely able to believe it. Braden caught me and twirled me around. The people who had stuck around exploded in applause and danced around the chambers. It hadn't seemed real.

It still didn't.

From his dog bed on the floor, I heard Noodle scratch his ear, which was his way of telling me he was ready for breakfast. Then I smelled pancakes.

I sat up in my bed. Noodle sat up in his bed. He shook his head and trotted to the door. I grabbed my robe and followed him downstairs to the kitchen.

Mom had set up bowls of mixed berries, whipped cream, Nutella, and home-made granola. She'd made French press coffee. A glass of fresh-squeezed orange juice had been placed on my placemat. Gluten-free pancakes steamed on a platter in the center of the table.

"Good morning!" Mom said, saluting me with her coffee mug. Her hair was in a messy bun, and she still had sleep in her eyes.

"What's all this? It's not my birthday."

"I'm not waiting until July to celebrate." Mom flipped another pancake.

I studied her face. Bags under her eyes. Dimples on her cheeks. She was happy. But Mom was an optimist. You didn't even need a glass half full for her to be ecstatic. Just a drop or two would suffice.

Mom pressed something on her tablet.

"Whoa, no devices at the table, Mom!"

Freddie Mercury's voice started coming from a nearby speaker, singing "We Are the Champions." Mom and I sang along. She shimmied and swung her hips. I tapped my foot and did a few simple rah-rah moves. Noodle barked.

Another text alert. I checked my phone. Braden again. Heart emojis in every color of the rainbow. I sent him back a blue butterfly and a kissing face and fireworks emojis. I texted the YouTube link to the Queen song.

I congratulated Mom. "You even got the slow wheels of government to speed up!"

"*We* did," she acknowledged. "You, Braden, and your friends, and your friends' friends . . . . See, I'm not BS-ing you when I tell you: You can accomplish anything you set out to do. Don't forget that."

My mind spun to some of the documents I'd found on the city's website during my research—letters that Mom had written in an official capacity to support prison reform, to urge environmental protections, to protect the elderly from abuse. In my head, I saw all the random people who stopped her on the street to share their problems or just to thank her for her help. I took stock of how, after all these years, she'd only forgotten to pick me up from school twice.

Then I saw my father. How he didn't believe in my diagnosis. How he had fought with Mom, and how she hadn't given up on me.

My mind shuffled the memories, and I landed hard on the times I'd yelled at Mom for making food I didn't like. How I argued with her about going to school. How I completely lost it that time and punched her.

Part of me collapsed in on itself.

Shaky, I slumped into my seat at the breakfast room table. "You give so much, Mom. You work so hard. You always try to do the right thing, even when it seems like the whole world is against you and you didn't have anyone."

"I always had you."

"I'm sorry, Mommy." I took in the breakfast spread. How many moms got up early, after they'd been at a long meeting the night before, and made a huge, beautiful breakfast for their kid? "I am so sorry."

Above it all, I agonized over the fact that I'd struck her. I couldn't even say it out loud. I was utterly ashamed. Yet she knew. She read my mind, because she's my mom.

"It's all forgotten, Rae, it's all forgiven. One bad decision doesn't define a life. It doesn't change the bond that we have and always will have."

I got up and hugged her. Then I took in a deep breath. The excitement returned as my mind jumped ahead to school. I let go of Mom and, of course, asked her to do something else for me. "Can you make more pancakes?"

"Well, yes, but I doubt we can finish these . . . ."

I shook my head. "I need enough for ten people. All boys, so you better make enough for fifteen."

"No problem!" Mom saluted me again with her coffee mug. "You need them 'to go'?"

43

BRADEN

I drove to school on the morning after the council vote, surprisingly energetic considering I'd gotten less than five hours' sleep. I cranked the radio, with thoughts of Rae on my mind.

Leaving the student parking lot, I saw Connor stuck in the middle of a pack of kids, all moving together like they were in a rugby scrum. "Wait up!" I called.

Connor pulled one earbud from his ear and faced me. The other kids rushed around him, in a hurry to get to homeroom before first period. Connor's eyes were at half-mast, like they were every morning. He had his gigantic thermos in his right hand.

"You refill that thing, or is it left over from yesterday?" I wondered out loud.

"Take a guess," he croaked.

"Foodborne illness is more common than you think," I said sternly. "The incubation period for bacteria can range from hours to days. So, if you find yourself with the shits, look no further than your trusty thermos."

Connor took a hearty gulp. "It's fresh brew," he assured me.

I took the thermos and opened it, wiped down the lip with my shirt, and helped myself to a few sips. "Too much sugar. What're you trying to do, get type II diabetes?"

"You should be a doctor, you know that?"

I *tsked*. "I almost fainted when they had to draw blood. I don't think I'm cut out for it, cuz."

"But no one else I know worries about diabetes. Or dengue fever. Or tearing their medial collateral ligament. Or—"

I cut him off. "Are you calling me a hypochondriac?" I placed my hand on my heart in mock horror.

"Actually, you've been a lot better lately. Still, isn't one person's hypochondriac another person's environmental activist?" Connor said, grinning.

"Some questions are not meant to have answers. For instance, should I question your sanity for showing up at school in uniform, risking your hard-earned reputation as a stoner musician?"

The morning bell rang, and we headed through the glass lobby doors. I recognized Detective Figueroa and Officer Stanten motoring past us. Figueroa moved swiftly for a big guy, and Stanten had to practically jog to keep up with him. I watched them push out the doors we'd just come through and wondered what was up.

Connor and I parted at the base of the stairs, with him heading to the new building and me to Life Skills in the older structure. For some reason, a school guard redirected two girls away from the hallway I wanted to cross. Not wanting to be tardy, I skirted around him, unnoticed.

The hallway was deserted, which was odd. My footsteps echoed through the corridor. Then finally someone appeared: my counselor, Ms. Nguyen, with her hand on Andy Jennings's arm, guiding him down the stairs.

Her eyes went wide when she saw me, like I'd accidentally opened the door to the women's restroom. She gave a curt nod and guided Andy in the opposite direction. Andy curled his lip in scorn. Strangely, he wore an oversized sweatshirt that seemed to be covering his usual button-down.

There was something weird about his posture, too. It was his hands. They were secured behind his back.

Andy Jennings was handcuffed.

I turned the corner, and the normal sounds of student chatter and lockers slamming returned. Three guys from the baseball team high-fived me. "Way to go, man. We did it!"

A couple of girls from Spanish class saw me and cooed, *"Eres lo mejor, guapo! Te amo, corazón!"*

Most people just hurried to class like it was any other day. A few definitely avoided eye contact altogether.

Through it all, a question nagged at me: Did Andy key my car? Maybe the detectives should be talking to *me* about that.

I quickly retraced my steps. Everyone else was in class by now, and I had long enough legs to cover ground when I wanted to. Across from student parking, I caught up to Ms. Nguyen, who was talking with Detective Figueroa.

"You again? You'll be late for first period," she said with a serious look, but I could see the glimmer in her eye. She was happy about something, maybe even happy with me.

"Busted," I said, realizing too late that was probably the wrong expression, considering that Andy now sat ten feet away, frowning in the back of an unmarked police car. I heard the engine start up. Officer Stanten was behind the wheel.

Detective Figueroa smiled at me. "Good morning, Braden!"

"Good morning. Can I ask you a question, Detective? Real quick!"

Detective Figueroa and Ms. Nguyen exchanged a quick look.

"Check your email when you get a second," Ms. Nguyen said to me before trotting up the stairs toward the school.

I nodded my chin in Andy's direction. "He have anything to do with keying my car?"

Figueroa gave me an amused tilt of the head.

"Sorry. I guess I shouldn't ask," I responded.

"Questions are good," the detective replied. "No need to apologize. So, I heard about the council vote last night. Maybe I'm not supposed to weigh in on these things, but oh well! I believe congratulations are in order."

"Wow. Okay, thanks. Word gets around fast."

"Pacific Crest is a very small town." He handed me his card. "Well, I better get going. And by the way, between you and me, those pesky false alarms shouldn't be bothering anyone anymore."

My eyes shifted to the police car. "*He's* the swatter?" Huh. I would not have guessed that. "How'd you find out?"

"Remember our chat? About students using Venmo for illegal activity?"

I remembered. "Sure. Kids hiring other kids to be their thugs."

I caught a faint smile on Figueroa's face. "Turns out, adults have caught on. They're using kids to do their dirty work, too."

"Wait, wait, wait. Detective Figueroa. You can't leave me hanging like this. An adult? Is it"—I lowered my voice—"his dad?"

He turned away and opened the door to the back seat. "You ask good questions. Ever consider becoming a detective?"

Andy stared straight ahead and I noticed his chin drop. You could tell he was on the verge of tears.

I couldn't wait for Advanced Journalism to tell Lucas that he was safe. No one was going to blame him for the trouble at school. Oh, and to break the difficult news to him that there would be no more unscheduled class cancellations.

Unlike Lucas, Rae hated the disruption during the day, and I knew she'd be relieved to know that was all over. For now, anyway. Andy and his dad weren't going to be bothering her anymore.

I still had almost four hours until lunch, when she and I were set to meet. Four hours! It felt like four thousand. I got a funny feeling in my stomach as images of the night before came to mind.

On the way to AP History, I checked my emails. The first one said I'd gotten an A-minus on my in-class essay, the one I'd barely prepared for. Message to self: Work less.

Another email, this one from Ms. Nguyen, asked if I wanted to stay on next year in Life Skills. She wrote that Ms. Hinojosa had made a special request for me.

No-brainer. Why wouldn't I want to hang out with my friends every morning and play games and watch videos and hear about the stuff that mattered?

When third period rolled around, I opened the door to the Life Skills room, expecting the guys, the loud voices, the usual energy. Simon did not disappoint, shouting, "Captain America!"

But the aroma of something delicious drifted over to me. Before I could identify the source, Simon, Jerome, and the rest of the boys began clapping and congratulating me on my "win."

I was so touched, it was almost too much. "Not just me. It was a team effort! Like at the Special Olympics, when you guys all worked together."

"I'm going to be able to say that I knew you when," Ms. Hinojosa said.

"Uh . . . ." My neck and cheeks started getting warm. I found the attention a little bit painful. "Hey, you guys are all my wingmen."

Then the door opened behind me, and there was Rae and that incredible, delicious smell. She had on a funky red lace skirt, black tights, and a denim jacket that I think might have been her mom's because it fit and wasn't two sizes too big. In each hand, she carried a large shopping bag. She took my breath away; she was so incredibly pretty.

"Ms. Hinojosa said it's okay if we have a little last-minute party," she said, looking directly at me.

"Yes!" Ms. Hinojosa agreed. "Boys, give Rae a hand, please."

The boys quickly forgot all about me and closed in on Rae, helping her with the bags and the unpacking. Then they sat down and went about the business of making maple syrup ponds on their paper plates. My stomach grumbled when Rae peeled back the foil on a mother lode of warm, fluffy pancakes. We piled them on each plate and watched the boys' expressions of pure joy.

"Just when I thought the day couldn't get any better," I said, snaking an arm around her waist and giving her a squeeze.

She squirmed, uncomfortable.

I dropped my arm. "Uh, whoops. Sorry!"

Rae took a breath. "Let's try that again."

I leaned in and this time, Rae anticipated the contact. "I've missed you," I whispered.

"It's only been a few hours since we were together," she said laughing. She brushed her lips lightly against my cheek, so don't ask me why my whole body lit up.

"Rules!" Simon got in my face like a referee. "No touching! No, no, no."

Rae's mouth twitched. "Sorry, Simon. My bad."

The boys polished off the pancakes in record time. When they literally licked their plates, nobody stopped them.

"Mmm," I said. "You flip a fluffy pancake."

"Mom made them this morning, but I do, in fact, flip a fluffy pancake."

"That reminds me," I said, scratching my chin. "When's the next council meeting?"

"Next month. Why? The vote is over. It's a done deal."

"I figure your mom comes home pretty late when she has those meetings. I'm thinking, I dunno, pancakes and a candlelight dinner for two?"

"Are you saying I have to wait a month for our next date?" she asked, pouting—definitely disappointed.

It was so cute when she took me literally. "Absolutely not. What're you doing tonight? And tomorrow? And the next day?"

Rae's mouth twitched, and I felt her soften. "What do you have in mind?"

"I'm a bright and cheerful lad. I'll come up with something."

I used to think I knew everything. I knew that getting good grades, being the editor of the school paper, and clinching a spot on varsity basketball would give me the key to getting into the right college, getting the right degrees, and living happily ever after.

That was fun while it lasted.

Well, true fact: Thinking I knew everything made me anxious as hell. It led me to believe I had run over dogs and been accused of cheating. It convinced me that losing my best friend, Hojun, in a fatal car accident meant disaster was always hiding around the next bend. It caused me to be completely uncomfortable in my own skin. All the endless preparation in advance of tests, the obsession over deadlines, the exhaustion from trying to avert disease and death—it did not make me happy.

Now I can freely admit: I'm not sure what I want to do with my life. Maybe I'll be a special needs teacher or a detective or a sports agent. Now I can accept that while I don't like uncertainty—not at all, actually—it's not going away. Not in this life. So for now, I do the best I can with the discomfort.

And I try not to let it win.

Meeting Rae was maybe the best thing that ever happened to me. She's passionate, caring, and sensitive. Her autism is a huge part of who she is and how she sees the world. I don't think of it as a flaw. She's the most honest person I've ever met. She's also stubborn and prickly. She's smart as hell. She is not normal. She is weird.

In the best possible way.

I still don't know if I was born with the worry gene or if I suffer anxiety because my parents are worriers and my best friend died suddenly. I do know that, like Rae's autism, there's no cure for my anxiety. It's a part of me, and even with therapy and my prescription, some days can be a lot of work. Some days feel unbearable.

But Rae has inspired me to keep facing it. She reminds me that as bad as I might be feeling one day is as good as I might be feeling the next—and that most of the time, I am pretty happy. Basically, she's magic.

Let's be straight about one thing, though: I am *not* magic. I just have the good sense to recognize it when I see it.

ACKNOWLEDGMENTS

Heartfelt thanks to:

Benee Knauer, world's best editor and cherished friend.

My niece Becca Lory Hector, best-selling author, award-winning autistic advocate.

Sydney Frank, neurodivergent artist.

Megan Amodeo, writer, autism self-advocate.

Jill Escher, past president, National Council on Severe Autism.

Detective Ubaldo Mendoza, Beverly Hills Police Department.

Ali Norman-Franks, Beverly Hills High School wellness coordinator.

Karen Winnick, children's author and artist.

Hayley Kaplan, sistah-friend-treasure.

Brent Kaplan, early reader and mirth maker.

My big bro, Greg Kaplan, psychic twin and trusted confidant.

Debbie Naiman, the compass every writer wishes they had.

Rhonda Stone, Julie Sayres, Renee Brook, Marni Traub, Elaine Maltzman, and Deborah Frank, longtime cherished cheerleaders.

Greenleaf publishing pros: Erin Brown, Benito Salazar, Laurie MacQueen, Diana Coe, Madelyn Myers, Jamie White, Amy Dorta McIlwaine, Justin Branch, Brittany Jones-Pugh, Jenny Cribb, Kyle Pearson, and Emma Watson.

Creative Breezie Castell, who infused my online presence with soul and warmth.

Writers group at mentor Barbara Bottner's Table: Cambria Gordon, Denise Doyen, Jim Cox, and Hillary Perelyubskiy.

Aaron Azizi, Mike Medina, and Jason Sleissenger, who told tales of high school glory days, informing my make-believe story.

Garrett Kaplan, fellow artist. You earned your place on Mt. Olympus.

My parents, Gloria and Laurence Kaplan, whose fierce love provided an unshakable foundation that continues to inspire me.

Hijos #1 and #2, for the wellspring of love.

My husband, Neal. With you.

RESOURCES

According to the National Institute of Mental Health, 31.9 percent of adolescents in the United States between the ages of thirteen and eighteen have an anxiety disorder. Anxiety disorders include panic disorder, generalized anxiety disorder, agoraphobia, specific phobia, social anxiety disorder, post-traumatic stress disorder, obsessive-compulsive disorder, and separation anxiety disorder.

In the United States, about one in thirty-six children has been identified with autism spectrum disorder (ASD) according to estimates from the Center for Disease Control's Autism and Developmental Disabilities Monitoring Network. ASD is nearly four times more common among boys than among girls.

If you or someone you know needs support, there are plenty of sources for help. The isolation of feeling like you don't belong or that something is wrong with you ends when you find your circle, your person, your team. Here are excellent books and organizations for you to consider:

Recommended Books

- *The Awesome Autistic Go-To Guide: A Practical Handbook for Autistic Teens and Tweens* by Yenn Purkis and Tanya Masterman

- *I Think I Might Be Autistic* by Cynthia Kim

- *Self-Care for Autistic People* by Dr. Megan Anna Neff

- *Unmasking Autism* by Devon Price, PhD

- *Uniquely Human* by Barry M. Privant, PhD, and Tom Fields-Meyer

- *Always Bring Your Sunglasses* by Becca Lory

- *Autism in Heels* by Jennifer Cook O'Toole

Organizations

- American Society for the Prevention of Cruelty to Animals: https://www.aspca.org/

- The Arc: https://thearc.org/

- Autistic Self Advocacy Network: https://autisticadvocacy.org/

- Autistic Women & Nonbinary Network: https://awnnetwork.org/

- Association for Autism and Neurodiversity: https://aane.org/

ABOUT THE AUTHOR

CYNTHIA BASEMAN is the author of the memoir *Love, Mom: A Mother's Journey from Loss to Hope*, which has been recommended by clinicians and bereaved mothers worldwide and has been excerpted in Barbara Seaman's *Voices of the Women's Health Movement*. She is the author of the children's illustrated book series *Lip Monsters*, which she created with Victoria Greenwood. She is a Nicholl Fellowship finalist for her first screenplay. Baseman earned an Emmy nomination as coproducer of a children's special on literacy, *Word Up!* She lives in Los Angeles with her husband, four chatty cockatiels, and rescue dog, Stella.

You can visit Cynthia Baseman at www.cynthiabaseman.com.